"D

Dea... ...eep voice penetrated the night. "Calley, I don't feel safe about you being down here alone."

He stepped onto the riverbank, his frame silhouetted against the sky and rising moon. Wordlessly he stripped off his shirt and then his jeans and stepped into the river. Calley shivered for him as he sucked in his breath. He was so magnificent, a superb physical specimen no woman alive would be able to ignore.

"I'm not shutting you out," she said when there was no ignoring his inexorable presence. "I just had to think about us. We aren't ready for what's happening. We don't know each other well enough."

"Not yet we don't." His eyes were relentless daggers heading straight for her heart. "But I think it's going to happen."

"You think we're going to become lovers?" Calley couldn't remember ever being this honest with anyone else.

"More than lovers I hope."

ABOUT THE AUTHOR

Vella Munn claims she has only one pseudonym—Mom. Originally from California, she resides in Oregon with her husband and two sons. Before turning to writing full-time, Vella penned more than fifty articles and a nonfiction book. She also worked as a reporter and a social worker.

Books by Vella Munn

HARLEQUIN AMERICAN ROMANCE

42–SUMMER SEASON
72–RIVER RAPTURE
96–THE HEART'S REWARD
115–WANDERLUST
164–BLACK MAGIC

HARLEQUIN INTRIGUE

6–TOUCH A WILD HEART

These books may be available at your local bookseller.

Don't miss any of our special offers. Write to us at the following address for information on our newest releases.

Harlequin Reader Service
901 Fuhrmann Blvd., P.O. Box 1397, Buffalo, NY 14240
Canadian address: P.O. Box 603,
Fort Erie, Ont. L2A 5X3

Wild and Free
Vella Munn

Harlequin Books

TORONTO • NEW YORK • LONDON
AMSTERDAM • PARIS • SYDNEY • HAMBURG
STOCKHOLM • ATHENS • TOKYO • MILAN

To Neil Diamond,
whose magic makes all moods possible.

Published January 1987

First printing November 1986

ISBN 0-373-16184-0

Copyright © 1987 by Vella Munn. All rights reserved.
Philippine copyright 1986. Australian copyright 1986.
Except for use in any review, the reproduction or utilization of this work in whole or in part in any form by any electronic, mechanical or other means, now known or hereafter invented, including xerography, photocopying and recording, or in any information storage or retrieval system, is forbidden without the permission of the publisher, Harlequin Enterprises Limited, 225 Duncan Mill Road, Don Mills, Ontario, Canada M3B 3K9.

All the characters in this book have no existence outside the imagination of the author and have no relation whatsoever to anyone bearing the same name or names. They are not even distantly inspired by any individual known or unknown to the author, and all incidents are pure invention.

The Harlequin trademarks, consisting of the words HARLEQUIN AMERICAN ROMANCE, HARLEQUIN AMERICAN ROMANCES, and the portrayal of a Harlequin, are trademarks of Harlequin Enterprises Limited; the portrayal of a Harlequin is registered in the United States Patent and Trademark Office and in the Canada Trade Marks Office.

Printed in Canada

Chapter One

Calley Stewart was back doing what she'd been trained for six years ago at Utah State University. She and Melinda Stone were crouched behind brush a few hundred yards from Highway 93, northwest of Missoula, waiting for daylight, waiting for what ancient Indians had once considered to be supernatural.

Neither woman spoke as the first fingers of dawn light touched the wooded drainage area that they faced. Although Calley's life had been one of too much tension during the past year, she hadn't forgotten. This morning, this place, the anticipated experience, was what she'd been born to. She could feel that fundamental fact in her soul.

Five minutes later the drainage area was light enough for Calley to make out the individual Western larches dotting the terrain. Silently she pointed toward one tree that was missing a slab of bark at least ten feet in length, which had been torn from it. Melinda nodded, acknowledging the work of the creatures they were waiting for and then cocked her head in a silent signal.

Calley heard it—the deep, dry cough rumbling out of the forest—an awesome signal echoing up from the ages. The grizzlies were here.

She rocked back onto her heels, her well-worn boots making no sound despite the strain she put them under as she reached for her camera with its 300mm lens. She knew she'd start shaking as soon as she heard the sound. As Mike had once said, "Anyone who isn't in awe of the grizzly is either an idiot or a damn fool." Beside her, Melinda was lifting her own camera into position. The other woman had her lips clamped between her teeth.

There were three of them—a full-grown female weighing perhaps 700 pounds and two immature youngsters ambling after her, swinging their noses along the ground and sniffing the crisp air as their heavy bodies rolled through thick grass that reached to their bellies. The power contained within their compact frames was evident despite the long, thick hair that covered everything except the tips of their noses.

If Calley was still breathing, she was unaware of it. Nothing mattered except concentrating on what was coming into focus through her camera lens. The sight of Nature's largest carnivorous land-based mammal wasn't something she'd ever become blasé about. The grizzlies were why she'd returned to her career.

Tears, which had nothing to do with the morning cold, touched her eyes. The Indians had been right. These creatures were to be treated with reverence—even with a kind of love.

Calley waited another two or three minutes until the bears' lackadaisical search for food—whether roots, tubers, mice or snakes—brought them close enough for the wind to introduce their pungent smell. For another moment she fought and then conquered a wave of panic that could be her undoing. Then she started running off camera shot after shot of the trio, thankful for the silent shutter that advanced the film without signaling that fact to her subjects. She thought, briefly, about the nearby highway. She doubted if anyone on it knew how close they were to the ultimate example of Montana's wilderness. As long as she and Melinda remained out of view and the breeze continued to blow from bears to humans, there was little danger that the bears, with their weak eyesight, would locate the intruders to their world.

And if Calley and Melinda were spotted, there was less than a fifty-fifty chance that they would be challenged. This wasn't a mother with young cubs to protect or a male during mating season. These grizzlies had stood their ground despite humans brought to their turf by Highway 93. The sight of a couple of women in their territory would probably only bring a loud snort of disgust and a quick fade into the forest.

Just the same, Calley didn't take her eyes off the bears for an instant; complacency in the presence of grizzlies could be a fatal mistake. Calley had more than a degree in wildlife management under her belt. She'd been part of the Border Grizzly Project, based at the University of Montana, for three years. She would have never come here, or allowed Melinda to accompany her, if either woman had been having her period. Neither woman wore any cosmetics; they'd both washed their hands with vinegar after filling the gas tank of her jeep. Those were things she'd learned not from textbooks but because she intended to stay alive.

The sight of three of Montana's grizzlies lasted no longer than five minutes, just long enough for Calley to use up her roll of film. She was delighted to see that the bears were in excellent physical condition. "Not bad for a morning's work," Calley said once she was certain that the bears would not be returning. "God, I'm still shaking. That's what a year away from them does to me. Did you get your pictures?"

The University of Montana research assistant nodded, her eyes shining with a light Calley knew was reflected in her own deep gray eyes. "We did it! We actually did it!" Melinda laughed. "Dean kept waving his pictures in my face, but they didn't mean that much to me. Not until now. I don't know if I'll ever be content to stay on campus doing paperwork for him anymore."

"Neither of us is going to be doing anything for the project if we don't get a move on. Our respective boss is going to have my hide if I don't get to the Flathead today," Calley pointed out, holding up her wrist, with its relentlessly moving watch, for emphasis. "This is crazy. I've been working for Dean Ramsey for two weeks now, and I still haven't seen the man."

"Yeah, you have," Melinda said as the women started trudging through the high grass back to where they'd left the jeep.

"I have not," Calley insisted. She glanced back, hoping for a final sight of the bears, although she wouldn't be responsible for the sounds that might come from her throat if they suddenly appeared. "He was in Yellowstone all last week and out on the Flathead River since he got back. The only proof I have of his existence is a phone call and a couple of letters."

Melinda winked. "You remember the bigger of those two young grizzlies? The one with the lighter coat. Put him on two feet and you have Dean Ramsey."

"Wonderful!" Calley pretended to shiver, her broad but slender shoulders moving easily under her limp cotton shirt. "Don't tell me he smells like a bear, too. I am definitely not ready to spend the summer working side by side with that."

"Of course he doesn't smell like a bear, although—" Melinda paused dramatically. "Maybe he does by now if he's been out setting snares for several days. What I mean is, he has this mess of dark brown hair and a beard that's kind of going tan instead of gray, like that one bear. When he smiles, he has these incredibly white teeth that show through all that hair, just like a bear with its mouth open."

"A bear's teeth are yellow," Calley pointed out, her eyes on the ground so she wouldn't trip over a hidden log.

"Minor point," Melinda countered. "Take my word for it, that man will make you think about everything positive that can be said about grizzlies. We don't have to meet him at any particular time, do we? We're going to be half the day just getting there, let alone finding where he and Steve are camped."

"No, the telegram from Bigfork just said he'd be looking for me on the twenty-fourth. You do have the map, don't you?"

"Of course." Melinda patted her back pocket. "Given the state of Dean's desk, that's no small accomplishment. I swear, the amount of time that man has had to spend trying to get funds for the project is unreal. I mean, he's a biologist, not a bureaucrat."

"He's not pushing pencils now," Calley said. "Thank goodness that extra funding came through. How do you think I was able to come back here?"

It was a poor choice of words. The reason for Calley's leaving the project last year had remained a subject that the two friends hadn't touched. Melinda was waiting for Calley to bring it up; Calley wasn't ready yet.

Calley shook off the past and concentrated on finding her footing in grass too thick to allow her to see the ground. The two women walked silently in single file until they'd covered the mile that took them back to Calley's jeep. They repacked their cameras and placed them on the floor behind their seats. After grabbing a thermos of coffee, they started north to where Dean Ramsey and Steve Bull hopefully were snaring bears as they collected data for the project.

It wasn't until Calley no longer had to fight to see around the sheen of a Montana sunrise that she broke the silence. For the past two weeks she'd been occupied with redefining the job, which was financed by the Endangered Species Act, finding a place to stay and having her jeep serviced. There'd been little opportunity to find out what Melinda was up to other than assisting Dean Ramsey. "Are you still entering those photography contests?" she asked. "If those shots of the grizzlies come out, you'll really have something."

A self-satisfied smile spread over the compact thirty-year-old's face, crinkling her eyes and seeming to turn her into a child again. "That's just what I was thinking. Why do you think I talked you into hooking up with me at four a.m.? And why do you think I'm trailing along on this trip out to the Flathead? I've got enough film in my camera case for shots of every grizzly south of the border."

"Your friend doesn't mind?" Calley asked with the boldness that came from learning that a year's absence hadn't destroyed a strong friendship.

"My friend, as you so charmingly call him, is used to my idiosyncrasies. Poor guy. If he thought he was hooking up with a lonely old maid, he sure was wrong. Calley, what would you say if I told you I was thinking of marrying Kirk?"

"Marriage? I don't know." Calley stumbled. It wasn't as if Melinda and Kirk's relationship was something still in the forming stages. They had been living together for almost two years now. But Calley had always thought of it as only that—living together. Melinda was a strongly independent woman, while Kirk fiercely guarded his personal space. They were hardly the typical couple walking hand in hand through the pathways of life. But maybe that was precisely why their relationship was working. Melinda and Kirk complemented each other without intruding.

"I don't know," Calley started again. "I've never given it any thought."

"Well, think about it. I am."

DEAN RAMSEY'S JEANS were caked with mud from the knees down. His boots squished with every step. He was sweating, cursing the life-style that made a beard and shaggy hair more a matter of lack of time for personal grooming than an attempt to imitate one of the creatures he'd spent the past ten years studying. He also needed a shower.

No, he felt as if he needed to be thrown into a hot, soapy washing machine and left on the wash cycle for an hour. The sleeves of his flannel shirt were rolled up, partly because he needed to feel air on his muscular forearms and partly because his elbows kept poking through the tears in the sleeves. He was sweating between his shoulder blades, under the extra layer of fabric formed by his bright orange vest. But he knew enough not to remove what should be proof to other humans that he wasn't something to be brought home to mount over a fireplace.

Behind him he could hear the labored breathing of biologist Steve Bull as the other man followed his lead along the transparent vein of water that snaked its way through the vast roll of mountains that made up the Flathead area. Dean first met the Sioux Indian while Steve had been working for the Yellowstone National Park bear-management program. Dean had spirited him away when additional money from public and private conservation groups became available for the Border Grizzly Project. Steve, who had never quite been able to adjust to the demands of tourists, had been a willing transplant. The twenty-six-year-old, who Dean thought of as a boy with an old man's wisdom of the wilderness, operated on the same wavelength as Dean. They sought out civilization only when their clothes would no longer come clean in a river and the food in their backpacks could no longer be supplemented with chokecherries, thimbleberry or trout.

Dean was pretty sure it was Wednesday. If it was, the newest member of the project team, Calley Stewart, would show up.

He hadn't given the woman much thought. Knowing that she'd worked for the project before, under its former director Mike Bailey, was all he needed to know. Despite having certain philosophical differences, Dean admitted that Bailey knew what he was doing. Bailey wouldn't have tolerated anyone who didn't understand that making peace between humans and grizzlies was the only way the great creatures were going to survive.

"I don't know why we have to drag this rotting meat around with us," Steve whispered. "The way the two of us stink, no bear's going to be able to smell anything else."

"You noticed." Dean wrinkled up his nose but he didn't turn around. They were getting close to the last of the seven snares they'd fastened to ponderosa pines yesterday. The first six had been empty, but already they could hear angry growls around the bend in the river. To an outsider, all bears probably sounded the same, but Dean already knew from what he heard that their prisoner was a black, not a grizzly. It wasn't what Dean wanted, but he could still learn something from the smaller bear.

A scruffy-looking male weighing just over three hundred pounds glared at Dean and Steve as they came around the bend. Its right rear foot was caught in a snug noose that wouldn't injure it unless the creature was left trapped long enough to become desperate. The two men had no intention of letting that happen. The black raised a free front paw at the humans, pointed its muzzle in their direction and angrily shook its coal-black body. The movement revealed a blaze of white adorning the bear's chest.

"Look at him," Steve pointed out. "I've seen healthier specimens."

"I agree." Dean noticed the strange way the bear kept shaking its head randomly as if the trapped foot wasn't the only thing on its mind.

Dean pushed closer through the underbrush hanging low over the river shallows until he was close enough for a good shot. Something he recognized all too well clawed its way into his throat and made breathing difficult, but Dean refused to let the emotion control him. He pulled the rifle out of his backpack and took aim, wincing as the dart found its target beneath the thick hide. Fascinated, Dean watched the bear snap its sharply curved teeth at the inaccessible dart. His body was drenched with sweat, which had nothing to do with the day's heat and might haunt him as long as he went into the woods. He sensed the Indian watching him, but Steve said nothing. Unless there was no alternative, neither man ever would.

Five minutes later the black was sleeping under the effects of a tranquilizer, its movements no longer taking Dean back fourteen months into hell. While Dean released the trapped foot, Steve started checking the animal for evidence of parasites. It wasn't until Dean parted the loose lips to check the animal's teeth for an estimate of its age that he located what had robbed the bear of its health. A lower fang was sheered off close to the gum line, leaving an infected stump.

"Bit off more than you could chew, did you, big fellow?" Dean asked his sleeping patient. Now he could relax. The teeth and claws and muscle were immobile. "I wouldn't be in a very good mood, either. Steve, you got those antibiotics? I think it's time we turned dentist."

Removing the stump with improvised tools took fifteen minutes and left the two men limp from the exertion. Finally, Steve applied medication to halt the infection, patted the snoring bear on the nose and then rocked to his feet. "Not a bad job, if I do say so myself. Of course, if it was a grizzly—"

"If it was a grizzly, we'd still be working on that tooth," Dean admitted. "I had to remove one once a few months after college. Biggest damn thing I've ever seen. I had it made into a footstool."

Dean's joke was lost on Steve, who was closely gauging the bear's breathing rate. "I think nap time is coming to an end. What say we mosey on down the road? Do you want to reset the snare?"

"Not this one," Dean answered. "There's too much of our scent around. Besides, we'd better start back to camp. It's not going to be light much longer."

Actually there were still three hours of light left, but it took most of that time for the men to tramp through the thick stands of ponderosa that clung to the ridges on their way back to the camp, which was situated some twenty miles out of Bigfork. As they walked, Dean took note of the long lenticular clouds floating downward to touch the mountain tops. Storms, he knew, could come with amazing speed.

Dean's and Steve's pup tents were set up side by side between supporting evergreens near the base of a valley that served as one of the wilderness's many drainage areas. They'd left enough space in the small clearing for Calley Stewart's tent to be put up when she arrived. They'd managed to buck Dean's battered pickup within a hundred feet of the campsite, which was to their benefit considering the amount of equipment needed for the Flathead study.

Neither man had taken time to set up a campfire, because they were never in camp long enough to sit around a fire and because the forest was summer-dry. Working efficiently, they went about their tasks of starting the Coleman stove, bringing buckets of water from the shallow river branch running past their camp and opening packages of dried beef and mashed potato flakes and preparing a rare hot meal.

They ate with the quick efficiency of men who saw food as a means of fueling their bodies, washed their plates with water warmed by the Coleman, and then Steve announced that he was going to wash up before it got much cooler. "Save some of the warm water. I may shave."

"Shave?" Dean frowned and buried leathery fingers in his beard. "I heard of that once. I'll have to try it someday. Don't take too long, will you? If I don't get into some different clothes, I'm not going to be able to stand myself."

"Yeah," Steve said with a wink. "Besides, we're going to have a female joining us. You wouldn't want to chase her off on the first night."

Dean gave the Sioux a puzzled look, not catching Steve's meaning until the younger man was heading toward the river. That was right. The newest member of the project was a woman; that would change things. He was a little surprised that Steve had mentioned that fact. Even after all the time the two men had spent together, women seldom entered their conversation.

He didn't even know how old Calley Stewart was, although the date of her graduation from college gave him a clue that she was probably still in her twenties. His predecessor, Mike Bailey, was barely thirty. The two, Dean knew, had more than age in common. Not that it had anything to do with Calley's qualifications for the job. What people did in private was their own business to Dean's way of thinking.

"Damn!" Dean heard Steve shout from the river and guessed that the Indian had stepped naked into the water and was regretting his action. Dean smiled and slipped into his tent to retrieve his log. Steve should try dunking in an Alaskan stream if he wanted to experience cold. Dean wrote by the light of a lantern until Steve returned, dressed in faded but clean jeans and a cotton shirt that looked as if it had been at the bottom of his sleeping bag for a week.

"Your turn," Steve said conversationally. "It's good for the soul. Besides, I'm going to make you sleep in the woods if you don't start smelling a hell of a lot better in a hurry."

Dean figured it would probably be a toss-up which man would win a wrestling match over sleeping spots, but he had no objection to ridding himself of the day's exertions. Steve was the shorter of the two, but with shoulders that took an extra large shirt, the same size Dean wore. The Indian's thighs were probably larger, but Dean had calves that pressed against whatever pants he wore. They both had big hands, a trait Dean decided was as important in their work as the equipment he'd collected over the years.

Dean pushed through the lower branches of the evergreens that stood between him and the river, instinct and keen hearing telling him better than a flashlight where the gentle slope leading to the river began. When he could smell the water, he stopped, stripped off his clothes and then walked forward until biting cold reached his knees. He'd learned from Steve's outcry. He was going to take the river inches at a time, washing from the feet up.

Dean was shivering but clean by the time he emerged from the river with a slippery bar of soap trapped in his right hand. He dropped the soap close to the pile of clean clothes he'd brought with him and quickly pulled on shorts, jeans and socks. Because he was in a hurry to return to camp, he didn't bother with a shirt or boots. His soap was covered with pine needles, but he was able to rub most of them off with the flannel shirt he'd been wearing for two days.

He'd spotted the light coming from the lantern and was tenderfooting his way through the pine needles when he heard the rumble of a vehicle. The vehicle stopped where he knew his pickup was parked; the sound of two feminine voices cut through the darkness.

The higher voice he recognized as belonging to his assistant, Melinda Stone. The deeper, quieter one sent a sudden shaft of electricity up his naked spine. He had no understanding of his reaction, only that it was intense.

Dean thought about slipping his shirt over his shoulders, but he was burdened with dirty clothes and the bar of soap. Instead, he stepped into the flickering light with his boots tied over his shoulder and bouncing lightly against his naked chest.

Calley heard the approach of the man before she saw him. A newcomer to the forest would have heard nothing, but Calley had been trained out-of-doors. She knew which sounds went with her surroundings and which didn't. The muffled thump told her that the man wasn't wearing boots and that he was packing close to two hundred pounds on his frame.

He came into the circle of light afforded by the lantern hanging from a branch. Calley's first impression was that the man had spent so many years around grizzlies that he was starting to blend in with them and take on their traits. Melinda had been right about the beard and the hair. It was too dark to see if there really was gray in the mass covering his face but not so dark that she couldn't see his eyes glinting like polished stones.

She waited, her hands held easily at her side, letting him make the first move. It was probably the setting, the night, the whispering from the river that was doing this to her, but there was no ignoring the pull she felt traveling from him to her.

Calley shook off the sensation. She didn't try to deny its existence, only its influence over her. This was only a man, a hard, competent man coming out of the environment he'd settled for in life.

"Calley Stewart. It must be Wednesday," Dean said. His words slackened his spell over her and gave her the freedom to breathe again.

The forest, Calley knew, had a way of stripping away a sense of time. The usual landmarks were missing in the agelessness of the wilderness. When mist settled into the mountain valleys, dawn and dusk became the same. "We're late," she made herself say as she drew closer to the flickering lamplight. The man belonged here. Maybe more so than anyone she'd ever known. "I broke a fan belt. It's a wonder we didn't get swallowed up in some of those potholes. I swear they were three feet deep."

Dean didn't speak until he was close to the light, showing her that there was indeed a skift of tan in the black beard. "Did you get it fixed?"

"Yes," she answered simply. Talking shouldn't be so hard. She knew what words should be said; all she had to do was open her mouth and let them come out. "That's what happens when you grow up driving tractors. You learn to carry spare fan belts."

"I hope you're good with brakes; mine have about had it." Dean turned from Calley, freeing her from his gaze. "What are you doing here, Melinda?" he asked.

"It was a joint decision," Calley explained. "Melinda and I go back several years. I knew her when I was working before for the university. She's quite a photographer."

"So I understand." Dean's glance swung back toward Calley. His eyes were a deep blue with flecks of black in their center. At least that's how they looked by the lamplight. "And she's hoping to get some shots of grizzlies. What about that paperwork I left on my desk?"

Melinda spoke for herself. "Paperwork can wait; grizzlies won't. Some fool called yesterday asking about some pictures I'd taken of a bull elk. He wanted directions to the place before hunting season. I'm afraid I wasn't able to oblige."

Dean smiled. Melinda was right, Calley decided. His teeth were white, very white. "I just hope the two of you aren't going to be disappointed," he continued. "All we have to show for our time so far is a black with a bad tooth. The signs of grizzlies are here, but no sightings so far."

Melinda winked broadly, which allowed Calley to think about something other than white teeth and flecks of black in blue eyes. "Do you think we should tell them?" Melinda asked.

It took Calley a moment to catch on to what Melinda was getting at. "It's as my father used to say," she said, noticing that Dean was able to stand comfortably in his stocking feet despite the rocky ground. "We knew hunters who would crawl all over the country looking for mule deer while we had them in with the cattle herd. 'Don't have to look for them,' Dad would say. 'They're right under our noses.'"

At Dean's puzzled look, Calley quickly explained how they'd spent the early morning. "It's strange, isn't it," she mused aloud, hoping Dean would understand without much explaining. "Some grizzlies retreat when man pushes them. Others stand their ground. These three decided to stay where they were. I first heard about that grizzly crossing back when I was in high school. Some people tried to film a commercial there once. A few of my friends and I drove out there and told them about the bears. Those cameramen didn't stay long."

Dean nodded. "There's two other grizzlies who hang out there," he explained. "A mature male and a female who I figure is barren. They're kind of like the deer in your father's fields. Not quite wild."

Dean did understand. Calley wanted to say more, but all thought stopped at the sight of lamplight glinting off his naked chest. Dean was hardened in the manner of men who needed to be fit for the kind of work they did. Black hairs curled away from smooth skin stretched over muscles. Except for the scar running from his right armpit down his rib cage, he was perfection.

Calley was still looking at the scar when Dean dropped his pile of dirty clothing and slid a fresh shirt over his shoulders. He touched the hard ridge. "I lost that argument," he said simply.

"Grizzly?" Calley asked, the untold story chilling her.

"Grizzly."

Calley nodded but didn't speak. She didn't know Dean Ramsey well enough to ask him questions about a foot-long scar and memories that maybe still invaded his dreams. He might have been friendly enough a few minutes ago, but now something had risen between them, closing off communication. There was no way she could vault the barrier. She turned away from the light given off by the overhead lamp and started toward her jeep. "We'll get our things. I'm still not sure how we got everything in there. I figure Melinda and I can both fit in my tent."

Steve offered to help unload the jeep, and after Dean put on his boots, he joined in carrying the fresh food supplies to the campsite. Within a half hour the women were set up for the night, and Melinda was filling Dean in on correspondence from a couple of private wildlife preservation organizations that had arrived during his absence from the office. Steve was reading a letter that his parents had sent to him in care of the university. Calley slid her spine down along the evergreen supporting her tent, found a smooth seat on the ground and listened silently.

She'd been here, or near here, before. With Mike. It had been their job to study the habits and habitat of the grizzlies. She knew how to collect hair, blood, urine and small premolar tooth samples from the animals as well as how to take readings of blood pressure, pulse rate and body temperature. That part of the expedition she was prepared for.

In a way, it was good that Dean and Steve and Melinda were here. Last year it had been just she and Mike. The presence of more voices, more bodies, took away the rawest edge of that memory. She concentrated on the differences between her companions. Melinda bubbled over with enthusiasm for everything. When she was wrapped up in what she was saying, her voice threatened to disturb the wilderness silence. By contrast, Steve said more with his eyes and body movements than with words. Calley wondered if he'd been raised by parents who didn't have much need for conversation.

"I understand you've done some work in Yellowstone," Dean was saying. "Steve put in his time there, too."

Calley latched on to the lifeline Dean was unknowingly throwing to her. Maybe she'd only imagined the space he'd placed between them. Her voice was almost lost in the whispering wind sliding through the trees, but she couldn't help that. "Yellowstone was a one-shot thing," she explained. "Vegetation maps sent to earth from the Landsat III satellite showed an unusually rich growth of cow parsnips that spring. The biological technician at the park was concerned that the plants might draw more grizzlies than usual to the avalanche slopes. Mike Bailey and I went there as consultants. We made the decision to close the trails and campgrounds in the area."

"Small world, isn't it?" Dean said in a tone that, like hers, almost lost the struggle with the wind. "Mike and I did some graduate work together several years ago. Polar bears that time."

"You know Mike?"

"Who do you think told me about the research director's job?" Dean asked. "Mike and I go back a long way. After all, there aren't that many of us who make our living off bears. We have a way of bumping into each other."

It made sense. Just as it made sense for Melinda to reach out and touch Calley's hand in a strength-giving squeeze.

Chapter Two

By morning Calley had regained enough control over herself that she was able to look back at the previous night and admit there'd been a strange, wispy, fluttering line existing between reality and entrance into a world ruled only by emotions. She was also able to admit feeling that way around Dean Ramsey didn't make sense. He wasn't any different from the other men in her world—intelligent, competent, self-contained, hard-bodied.

"I went to Washington last year," Dean was saying as they were cleaning up after breakfast. His tone was friendly and yet reserved, as she would expect from someone she'd just met. "I had to testify at a hearing while Congress was trying to decide how much money to earmark for wildlife research. That was my fourth trip back there. Damnedest mess I ever saw."

"You don't like going to D.C.?" Calley asked. She sat down to wipe off the bottom of her socks as she reached for her boots. "I'd think it would be exciting to see how Congress works."

"That part was okay," Dean said with a shrug, "but most of what I saw was the airport, some taxies and a bunch of dark, smoky rooms. I didn't get to say half of what I wanted to about what we're trying to accomplish here. That bothered me. Besides that—" a faint smile touched his eyes "—I don't think half of those congressmen had any idea what points I was trying to get across. They're thousands of miles away from the grizzly's last toehold in America."

"They don't understand that grizzlies need their own space," Steve said as he emerged from his tent. "Them and some people."

At Steve's words Dean's smile grew. "They see deer and other wild animals adapting to the presence of man. They don't understand how it is for the grizzly. Tell me, Calley, how did you get interested in grizzly research? There aren't that many women doing this."

Calley finished lacing her boot and then wrapped her arms around her knees, hugging her legs close to her body. Her eyes never left Dean's as she spoke. "I touched on that a little last night. My father's a Montana rancher. I love this state as much as I could love anything. I'd probably be a rancher myself except I was more interested in wildlife than cattle." Her eyes softened. "Mule deer, wolves and coyotes were what fascinated me as a child. Although there were times when Dad could do without any of them, I guess—" Calley paused, thinking. "I realized there wasn't anything I wanted more than being out-of-doors. I wasn't too crazy about having to take science and biology courses, but I knew I wasn't going to get anywhere without a degree in wildlife management. Anyway, like most teenagers, I had some idea of what I wanted. I just wasn't aware of everything that was entailed. The rest I've learned through the school of hard knocks."

"And you wound up at the University of Montana. What did you do before you became involved in this project?"

Calley didn't know whether Dean was simply making conversation or if he really cared, but she had no objections to answering his questions. "The usual," she said with a laugh. "When I heard about the research that was going on with the grizzlies, I decided I wanted to do more with my education than telling tourists not to stick their hands outside a car when there's a bear around." She winked at Steve to show she shared his sentiments.

"You left the project for a year." Dean was ready to leave camp now, but he was making no move in that direction. Instead, he was focusing his entire concentration on Calley. "Why?"

It had to come down to this. Sooner or later they would have reached this point. Calley would have preferred to have more time to pull her thoughts and emotions together, but maybe that wouldn't help, either. "That's personal," she said, fighting to keep her tone even. For the first time since they started talking, she couldn't meet Dean's eyes. "I'm back. Can we leave it at that?"

"For now." Dean reached for his day pack, his eyes never leaving Calley's face.

What if I don't agree with that? Calley thought as she slipped her own pack over her shoulders. Certain things were no one else's business.

At Dean's suggestion Steve took Melinda with him to a vantage point overlooking a stretch of the Flathead where Dean and Steve had found grizzly sign last week. Melinda was weighed down with her camera equipment but so delighted to have the Indian serve as her guide that she insisted on carrying all the equipment herself. That left Calley and Dean to return to the snares the men had set earlier.

"I don't like using snares. I wish there was a better way of accomplishing this short of spending weeks stalking bears to get close enough to tranquilize them," Dean explained as he secured the opening to his tent. "I believe that a grizzly that has been touched by a human is somehow changed. But there are certain facts that can't be ascertained from looking at a bear through binoculars."

Calley didn't need to have Dean tell her what that was. She'd been working with Mike when the first stages of the study were being developed. The researchers were in the process of checking bears over a period of several years to determine how much the creatures ranged in their search for food. The question of when and under what conditions grizzlies retreated from human advancement could only be answered by fitting the bears with radio transmitters and tracking their movements.

"Have you fitted enough bears to have much of a sampling?" Calley asked as she fell in line behind Dean.

"Not really. That's why I'm out here for two weeks." Because the breeze was blowing from Calley to Dean, she had a hard time catching his words. "I had to postpone a graduate-level class I was teaching to finish the sampling, but hopefully I'll be bringing enough back to the students to make it worth the delay. So you're a rancher's daughter. Any brothers or sisters?"

Calley told Dean about an older sister now married and raising her own farmhands on the spread that had been in her husband's family for generations. She explained that she'd finally made her peace with her high-energy younger brother after years of having him trail along after her wherever she went. "For years my dad thought Jack would never get off a horse long enough to learn the ranching business, but it looks like he's going to take over the spread when Dad retires." It seemed like such a simple statement now. It was almost as if the months of living with uncertainty had never happened.

"Do you think you'll ever go back to ranching?"

"I haven't given it much thought," Calley admitted. "I love what I'm doing now."

"You left it once."

"We do what we have to," she answered, glad that she only had his back to look at. "Tell me something," she pushed back. "Is this what you want to do with your life?"

"Would I want to do anything except bear research?" Dean shrugged his broad shoulders but didn't stop walking. "Maybe. I thought about it, but I have to go with what feels right for me. I like what I'm doing, my life-style. I guess if the day comes when I don't like it anymore, I'll find something else."

Calley couldn't imagine that ever happening to Dean. Oh, yes, the time might come when the project was completed and the answers had been found for the grizzly. But there would always be something in the wild calling to the man walking ahead of her. "I don't think so," she said softly around the conviction she had about a man she barely knew. "They'll never bring you indoors."

"Maybe not." Dean paused long enough to turn around and look at Calley, but his expression told her nothing. "It's funny how some people instinctively know what's right for them. I grew up going on camping trips with my folks and Dad's brothers. We didn't have a ranch, but Dad did a lot of mountain climbing. He even led expeditions. That's when he was happiest. It made it possible for him to stick with earning a living instead of riding the rails. I guess it rubbed off on me."

"Do you still do any mountain climbing?" Calley asked. She liked the sound of his voice. That had to be why she wanted to keep him talking.

Dean had gone back to breaking trail. "No time right now," he said over his shoulder. "But maybe this fall. I'm thinking about tackling Glacier Peak in Washington state. I don't have the kind of responsibilities that keep most men at home. No personal commitments."

Calley wasn't sure. It might have simply been because the wind was part of the conversation, but she sensed that Dean didn't see his single status as being as positive as he was trying to paint it. She wondered, despite herself, if he was lonely.

"I've never tried mountain climbing," she said, "but I think I might like it."

"Give it a try. I think it's the biggest damn challenge a person can give himself."

"And you think challenges are necessary?"

"Don't you? Don't you want to know what you're made of?" Dean stopped and faced her. "You must, or you wouldn't be out here. We aren't doing this just so we can collect a paycheck."

"You're right about that," Calley said with a laugh. "I'm a lot like Steve, I guess. The paycheck is almost anticlimactic." It wasn't easy meeting Dean's eyes because of the intensity she saw in them, but Calley accepted the challenge. "I think that's why my dad stayed with ranching. It hadn't been easy, but it was the biggest damn challenge he could find."

"And studying grizzlies is yours?"

Dean wasn't going to let up. Calley sensed that he wanted, maybe needed, to learn all that he could about her and that he didn't much care how he went about gaining that knowledge. It could simply be because he'd hired her sight unseen and was making up for lost time. Calley didn't mind. Someday their survival might depend on how much they knew about each other. "I'm not sure whether stalking grizzlies is the most I could ever ask of myself," she explained. "There are other experiences that have required a lot of me emotionally. However, this is the biggest physical challenge."

Calley had no forewarning that Dean was going to touch her. It was a simple gesture, a gentle touch of his fingers against her temples as he brushed her long, softly waving hair away from her eyes. She forced herself to stand motionless as he secured an amber lock behind her ear, but that touch changed things between them.

When they started walking again, the distance between them wasn't as great as it had been before. Calley wanted to be closer to Dean. She didn't believe it had anything to do with physical attraction, even though she was aware of his masculinity. Rather, he was no longer someone she'd simply shaken hands with. They had shared something personal. He knew about her childhood; she knew of his love for mountain climbing.

She reached out and snipped a few pine needles off a tree as they passed under it. She brought the long needles close and drank in the strong scent of pitch. It was a scent with the power to reach deep into her subconscious and touch fibers of the past. It wasn't just the days that melted together in the forest; the years blended, as well.

Calley started telling Dean about the grizzlies she and Melinda had seen the day before. From there the conversation turned to the work Dean had done with polar bears, of winters in the far north and the pros and cons of different types of cold-weather clothing, subjects that gave Calley more than the weight of her day pack to think about. She fixed her gaze on Dean's back, concentrating on the deep sound of his voice, enjoying the enthusiasm he brought to everything he talked about. She barely knew the man, and yet she knew he was the right one to replace Mike on the project.

When they reached the area where Dean and Steve had set snares, they lapsed into silence. Calley walked with an eye to the ground in order to minimize any noise she might make. Her ears were alert to sounds that didn't blend in with the forest's melody. She acknowledged the prickling along her spine; they were in grizzly country, and Dean was depending on her to play her own role in this experience. She didn't dare think about anything else.

Slung across Dean's back was a tranquilizer rifle, but they had no other weapons. Calley knew that their quarry was the only creature in the forest that wouldn't automatically flee at the sight of a human. There was no reason why a grizzly should. The carnivores had no natural enemies. Calley's mother had never understood why her daughter was drawn to the danger-filled study of creatures with skulls so thick that high-powered rifle slugs ricocheted off them. Calley wasn't sure she understood it, either.

Dean stopped so abruptly that Calley nearly ran into him. Now his only signal was a sharp forward jerk of his head. Calley tensed, senses alert. Then she heard what had brought Dean to a halt. The distant roar was angry, puzzled, maybe even a little frightened. She didn't need to have Dean say it; they'd trapped a bear.

Dean led the way to the brush-filled area near the river he'd salted with spoiled meat the day before. From their vantage point a few feet above the spot they could see the imprisoned bear and the wreckage around it. Dean had been careful to cover the snare with branches from a fallen tree, but now the snare was visible, torn from its covering by the violent movements of a magnificent grizzly with the white-tipped hairs responsible for the creature's name. What shrubbery there was within the bear's grasp had been torn up by the roots; the carpeting of pine needles on the ground was scattered in all directions. The bear was flailing about like a child weary of the toys in its playpen.

"Too bad Melinda isn't here," Dean said over the bear's growls. "She could really get some great close-up shots."

Calley breathed in the scent of bear and forest, very much aware of how rare the sight below her was. She felt the hair on the back of her neck raise and tears well up in her eyes. Thousands of tourists could go through Yellowstone and not see what she was privileged to see. "A million years. They've been on earth for a million years," she whispered. "I wonder how much longer they'll be here."

Dean turned toward Calley, attracted by the note of awe in her voice. What he saw was a woman who would never be able to take for granted one of the great mysteries of life. Just because she'd already seen more bears than most people dream of didn't mean the experience no longer affected her. Dean hadn't often put that sense of wonder into words, but that, basically, was why he was doing what he was with his life.

Last night it had bothered him that Calley wasn't a physically powerful woman, but that was before he'd seen strength and commitment in her eyes. Waina was the only other woman he'd known with that look. But her commitment had been to something else.

The bear roared its defiance at the world and put an end to the silent communication between the man and woman. The grizzly had spotted the humans and was challenging them with an energy that couldn't be denied. Free, the bear would tear the humans apart. Dean pulled his rifle off his back and stepped closer. As he did so, he admitted to himself that he was taking unfair advantage; in an honest confrontation Dean would pay with his life.

Dean didn't put himself in position for a shot until he was certain that the leg hold was going to remain intact and give the drug time to take effect. He aimed at the bear's powerful shoulder hump and fired. The grizzly shook its massive body, tried to bite at the dart and then lifted its paw with its four-inch-long claws extended in Dean's direction.

Dean didn't want to face the bear. He wanted to avoid the eye contact that caused the memory of a slashing pain to eat away at his side; but the bear knew. Dean's vulnerability had been exposed.

A minute later the grizzly settled sluggishly on its side, eyes closed.

Dean reached the bear first. He stood over it, his muscles taut knots ready for futile flight. If the animal moved— No, the drug had done its job. Before Calley could guess at the struggle that was going on inside him, Dean sat on his haunches, watching the quiet animal, the persistent, if impossible, desire to ask the bruin to trust him waging a war with other emotions.

"It's a female with cubs," Calley pointed out. He nodded in agreement as she pushed away the thick matt of hair to reveal swollen breasts. When Calley's hand moved to the bear's small ear and scratched the animal gently and lovingly, Dean watched with wonder. She wasn't afraid; it was so simple for her. He both envied and hated her for that courage. She wasn't repulsed by the creature's pungent smell, the deadly claws, the fangs slipping through slack lips. To Calley Stewart this was simply the proud survivor of a world once teeming with saber-toothed tigers and mastodons.

"She's worth ten thousand dollars to a poacher," he said, trying to sort out his emotions.

"She's worth a hell of a lot more to her cubs." Calley lifted a huge limp paw in both her hands and rested the solid weight on her thighs as she knelt beside the animal. She spread the paw, running a finger over the worn granitelike nails. "Sometimes I think we have no right invading their privacy," she whispered. "We talk about needing to study them, but sometimes I wonder. I wish they could be left alone."

Dean's voice was just as soft, but he didn't seem able to make it stronger. The need to begrudge her her courage was already fading. She hadn't been through what he had; she could be forgiven. "I don't know if we can ever manage bears. Maybe we have to back off."

Calley's eyes left the unconscious bear and sought Dean's face. He felt the moment coming, but despite the danger inherent in the contact, it was too precious to avoid. When their eyes locked, he knew she felt it, too.

They were on the same wavelength. They were probably the only humans for miles around, and for this moment, at least, they were thinking as one. The knowledge rocked him and made it necessary for him to touch her again. He started by covering the hand that held the bear's paw with his own, but a minute later his fingers were traveling upward, touching a cheek that had been scratched and sunburned and attacked by insects and yet was still young and lovely. He'd made love to a model once, a beautiful creature with satin flesh and a flawless complexion who smelled as if she'd just stepped out of a lady's boudoir. This was better.

"We think alike," he managed to say.

"Maybe. Dean?" Calley was staring at him, trembling a little.

He was taking her places she wasn't ready to go, risking their fragile relationship. He could sense that. But her needs weren't the only ones being buffeted by the emotions of the moment. Dean Ramsey had needs of his own that had been buried in recent months. They were coming alive; he didn't know how to handle them. He'd been conscious of her femininity from the moment he met her, but this was the first time he'd allowed himself to acknowledge that.

"I'm not going to do anything you don't want me to," he said.

"I know."

But maybe she didn't. If he wanted to take advantage of the situation, there wouldn't be much Calley could do about it. He outweighed her by at least seventy-five pounds, and despite her having been conditioned by an outdoor life, his strength was more than it had to be if he wanted to overpower her. That was the last thing he wanted her to have to think about.

"I think we better check this old girl out before her kids start missing her," Dean said. He didn't know where the strength to say that came from. He removed his hand from her and reached for his day pack. His fingers still carried the message given off by her flesh.

Throughout the process of checking the grizzly's general health and clamping the radio-equipped collar securely around the animal's neck, Calley scrupulously maintained an outwardly professional demeanor toward Dean. Although there had been men since Mike in her life, none of those men had affected her in a deeply personal way.

Not until today. It would have been easier to tell herself that she hadn't expected the head of the project to break through the professionally prescribed barriers. She could have told herself that she was reading too much into a simple touch. But if she'd done either of those things, she would have been lying to herself. Dean Ramsey had touched her because there was something he wanted to share that couldn't be communicated with words.

Calley stopped her thoughts. She hadn't known Dean twenty-four hours yet.

She didn't try to speak until they were finished working over the inert grizzly. As Dean released its massive rear paw, she moved back, gathering up her pack and waiting for him to join her. She didn't need him to tell her that they had to leave quickly before an enraged bear regained consciousness.

"It was a healthy specimen," Dean said a few minutes later when they were once again back on the ridge overlooking the unconscious grizzly. "Steve's kind of bear. She'll be able to raise her cubs without any trouble."

"I wish we could have seen them. It's late enough in the year that they're out and about." Calley smiled at a memory. "Once, when I was in Yellowstone, I spent a whole day watching a couple of cubs fighting over a jacket they'd found. There wasn't enough left of that jacket to make a pile of lint by the time they were done, but they had a marvelous time. It wasn't until the bears left that I discovered it was my own coat."

"I don't like thinking about grizzlies becoming extinct in the United States," Dean said as they started retracing their steps. "Cubs should be able to grow up anywhere they want to."

Dean was doing it again, saying things, feeling things, that dovetailed with her emotions. "I really was lucky that time," she explained. "I'd gone camping by myself. I was taking a busman's holiday by spending my days off hiking the back country. I had no idea where the mother bear was." She shook her head. "It's a wonder I survived. Since then I've gotten a lot smarter about grizzlies."

"I'm not going to tell you how many times I've been treed by a bear," Dean said conversationally. "Some experts say to hightail it for the nearest tree. Others advocate standing one's ground, calling the bear's bluff. Frankly, my nervous system isn't made for that kind of a confrontation."

Calley acknowledged Dean's admission that he was human and not Daniel Boone reincarnated. "I have no qualms about admitting I'm very cautious around those creatures," she said, her ears tuned to any sounds behind them should the bear regain consciousness sooner than anticipated. "I'm not afraid, but anything that can cover a hundred feet in two seconds has my utmost respect."

Their conversation was general in nature for the rest of the time it took them to get back to camp. Melinda and Steve hadn't returned, but Melinda had left enough paperwork to keep Dean busy. Calley occupied herself by reading the daily log Dean had been keeping since taking over directorship of the project. Much of his writing was devoted to the logistics of fulfilling the requirements of the various state and federal funding bodies, but occasionally his personality shone through.

Calley particularly enjoyed his observations on the grizzly's diet. According to Dean, a bear was a far cry from a gourmet. "Their reputation as carnivores is vastly overrated," he wrote, "unless one counts mice, birds' eggs and insects. Their appetite for nuts, roots, grasses and of course berries is proof that bears will tackle anything edible in the never-ending attempt to pad their bodies with the necessary layers of fat. However, unless they have no other choice, they avoid true hunting and killing."

She was still reading when a squawk from the CB on Dean's pickup put an end to the comfortable silence. A few minutes later, Dean returned to fill her in on the conversation. According to the message relayed in from a park ranger, there was an injured black bear in Yellowstone who had so far been able to elude those trying to capture it. Would Dean, or anyone working for him, be willing to lend a hand?

"Damn. I really can't leave here," Dean groaned. "The park's shorthanded, or they wouldn't have gotten in touch with me."

"Can't you send Steve or me? We both know Yellowstone, and I've never been involved in helicopter transport. That's something I've always wanted to do," Calley pressed.

"I don't know my way around this part of the Flathead as well as you do. I don't know where the snares are. I wouldn't be much use left here on my own."

"I'm not going to leave you alone. Nor am I going to pull you off the project at this point," Dean said in a tone that effectively shut down any argument. "Maybe I'll send Steve. I'll see if I can talk him into going."

It was another hour before Steve and Melinda returned to camp. During that time Calley resigned herself to Dean's logic. Just because she was excited by the prospect of taking part in a rescue was no excuse for abandoning what she'd been hired to do. Maybe another time.

Melinda's disappointment at not having seen any grizzlies turned to anticipation at the prospect of accompanying either Dean or Steve into Yellowstone to attend to the injured bear the park staff was trying to save. "Please, Steve," she begged, "let me go with you. I'll stay out of the way."

As easily as that, the decision was made. Steve and Dean decided that capturing the bear wouldn't take both of them, and there was no need for Dean to abort his current study. "We'll leave as soon as it gets light," Steve announced. "But I hope to be back in a couple of days. All those people running around Yellowstone get to me."

"Yeah," Dean said with a chuckle. "They won't leave the place to you."

It wasn't until after dinner that Melinda drew Calley aside. On the pretext of wanting Calley to accompany her down to the river, Melinda waited until they were out of earshot and then put an arm around her friend's shoulders, looking closely at Calley's face. "Are you sure you don't mind being left alone with Dean?"

"Why should I?" Calley asked. "He won't make me carry both packs."

"That isn't what I'm talking about, and I think you know it. Besides, what you do is none of my business." Melinda screwed up her face to reinforce her words. "But, Cal, that man over there is special. When I told him I was thinking of getting married, we wound up talking for a couple of hours. He wanted to be sure I was going into it with my eyes open. He, well, he sounded like the voice of experience. He knows about a lot of the pitfalls of a relationship. He's intense. That's the best way I can put it, intense. I just want you to be aware of what you could be getting into."

"I'm not going to get into anything," Calley said. "I'm not sure I've put Mike to rest."

"That's why—maybe you'd like me to stay here," Melinda was offering.

"Thank you," Calley said with a laugh. "I appreciate it, really, but I don't want a keeper."

"He is special, isn't he?"

"Who?" Calley asked, although she knew where her friend's question was leading.

"Dean. He isn't one of those stuffy bureaucrats, and he isn't into grizzlies because he wants to make a name for himself. How much he cares comes through in everything he says and is. How can someone not be attracted to a man like that?"

"You make him sound like a saint," Calley pointed out. "I don't suppose you've noticed that he has big feet and probably wouldn't be allowed inside a barbershop."

"So you noticed his big feet. I don't suppose you've noticed his voice, too. Damn sexy, isn't it?"

Calley had noticed. "A low voice helps in the forest. Are you sure you don't have a crush on him yourself?"

Despite the dark, Calley could see Melinda's smile. "It's no crime. Yes, I have a man. Just the same, there's no harm in a little hero-worship, is there? I'm too old to moon after a rock star, and besides, Dean has more muscles and intelligence than those characters."

Calley laughed again, relieved to have the conversation take a light turn. "Like they say, he puts on his pants one leg at a time," she said as she started back toward the campsite. "I'm not as gullible as I once was," she said over her shoulder.

"Maybe," Melinda said from behind her. "Any maybe you're a lot more vulnerable."

Melinda was wrong. So much had happened in the past year. Mike was only a minor part of that.

Steve and Melinda left as soon as it was light the next morning. Calley was sorry to see them go, because she hadn't had time to get to know Steve, and having another woman around to talk to after the difficult year she'd been through was something she'd been enjoying. But there was enough for her and Dean to do to keep her busy.

As they were cleaning up after breakfast, Dean outlined what he wanted to accomplish for the day. In the rush to set up snares for the bears, neither he nor Steve had taken time to catalog the types and availability of vegetation. "It's not one of the most interesting aspects of the study," Dean admitted. "But if you're game, I'd like to get it out of the way."

Calley suggested that they split up in order to speed up the process. As she explained, she had considerable experience in identifying trees and plants and knew how to describe a region adequately for future reference. "Do you want to flip to see which of us takes which side of the river?" she asked.

"Not so fast." Dean stopped her. "You're not going anywhere until we've set up a communication system. I assume you know how to work a walkie-talkie."

Calley had no objection to what Dean was suggesting. Going out in bear country without a way of communicating was foolhardy. He stood close to her while she demonstrated her proficiency with the walkie-talkie. She was aware of his warmth radiating out toward her, his eyes on her hands, his breath disturbing the hairs along the side of her temple.

"You'll be careful?" Dean asked in the gentle tone Melinda had spoken about last night. "I want you back here before dark."

Calley looked up at him. "Yes, boss."

"I'm not your boss. At least I don't think of myself as anyone's boss. Just do what I say, please."

He wasn't giving orders or taking advantage of any male dominance. She was grateful for a man who allowed her the freedom to dictate her own life but at the same time asked that she be aware of his wishes and desires.

"I'll be back before you are. And I'll be careful if you are," she said.

Dean let her go then. He should be slipping into his own day pack and taking off toward the new growth a mile away, which was slowly hiding the scars of a small forest fire, but he wasn't. Instead, he stood watching Calley's retreating back until he could no longer see the easy sway of her hips, her long strides, the windblown hair trailing over her shoulders. He hadn't watched a woman's walk since Waina.

The two looked nothing alike. Whereas Waina boldly carried her dark heritage, Calley's color came from the elements. Her broad shoulders gave the illusion that there was more to the woman than there actually was. She was slim in the hips, with a waist he could encompass with his hands. Her breasts, he guessed, were small and soft. Her strong jaw and narrow nose gave her face definition. Softness and strong angles—he liked the way it all came together.

He should have asked Mike what Calley Stewart was like before luring her back to the project. Damn it, he should have his head examined for not thinking about what he might be getting himself into. But then Mike probably wouldn't have said much of a personal nature about the woman who'd once been his girlfriend.

That fact didn't bother Dean. He believed in giving others their personal space. What they'd done with their lives was their business. Maybe because he spent so much time alone, Dean enjoyed being given glimpses into the personal lives of the people he worked with, but he never made judgments about those lives. He'd learned from Mike that his old friend and Calley Stewart had been lovers.

That was all he knew.

Chapter Three

For the first hour on her own, Calley was occupied with getting a feel for her surroundings, but at length she found an excuse for getting in touch with Dean. She pressed the talk button on her walkie-talkie and waited for him to respond. "Do you hunt?" she asked as she tried to picture where he was and what he was doing.

"I haven't for years," Dean answered. Static caused by the distance separating them stripped his voice of much of its character. "I kind of lost my taste for it. Why?"

"Because I'm watching a magnificent four-point buck who's watching me," Calley explained as the large mule deer, some fifty yards away and higher up the mountain, lowered his head for a better view of her. Although she thought she knew what Dean's answer was going to be, even if it meant risking spooking the buck, it was nice hearing it from him. "He certainly is master of all he surveys. I think he knows it isn't hunting season."

"You be careful," Dean warned.

"Of what? A deer? I don't believe I live up to his standards. He doesn't seem to have any intention of adding me to his harem." Calley shifted her weight, careful not to bring her boots down on any dry twigs or needles. The buck was someone to share the day with; she didn't want to lose the sense of silent communication.

"You know what I'm talking about," Dean said in the same take-charge tone he'd used earlier today before sending her off. "It'd take me an hour to get to you if you got into trouble."

"Don't worry about me, Dean Ramsey," Calley replied with mock irritation. She was enjoying her encounter with the deer too much to be angry at anyone. Its large ears, which were responsible for the species' name, were dwarfed by the heavy, evenly forked antlers. The creature carried himself with a casual arrogance that stirred Calley's senses.

"We had deer everywhere on the farm," she went on, caught up in the mood created by the buck's presence. "They would eat the hay we set out for the cattle and then jump the fences, leaving the cattle wondering how they did it." She paused a minute as she collected her thoughts. "This is different. I always thought of the deer on the ranch as pets, or attractive nuisances. There were a few old does who practically ate out of my hand. This fellow—" She paused again. "This buck is special. He has to be pretty wise in the way of man, or he wouldn't have gotten to the size he is. He probably has his pick of the females. I'm glad you don't hunt."

Calley heard Dean draw in a long breath. "I'm glad I don't, either," he answered slowly. "I probably had buck fever as bad as any teenager, but then I killed one. I'll never forget those eyes. I don't think I could ever do it again. What's your friend doing now?"

Calley studied the buck for a moment. She wished Dean were here with her instead of on the other side of the river. She wanted to see the look in his eyes as he told her why he'd never hunt again. He would appreciate the buck's rich brownish-red coat, the dark nose and band around its muzzle, the white face and thick throat that told her he was in his prime and eager to prove the point to every doe in the mountains. Like her, Dean's eyes would be drawn to the heavy antlers topping off a two-hundred-pound body. "He's letting the rest of the world know he's king of the heap," she explained. "He has his head held high, and his tail is extended straight back. That's his way of telling any other bucks in the area that he's the big cheese and they'd better not mess with him."

There was static from Dean's end, but she could still make out his words. "You know a lot about deer."

"Of course I do," Calley said, interjecting an overdose of confidence into her voice. "This isn't just any old hick you hired off the streets, you know. When it comes to deer, I know my stuff. Do you want to learn more?" she asked, and then continued before he had a chance to comment. "Not many people know how to tell when a doe is ready to breed. It's all in her tail. If it's held stiffly out to one side, that means she's in heat and ready for service." It wasn't until she'd finished speaking that Calley realized what she'd said. Although it was a four-legged creature she was talking about, it was a rather intimate matter to be discussing with a disembodied voice.

"And where did you learn that?" Dean asked, his voice unmistakenly laced with humor.

"I just did. Don't make fun of me. Did you know that the smaller bucks tuck their tails between their legs when they come across a dominant buck?" Calley asked in an attempt to turn the conversation in a less sticky direction. "It's their sign that they know where they stand in the pecking order. They don't want the big guys taking them on."

"About this servicing business. Have you ever seen a buck and doe in action?" Despite the distance between them, there was no denying that Dean held the upper hand in the conversation.

Calley took a deep breath to give herself courage. "Once. At the ranch years ago. You're baiting me, aren't you?"

The walkie-talkie hissed again. "You have to admit you walked into that one. And I'm not baiting you, Calley. I really was curious."

"Don't you have anything better to do than waste my time?" Calley snapped in mock anger. "Besides, I think this buck is getting bored with me. I'm not going to make his harem this year. He's taking off." Calley lifted her hand in a salute to the buck's supremacy. He bore his solitude as easily as he bore the antlers he would be using in tests of strength during the autumn breeding season.

"In case you forgot, you're the one who started this conversation," Dean pointed out. "Any bear signs?"

Calley reported that although she'd spotted a few old bear droppings, she and the big buck seemed to have the area to themselves. She promised to be careful, listened as Dean told her about some beaver-stripped trees he'd come across and then agreed to meet back at camp in another three hours.

After mentioning a few nearby landmarks so Dean had a good idea of where she was, Calley replaced her walkie-talkie on her belt and continued her silent journey. She was hoping for another view of the buck; instead, in the space of an hour she spotted a doe with its half-grown fawn, put up with a general scolding from an evil-tempered jay and watched a buildup of clouds coming in from the north. By the time she'd made the decision to head back toward camp with the help of her compass, she was sure the clouds were more than an idle threat. She could actually smell the approaching rain.

Dean had reached camp before her. Calley stood on a ridge overlooking the camp for a few minutes, watching the man through her binoculars as he went about the business of preparing some kind of stew.

There was no wasted movement as Dean peeled potatoes and carrots and then buried the skins in the pit he and Steve had dug. Calley was fascinated by the comfortable way he squatted on his haunches over the blackened pot while stirring their dinner. She'd never been able to do that for more than a few minutes at a time because the position cut off the circulation in her lower legs, but Dean apparently found squatting as comfortable as sitting.

It reminded her of pictures she'd seen of Indians hunched over their cooking fires. Except for his full beard and modern dress she would have accepted Dean as a link with the prehistoric past. Although she wasn't close enough to be sure, she guessed that he was also testing the humidity of the heavy air, his ears tuned for her approach. Honing her senses was something Calley had learned to do as part of growing up responsible for creatures without the power of speech. Although not a product of farm life, obviously Dean had mastered the same skill.

It gave them something more in common, a way of communicating without having to put certain emotions into words. Understanding that made it easier for Calley to leave the shelter of the woods and walk into camp.

"You'll make some woman happy someday," Calley said as she stepped into the clearing. She nodded in the direction of the stew.

"That's what my mother told me," Dean said. He came to her and helped her out of her day pack, his hands on her shoulders impersonal and not possessive. "She couldn't believe the change in me when I took my folks camping a couple of years ago. For a kid who couldn't boil water, I've turned into a serviceable cook."

Calley didn't move away from the big man standing near her. He smelled of sweat and pine and wood smoke, smells that were buried deep in Calley's subconscious. "I'd call that more than serviceable," she said. "Dinner smells delicious."

"An old family recipe. The secret ingredient is an army-ration meat bar mixed in with the vegetables." Dean wasn't moving either. He wasn't touching her, but the inch separating them was more significant than if he had put his arms around her.

"I'll have to remember that," Calley said lamely. She could sense herself drawing closer to him.

"You hungry?" With a jerk Dean turned away, his whole focus now on the simmering stew.

Calley didn't need words to understand what he'd done. He'd sensed the pregnant moment just as she had. But now he was moving about, getting out their metal plates, unrolling squares of paper towelling to be used as napkins. Calley busied herself by putting away her walkie-talkie and exchanging her hiking boots for comfortable tennis shoes. She used a little of the warm water to splash away the tingling sensation on her face and washed her hands. She would have to put on cream soon to ease the sunburn on her cheeks, but Calley had had her flesh touched by the elements so many times that she was able to dismiss the discomfort for the time being. When she finally walked over to accept the steaming plate, she'd had time to remind herself that this was Dean Ramsey, director of the university-based grizzly project.

"Not bad," Calley admitted as she concentrated on her meal. Even now her voice sounded strangely disembodied. She wasn't sure if it was because she'd used her voice so little today. "I don't think any of the finer restaurants are going to steal your recipe, but it's a real treat after the granola bar I had for lunch."

"You know what that means, don't you?" Dean teased. "Dinner tomorrow is your department. You can cook, can't you?"

Calley glanced up at the now leaden sky. "If I do, it might be soup. Very watery soup." This wasn't so hard, she thought. She could carry on a decent conversation with Dean. "What if it rains tonight?"

"Then we get wet," Dean said with a shrug. Obviously physical comfort was a minor concern to him. He'd stripped off his flannel shirt and now wore only a T-shirt. Calley could make out the smooth interplay of muscle and bone as he moved his shoulders. "Our tents are waterproof. We might not be very comfortable, but we'll be dry."

Calley made a quick assessment of the situation. Dean's pup tent was barely large enough for him to sleep in, let alone move around in while the one she'd brought for her and Melinda's use was large enough to allow two people to sit in relative comfort. She mentioned that without first weighing the consequences. "I suggest we share mine if this storm lasts as long as I think it's going to. I've slept in enough pup tents to know they get cramped in a hurry."

Dean watched her longer and closer than she felt comfortable with. "Are you sure?"

Calley didn't have to be told what was on Dean's mind. The question might have dealt with two individuals sharing limited space while the elements held them prisoner, but she knew it went deeper than that. Something could happen between them tonight that would change what they were to each other.

But Calley knew herself better than that. She had enough years under her belt, enough experience, that she knew how to handle impulse. If nothing else, Calley was a self-controlled woman. "We're not a couple of teenagers," she pointed out. "I'm offering you use of my tent. It would be selfish of me not to."

Dean wasn't sure he believed her, but he didn't turn down the offer. It wasn't because he objected to waiting out a storm while lying on his back in a pup tent. He'd done that more than once. He agreed to sharing the larger tent because experiencing a storm together could turn into a rare opportunity to get to know this young woman better. It could also lead to talk about more personal matters.

It bothered Dean to know what he did about Calley and Mike. He didn't have all the facts. The woman might have had reasons other than a spoiled love affair for leaving the project, but if she'd run away from the responsibilities of her job because of a man, Dean wasn't sure he wanted her doing field work with him. That might be a hard-line approach, but Dean wasn't going to apologize for it. The job, their very lives, could depend on each other's commitment and stability. His co-workers had to be ruled by their heads and not their emotions. They had to have staying power. That was what he still needed to learn about Calley Stewart.

After dinner, Dean helped Calley put up the canvas covering on her jeep and secure her belongings. He brought some reading material from his tent to hers along with his sleeping bag. "Zane Grey," he admitted when Calley asked about the book. "I'm trying to make up for what there wasn't time for during my childhood. I was going to read Zane Grey then, but I always found something more interesting to do outside."

Calley showed him the book she'd tucked into a corner of her tent. The illustrated nonfiction was a series of diaries and letters written by pioneer women. "They wrote so simply," Calley explained. "Just a few words to describe a birth or death. And yet they were the right words. I really think the women in the covered wagons were shell-shocked. Can you imagine women today crossing the country on foot with babies in their arms, wondering if those babies would be alive by the time they reached their destination?"

"I can't imagine anyone doing that," Dean admitted. "We don't understand enough about what motivated the pioneers. I think I'm doing pretty well with this back-to-nature business, but I got here in a truck, sleep in a tent I bought at a sporting goods store and eat prepackaged foods. I'm hooked up to the rest of the world with a CB. I've seen the trail taken by miners during the Klondike gold rush. The Golden Stairs was a misnomer if I've ever heard one." He shook his head. "You're right. Our ancestors looked pretty brave in those old Western movies, but I don't believe that was how it was at all."

Calley liked hearing Dean admit that he was dependent on modern technology. Not every man would own up to that. True, she enjoyed watching him go about his work while she pretended that he was a mountain man or Indian, but he wasn't losing himself in a romantic image of what he was doing. "You like the idea of a medic pulling up in a four-wheel drive in case you break your leg, don't you?" she teased.

"I don't ask for that much. Some things I've had to learn to do on my own. I hate to tell you this but—" Dean lifted his head skyward. "It looks like we're in for it."

Calley and Dean were in for more than a rainstorm. Although their view of the sky was limited by the surrounding trees, enough of the powerful, sudden lightning lit up the sky to impress them both. Calley was aware that a forest fire could start as a result of the lightning unless it started raining soon, but worrying about that wouldn't erase the possibility.

Instead, she sat curled up near the opening to her tent and peered out at the jagged slashes of silver that transformed the sky into a thing of both potency and beauty. She slipped out of her tennis shoes and wriggled her toes in relief. She felt the vibrations from the thunder as it rocked the earth beneath her almost as clearly as she heard it shatter the forest stillness.

Even as a child, thunder and lightning had fascinated but not frightened Calley. It reminded her that there were still things left in the universe that were beyond the ability of man to harness. Maybe it was the electricity given off by the lightning; maybe it was the way her body accepted the shock waves from the thunder; at any rate, she was being filled with the force of nature's energy.

Calley leaned forward, sticking her head outside the tent, and accepted the first tentative splashes of rain on her uplifted face. Tonight was a segment cut away from the reality of life. The rest of the world couldn't touch her; she felt no loyalty or ties to that world.

"I take it this isn't your first storm," Dean said as drops became a downpour. His body was inclined toward her so he could be heard.

"Hardly. The cattle on the ranch would go crazy when it stormed like this." Calley closed her eyes, remembering. "I was so busy trying to contain them that there wasn't time to be afraid myself. I—" She laughed softly. "I used to get so wet that the water would pour out of my boots. I ruined more than one saddle because I'd be out in it for hours."

"Do you ever go back to the ranch these days?"

Calley opened her eyes. Already the ponderosas were shedding their wet load. The ground quickly absorbed what the trees couldn't hold. "I lived there for the past year. But it wasn't the same. Nothing was the same."

"Because you're not a child anymore?"

Calley appreciated the tenderness in Dean's voice. "Because my parents had changed. Or maybe I was seeing them through adult eyes for the first time. I'm sorry." She drew into herself. "I really don't want to talk about that."

As Dean slid closer to her at the tent opening, Calley turned toward him. Raindrops thudded angrily against their canvas roof, daring them to venture out. He'd put his wool shirt back on, but it hung open in front, which let her see the fine ridges of his ribs. He didn't jump when the thunder rolled; he accepted it in the same way she did. "It's awesome," she said during a break between thunderclaps. "I keep wishing I had a better way of describing a storm like this, but all I can think of is awesome."

"It's a statement of nature's dominance." Dean was looking at her and not the sky. "We'll never be able to control that. At least I hope to God we won't."

"Why wouldn't you want to harness this power?" Calley challenged. She was wise enough not to risk meeting Dean's eyes. Not many men felt comfortable enough about themselves to expose their most basic emotions. Dean was coming to that point; she didn't want to risk their losing that intimacy. "There's so much potential here."

"Because I believe there are some things that should remain greater than man." He was looking at Calley's hands as they rested on her knees. "I don't believe man was destined to rule his environment. We don't have the wisdom."

This time Calley risked a closer look at the man who was sharing nature's show with her. If anything, the sense that they stood apart from everything that could be called civilization was growing. They were on their own, cut off. Nothing existed beyond this spot in the forest. When lightning cut a swath of gold over Dean's face, she acknowledged the intelligence glimmering deep in his eyes. She might not know much about Dean Ramsey yet, but she felt united with him in their isolation.

When once again she looked at him, his eyes were watching her. "It might rain all night," he said, touching her hands.

"But not the thunder and lightning. That part of the storm is going to exhaust itself soon." Calley didn't have to say that another storm was coming to life inside the tent. His hands on hers were a simple gesture but one with limitless potential.

Dean turned Calley's hands over, examining them closely. "Your hands are what I expected," he said in a voice that reached her more as a vibration than as words. "They'd be softer if you had an indoor job."

Calley accepted what she knew to be a compliment. "My father has the most expressive hands I've ever seen on a human being," she explained. "They were made for a farmer. Big, with calluses that have been there for thirty years. He— he's fought so hard for that damn ranch."

Before she'd finished speaking, Dean had lifted her hands to his lips and was moving his mouth over her palms. She was aware of the contrast between his soft lips and thickened flesh at the base of her fingers. She wasn't sure having him touch her like this was safe, but she didn't pull away. "You have your father's hands," he said.

"Thank you," Calley whispered, touched by what he said. She leaned closer to Dean, accepting his slow, gentle exploration of her hands. Although she'd never had a man do that before, his lips on her palms felt as intimate as a lover's hands on her breasts. "Dad's stubborn, and he doesn't know how to let his emotions out, but I've always respected him."

"You fascinate me," Dean said.

"Why?" A spasm of emotion passed through Calley, but it was lost in the greater force of a thunderclap.

"I'm not sure." Dean met her eyes in honest confusion. "Part of it is, I guess, because you're doing things with your life that not many women would want to. Or at least they'd only daydream."

"And the rest of it?" Calley ventured. She realized that she'd been looking intently at Dean for close to a minute now, although she could see his face only when lightning flung away the forest-deep darkness.

"I'll tell you that when I understand it a little better myself."

When Dean dropped her hands, Calley again draped them over her knees. She was sitting cross-legged, her knee grazing the side of his thigh. "I saw a doe and her fawn today," she said after several minutes of silence. "The fawn still had spots. The doe was a little scared, but they were both fat and sleek."

"So was the raccoon I came across. I'm guessing he weighed over forty pounds. It's been a good summer for animals."

"It could also mean he's putting on a lot of fat for a long winter. A raccoon out in the daylight?" Calley questioned. "It must have known it was going to rain and there'd be no hunting tonight."

Dean frowned as if considering the possibility. "It could also be because I tripped over his log home, but he didn't stick around long enough for me to ask many questions."

Calley liked the direction the conversation had taken. She helped it continue in that vein. "Animal instinct is a lot better than ours."

"True." Dean laughed. "He knew enough not to hang around me."

Calley cocked her head, pretending to be pondering his last statement. "I hope he doesn't know something I should."

"You don't have to be afraid of me, Calley."

If she hadn't caught the somber note in his voice, Calley might have kept up the light conversation. But Dean, perhaps unwittingly, was telling her something about himself. Something precious. "I know that" was all she could manage to get out.

"I hope so." Calley thought Dean was going to touch her hands again, but he didn't. "I wasn't sure how you felt about being here alone with me."

"Dean?" She touched his cheek in an attempt to bridge whatever gap existed between them. "Out here we don't have any choice but to trust each other."

Dean covered her hand with his, pulling her toward him. The savage light show was cloaking his face with a vibrant mix of glitter and shadow. She wasn't ready to have the mood change so quickly, so radically, but when it did, she didn't try to fight.

Calley leaned forward to meet Dean's seeking mouth. The contact was awkward and not intimate enough to be very satisfying. But Calley knew that he could make her forget the strong gusts of wind that blew fat raindrops onto her face and hair. Dean's lips were more than soft, warm flesh. They were promise and hope and the capacity to kindle something. Calley was ready to explore what that something could be.

"That's not going to work," Dean said before gripping her shoulders and pulling her against him. "There," he whispered. Then, with the rain-laden wind blowing her hair back from her face, Calley surrendered herself to emotion. Tomorrow, in the sunlight, she would rediscover the woman she recognized.

Tonight she didn't care. Her outer thigh was touching Dean's but the contact went further than that. He wrapped a work-tempered arm around her shoulder and brought her against his warmth. Before he took her chin in his free hand and turned her face toward him, Calley reached out with her tongue, bringing into her mouth the taste of a wilderness storm.

The cool raindrops slid to the back of her throat as Calley closed her eyes, ready for the lips that would make her warm. Their kiss was what she expected and more. Despite the mountain-tempered hardness of the rest of his body, Dean's lips were incredibly silken. Or maybe they only seemed that way because Calley needed to be touched by something that would take her away from her surroundings. The storm exploded around them, shaking the ground with a force that caused the creatures of the forest to crouch low to the ground. But Calley barely noticed Nature's fury.

She was experiencing an explosion of her own, less fierce, perhaps, but just as consuming. The lightning cascading throughout the heavens seemed to be taking its cue from an electrical current that burst to life inside her. She could tell herself that she was sensitive to the storm raging around her. She could tell herself that the cramped quarters and the body next to her were responsible for this moment.

Calley did neither of those things. She was unaware of any impressions other than the desire to take what Dean Ramsey was offering her.

Although his kiss was gentle, Calley sensed that he was holding back with an effort. She was vaguely aware of the fat raindrops landing with loud splats on the canvas roof, but it wasn't until the sound escalated that she swam back to reality. Until the moment when the heavens burst forth with its promised burden, Calley was aware of nothing save what was happening to her. She felt as if she were two people, one a seasoned woman, the other a trusting child. There was no war with the two emotions; they were capable of existing side by side.

Calley moved her hands from their hold on Dean's shoulders and boldly explored the mass of curly hair covering his cheeks. It was a delight to bury her fingers in the thick tangles. *I could spend the rest of my life doing this,* she thought. The coarseness of his beard fascinated her because it reminded her, just a little, of the matt of fur covering a bruin.

Her thoughts were shoved aside by the power from above. As they'd been threatening to do for some time now, the potent raindrops transformed themselves into a driving force that pressed against the tent roof and, whipped on by the wind, slapped at the two sitting by the entrance.

Dean whispered, his mouth no more than an inch from hers. "We're going to get soaked."

I don't care. No, that wasn't right. She should care about such things. "The flap's still tied up. We can't get it down without having to go out into the rain," she said with what she hoped was a degree of intelligence.

Dean rocked to his knees, gripped Calley by her shoulders and started to pull her back toward the middle of the tent as if she were some lifeless bundle he didn't want to get wet. "Then I guess the only thing to do is get out of the way," he explained when she muttered a complaint at the way she was being handled. When another shaft of lightning lit up the tent, he spoke again. "Your hair is soaked. It looks like you have diamonds in it."

Calley positioned herself so that she was sitting on her sleeping bag and waited for Dean to join her on the narrow cushion. She was glad he hadn't tried to close the tent flap. Despite the cold, she didn't want to be cut off from the storm. "I'd like to have diamonds in my hair sometime."

"Would you, really?"

"Of course not," she said with a laugh. "I'd much rather have raindrops." She was thinking a little more clearly now that he wasn't touching her, but she still couldn't remember anything of the past or think forward to the future. This moment was all that existed.

Dean's voice dropped to a whisper. Calley could barely hear him over the sound of rain beating down around them. "You don't have a lot of daydreams, do you? You're content with reality."

Calley wanted to take the words and wrap them around her heart, but the emotion died before it could blossom. Answering him would have to wait until she knew him better. "I'm glad it's dark," she said instead. "I'd never win a beauty contest."

Gently, reverently even, Dean brushed her hair back from her wet cheeks. Calley felt herself moving with the gesture, drawing closer to him. She was starting to shiver but wasn't sure whether the storm outside was responsible for what she was feeling. "I'm not interested in beauty contests," she heard him say before she surrendered to what he was offering her.

This time it was no chaste first kiss. Dean slid around until they were sitting side by side and then turned toward her, wrapping his arms boldly around her. She didn't protest when he stretched her out on the sleeping bag and leaned over her, sealing their lips together. This time his mouth was open.

Calley felt his fingers lace their way through the hair along her temples, touching her pulse before securing a thick lock. She sensed a moan growing deep inside her and stopped it only with a supreme effort. If she touched him at all, she should have confined herself to wrapping her hands around his neck. Instead, she reached for his waist and burrowed past his shirt until her fingers were over the ribs that were separated from her only by a thin layer of cotton.

His flesh was warm, softer, she knew, than the skin exposed to the elements. She heard his quick intake of breath and took that as her warning. He was defining the limits of their exploration. Maybe, if the storm hadn't taken over every other sound, she might have been able to remain in contact with some element of reality. But there was nothing but pounding rain, thunder shuddering through the forest, occasional flashes of light invading the space behind her closed eyes. Even the tent and sleeping bag ceased to have any meaning. Only one other emotion reached her.

"I'm freezing," she said simply.

She might be too cold to react to him in any other fashion than for warmth, but Dean wasn't so protected from the other sensations his body was capable of. He felt her hardened nipples against his chest, her cold toes curling around his ankles, and turned his head away from her so he could concentrate on bringing cool air into his lungs.

Dean lifted himself up on one elbow and again brushed the hair back from Calley's temples. She was gazing at him through half-opened eyes, but he wasn't sure she was seeing him at all. He could believe that she was lost somewhere deep in her own thoughts, perhaps trying to pull herself together, just as he was trying to comprehend his own emotions. He couldn't remember stretching her out on the sleeping bag.

Chapter Four

Like tiny blips on a blank screen, Calley slowly became conscious that something was replacing the peace that existed within the tent. For another minute she struggled to stay within the cocoon of sleep, but there was no wishing away the persistent staccato sounds.

She opened her eyes and lifted her head until her sleeping bag was no longer over her ear, but she didn't ease herself out of bed until she was sure that the sound was coming from Dean and not from some nameless and potentially dangerous source outside the tent. On hands and knees she crept the few feet that separated her from Dean and rocked back on her heels. He was in the depths of a dream.

It wasn't a pleasant dream. The way his breath came out in blasts, the quick, hard movements of his body within the sleeping bag, told her that. He was in some kind of emotional pain, that much was clear. Calley wanted to wake him in an attempt to bring him back to reality, but wasn't sure that was the right thing to do. A sudden intrusion from the outside world might be too much of an assault on his nervous system.

Maybe the dream wouldn't last long. Calley repositioned herself until she was sitting cross-legged beside him, waiting out the inner storm. She supposed she could shake him if the dream became a full-blown nightmare, but a man Dean's age had to have his own ways of dealing with whatever it was that tormented his subconscious.

The storm around the Flathead had become a steady downpour, but without the earlier wind that threatened to cave in the sides of the tent. Shivering slightly, Calley closed her eyes and wrapped her hands around her upper arms. Sleep pulled at her, erasing the edges of reality. She was a child again, sleeping in the upstairs bedroom of the family ranch house. Her world was secure and serene. In the morning she would scurry down the stairs to the warm living room to dress in front of the fireplace. Her mother would have breakfast waiting, French toast and hot chocolate. She would slip her hands into knitted mittens, wait for her mother to button her coat high around her neck and trot out with her brothers to the lean-to that served as a bus stop. At school she would huddle with her girlfriends, talking about horses and boys or their favorite country and western songs.

That seemed as if it were a thousand years ago. She quickly straightened and leaned forward. Dean was breathing deeply now, his chest moving with a slow pace that fascinated her. Once again she fought off the urge to touch him and instead crawled back into her warm sleeping bag. How like a child he was in sleep, she thought as her head sought a soft spot on her pillow. So many responsibilities settled on him during the day, but secure in the shelter of a tent in the middle of a forest, he was able to cast off those duties. And sleep.

Or could he? Calley was dozing off when Dean let out a sharp hiss of breath that gripped her nerves. "No. No!" Groaning, he jerked around until he was on his back, arms thrust outside the sleeping bag.

Calley sat up again, but this time she didn't get out of bed. Yes, they'd shared a wilderness storm. Yes, they'd shared a kiss. But nightmares were private things. "It's all right, Dean. It's only a dream," she whispered, hoping that at least the essence of what she was saying would reach his subconscious. "Sleep. We'll talk about it in the morning."

Dean groaned again; his hands gripped the sleeping bag. Although the tent was night black, she could reach out and feel the tension in his body. His head rolled back and forth rapidly; short, wordless sounds filled the air. This was no dream of monsters and ghosts. This was something Dean was living or had lived.

"Please sleep," Calley repeated. Her voice was a little stronger this time. She had to break through whatever terror gripped Dean. "It's all right. I'm here. It's all right."

He sighed; Calley felt the strain leave him. "Sleep," she repeated. "We'll talk about it in the morning."

But they didn't. Calley rose when the newborn sun was just fighting its way over the horizon, and she dressed before turning on the Coleman stove to fix their breakfast. Although it was chilly, there wasn't any dry wood for making a fire. To compensate, Calley started heating water and did jumping exercises while wearing her jacket. She was mixing instant coffee into a mug of steaming water when Dean emerged from the tent.

"Ah, the little woman's being domestic."

Scowling, Calley turned on him. She was ready to give him a piece of her mind when she noticed that the corner of his mouth was twitching. "That's as far as my domestic talent goes," she said as she brought the cup to her lips. "If you want coffee, you're on your own."

"That's the trouble with women these days." Dean sat on a stump so he could pull on his boots. He was already wearing jeans and a flannel shirt. "They don't know their place."

"You're in a fine mood." Calley had located Dean's cup, and despite her threat, was measuring out coffee for him. "Do you always start the day by reminding your assistants of their place?"

"When it's necessary." Dean reached up for the cup as Calley handed it to him. "How did you sleep? Were you warm enough?"

"Fine. I paid through the nose for my down sleeping bag, but it's worth it." Calley turned back to the stove to stir the hot cereal that would constitute their breakfast. "You had a nightmare." She waited, wishing she could see the expression on his face but guessing that he needed privacy.

"What about?"

"How should I know?" She laughed. "It was your nightmare."

"Did I say anything?"

Calley thought for a moment. "You said no a couple of times, but that's about it." She put down her stirring spoon and turned around slowly enough that she hoped he wouldn't feel he had to have his defenses up. "Do you remember anything about it?"

Dean's brow furrowed. "No. How much longer until breakfast?"

He does, too, remember. He just doesn't want to talk about it. "About five minutes. Why? Did you have to do something?"

Dean mumbled about having to clean his binoculars and disappeared into his tent while Calley went about selecting bowls for their meal. Dry milk mixed with river water wasn't quite the same as fresh, but it would do. Besides, breakfast wasn't what was on her mind.

"About last night," she started when Dean rejoined her. "I don't—"

"I don't know either. I didn't know I was going to do that."

Calley realized that they were talking about a kiss, not a nightmare. Calley shrugged. "It was the storm. A little too much electricity in the air."

Dean waited until Calley handed him his cereal. "Do you really believe that?"

"I think that's what we better believe, Dean," Calley said with the strength that had escaped her last night. "I'm sorry."

"You're sorry it happened?"

Was he? "I don't make a habit of kissing men I've just met. Especially men who happen to be my boss." She concentrated on her cereal, wishing there was somewhere else for her to sit except on the same fallen log with him.

"Mike was your boss."

Calley flinched. She was afraid to ask how much Dean knew of her romance with the man who preceded him at the project. "That was uncalled for." Her words were clipped, her body stiff.

"Maybe and maybe not." Dean was looking at her and not at his breakfast. "Look, Calley, we're going to be spending a lot of time in each other's presence. We can either spend it tiptoeing around each other, or we can start with honesty and let it go from there."

Calley didn't want to tiptoe around Dean; but neither was she ready to lay her heart out in front of him. She shouldn't have given in to her need to feel his lips on hers last night. Their relationship was progressing much faster than either of them was ready for. "So you want honesty, do you?" she asked. "Why don't you start by telling me what your nightmare was about?"

"I told you. I don't remember."

"And I'm telling you I don't believe you. I'm sorry," Calley relented. "I didn't handle that very well, did I? It's just that my relationship with Mike was rather—complicated. When—" She paused, sensing the web of the past that threatened to engulf her. "When you sprang his name on me, it took me by surprise."

"I shouldn't have." Dean hadn't finished his cereal, but he rose and walked over to the small table holding the Coleman stove. "I think it's an occupational hazard. I spend so much of my time alone that my social skills aren't what they should be. You're right. Your personal life is none of my business unless you care to make it so. What if we start over? You tell me a little about yourself, and I'll do the same. Neither of us will draw any conclusions or make any judgments."

Calley wanted to tell Dean that the moments they'd spent in each other's arms last night made starting over impossible, but things had happened too fast. They had to slow down, redefine their relationship. "Do you want a blow-by-blow from the day one?" she asked. "I was born on a cold wintry morning with a foot of new snow, making the race with the stork a lot more nerve-racking than it should have been."

"Who won?"

"Who won what?"

"The race." Dean shook his head. "You or the stork?"

Calley laughed. "That's not how it goes. The stork and the baby are supposed to get there at the same time. For the record, Mom had been logged in at the hospital for twenty-three minutes when I made my appearance."

Two days later Calley had told Dean everything there was to tell about growing up on a ranch; he'd responded with a lengthy account of his own rural existence, interrupted only during his college years. In that time they'd covered dozens of miles, identified every life-form in that area of the river and exhausted all possibility for variety in their diets.

And yet, because Dean was once again sleeping in his own tent, Calley knew their relationship had been put on hold through mutual agreement. Dean hadn't touched her in a personal way since the night of the storm. And she hadn't given him any indication that she wanted him to.

"I really do envy you. I've always wanted to go to Alaska," Calley told him as they were relaxing at the end of the day. "I almost made it two years ago with a group of biologists, but the trip to Sitka National Historical Park fell through at the last moment when the plane we were going to use developed some major engine problems. We searched everywhere for a replacement, but most of the available planes weren't big enough for all of us. I was terribly disappointed."

"Maybe you'll make it one day," Dean reassured her. He'd removed his hiking boots and, like her, was walking around in comfortable tennis shoes. "It really is the opportunity of a lifetime if it's done right. But don't go to the cities. They don't tell you anything about the state."

"That's what I've decided. If I ever get there, I'd love to get off the beaten track. What would you suggest?" Calley was sitting with the daily log open on her lap, but she was watching Dean wrap dough around green switches for snake bread. "Keep in mind that my finances are limited and I might not have much time for a trip."

"Flying's the only way to go." Dean squeezed the dough firmly around the switches he'd cut a few minutes earlier and then held them over the small campfire they felt safe having now that the rain had lessened the fire danger. "But if I were you, I wouldn't spend a lot of time at any of the national parks."

"Why not?" Calley knew she should be helping with dinner, but she'd been on her feet for the past twelve hours. Heat from the fire was warming her hands and face, seeping into her bones. "There's nothing wrong with a busman's holiday. I'd love to talk to the biologists there and explore the parks—compare what they're doing there with what's being practiced at Yellowstone. I'd probably go through a dozen rolls of film."

"Save your film for some of the native communities." Dean stuck the ends of the switches in the ground near the campfire before coming to sit next to Calley. Like her, he was using an evergreen as a backrest. "That's where you'll get a real sense of what Alaska is like," he went on. His voice took on a retrospective tone. "Angoon, Kake, Klawock—those are some of the communities that still cling to the traditional ways. If you go there, you'll understand why the Indians have clans named Raven, Dog, Salmon, Eagle, Bear. The seasons control their lives. In the spring the herring come to spawn, and the natives put an end to the long winter. They fish for halibut and salmon during the summer and spend fall preparing food for winter."

"What do they do in winter?" Calley closed her eyes and leaned her head against the back of the tree. They weren't in a remote Alaskan village, but she could understand what Dean said about seasons and elements controlling the ebb and flow of one's life. "That's the part I don't think I could handle," she admitted. "The sun doesn't even rise over the horizon."

"That's hard for a lot of people." His words came to her as a disembodied rumble. "But I don't think it's like that for those who cling to the old ways. They're used to it. The art of the natives reflects their reverence for tradition. That's what winter is for. They still make ceremonial costumes and their own clothing. There are isolated places you can go to watch Tlingit and Haida craftsmen working in wool, wood and silver. What impressed me the most is that this is still their way of life. They're not making trinkets to sell to the tourists. They guard their privacy; it isn't easy to be accepted enough to be given a glimpse of their culture. A Haida woman made me a silver bracelet with her clan emblem on it. It's something I cherish. I'd like to show it to you sometime."

"I'd like that," Calley said dreamily. "Have you been to all those villages you mentioned?"

"Yes." Dean got up to turn the slowly baking bread before continuing. "But the most haunting experience wasn't at any of those communities."

Calley opened her eyes. Dean was standing over her, the darkening forest giving her nothing to focus on except him. She waited, knowing he'd continue when he was ready.

"The woman I told you about. The one from the Haida tribe. She took me to Cape Muzon, which is on Dall Island. She wanted to show me what remained of Kaigani, a Haida settlement that had been deserted over fifty years ago. Nothing remained except a few hand-hewn timbers that had been the corner posts for houses. I still don't understand why the Haida people had lived there in the first place. It was so remote, the elements so cruel. I could hear the tide, but the silence was so eerie that I felt as if I was at a shrine." Dean actually shuddered.

"Oh, Dean," Calley breathed. Dean's description charged her with instant restlessness. "What an experience! You're right. That's what I should try to see."

"That isn't all." Dean sat down again. He reached for Calley's hand and laid it on his flexed knee. She wondered if he was aware of what he was doing or whether he somehow needed to make contact without knowing it. "While we were there, I found a human skull. Why was it there? Why had it been left behind? Whose was it? I wanted to learn the story of that man or woman. Learn what that person's life had been like."

"Dean," Calley breathed again. She felt so close to him that the emotion frightened her. "That was someone who probably lived the way his ancestors had for thousands of years. He could have told you so much."

Dean sighed. "I left the skull there. That's where it belonged."

For a minute there was no need to say anything. Calley's thoughts were on a man who could look at what remained of a human being and see not something to avoid but a timeless reminder of a way of life that no longer existed. It moved her to realize that Dean had that kind of perception, to know that she was capable of the same kind of thinking. "I wonder if it's still there," she said softly.

"Why?"

"Because I think I'd like to go there someday. There wasn't anyone else there?"

"Just me and Waina."

It was in the way Dean said the name. Waina was more than simply Dean's guide and a woman who made native jewelry. Calley got to her feet and tried to warm her hands over the fire. A minute later she turned her back to it and looked down at Dean. The man had experienced so many things, had been touched by so many emotions. He was sitting in the forest with her, but he was a product of everything he'd done and seen before they met. Just as she was. It seemed both incredible and very right that their paths should be crossing in this way. "I was thinking—" Calley started slowly. "I was thinking about everything that happens to people in the course of a life. A mother holds her baby and thinks of everything she wants for that child, but so much happens without anyone planning it."

Dean was staring up at her. "Such as?"

"Oh, I don't know, really." Calley shrugged. "I mean, when you were five, could anyone look at you and say you were going to spend your life trying to save grizzly bears or walk through a deserted Indian village in Alaska?"

"Probably not," Dean said softly. "I don't imagine your parents had any inkling that you'd be out here, either."

Calley laughed. In her mind's eye was the picture of a small child skipping beside her father as he walked from the house to the barn before dawn on Thanksgiving day. In the house her mother and grandmother and two aunts were stuffing the turkey and baking pies, but even at that age Calley would rather be outside helping her father feed cattle than watching the activities in the kitchen. "Oh, I think my father had a pretty good idea that they'd never turn me into a farm wife."

"What about another kind of wife?"

Even though it was personal, Calley didn't shy away from Dean's question. He never pushed her further or faster than she wanted to go when it came to opening up about herself. As a consequence, she knew she could speak around him and not wind up revealing more than she had intended to. "That hasn't happened yet. Maybe someday."

"It'll happen, Calley. You're a beautiful young woman."

Calley had been called beautiful before, but the word had never taken on that special meaning. "It's strange, isn't it," she said softly. "Even with women's lib, a woman's chances on the marriage market are still tied to her looks."

"Did I say something wrong?"

"No." Calley sat back down beside Dean. She felt philosophical and hoped he wouldn't mind her mood. "You didn't say anything wrong. I was just making an observation on our society. A woman has to be attractive, and a man has to have money before they can call the shots. Or at least that's the message we're given. I just wish—I guess I wish we weren't so obsessed with the externals or material wealth."

"More like the Eskimos. Women with strong teeth for chewing hide were the prized ones."

Calley laughed and bared her teeth. "Given that criteria, I should have a half-dozen whale hunters vying for my hand. No cavities."

Dean took her hand for the second time since they'd come into camp. "You'll get married when you're ready to, Calley. You don't need to be Mrs. anyone to give your life definition. You're capable of doing that on your own."

"Thank you." Calley rested her head on Dean's shoulder. She could smell baking bread and wood smoke and pine. She could tell Dean that she appreciated his vote of confidence. "I think I got that from my father. He shaped me in so many ways. He always told me I could be whoever and whatever I wanted. He said the only limits were the ones I placed on myself."

"Your father's a wise man." Dean turned his head so that his lips were touching her hair. "I'd like to meet him someday."

"He'd like you."

Calley hadn't changed her mind by the next morning. They'd spent the most relaxed evening since they'd met talking about everything and nothing, working in tandem to fix the rest of dinner and prepare for the next day's activities. Although once again Dean spent the night in his own tent, Calley didn't feel as if he'd left her. He'd awakened her once during the night with another nightmare, but by now Calley understood that it was one part of himself he wasn't ready to share with her.

Today they were traveling together. Yesterday they'd come across fresh bear droppings and had hopes that this bear wasn't the same one they'd tranquilized. An hour out of camp, Dean touched Calley's shoulder and cocked his head at an eagle perched high overhead. Although she couldn't see them, Calley could hear smaller birds calling a warning to each other. "It sounds like a zoo around here," Calley said. "I love watching when the smaller birds gang up on one of the big ones. If there's enough of them, they can get an eagle on the run. I talked to a hunting guide once. He agreed that the woods feel different when there's a bear in it."

"Nothing else moves."

Calley acknowledged a shiver running down her spine. It wasn't that she was afraid; rather, something in Dean's tone had touched deep running nerves. "The forest is silent," she continued. "There's a sense. A presence."

"There is for those who know how to listen to it," Dean said as they started moving again. "Too many people go into the woods with no idea what they're doing."

"That's when Search and Rescue gets called into service." Calley laughed before telling Dean about a group of Boy Scouts who'd become lost on the fringes of her parent's ranch. It took two dozen volunteers and a helicopter to locate the boys and their embarrassed scoutmaster huddled in a cabin used by ranchers during roundups. "They could have followed one of the fence lines for a couple of miles to a telephone, but one of the boys had broken his leg, and the scoutmaster was afraid to leave him alone with the other kids long enough to go for help. That little outing of theirs wound up costing thousands. I don't know who paid the bill for that one."

"Sometimes it can't be helped. There are times when the best woodsman needs help."

Wild and Free

"I know that," Calley said seriously. "I'm just saying that this poor guy had almost no survival training. They're just lucky they weren't far from civilization."

Dean acknowledged her logic with a grunt but didn't pick up the threads of the conversation. Calley guessed that he was lost in thoughts of his own. She didn't attempt to break through those thoughts with unnecessary conversation. A few minutes later they topped a rise and reached for their binoculars. Ahead of them stretched several miles of high valley land. Only a few snags from an old forest fire remained of what had once been a lush timber stand, but already new growth carpeted the ground. Calley was pleased to see a large number of seedlings reaching for sunlight.

Through the powerful binoculars Calley made out a couple of grazing deer and a movement close to the ground that was probably some kind of rodent. When Dean pointed at a spot to her left about a half mile away, Calley zeroed in on the unmistakable shape of a lean, long-limbed coyote.

"I don't think she's alone," Calley whispered a minute later. "Look behind her in the bushes."

Dean grunted. "Pups. I can't tell if she has two or three."

"Three. They look about half grown. Dean, take a close look at them. I don't think the pups are full-blooded."

"You're right." Dean inched closer to Calley, his voice low. "They're darker than the female, and their hind quarters are too solid to be pure wolf."

It was Calley's turn to grunt. "Something tells me a dog got to her. What do you think? German shepherd?"

"Probably," Dean observed. "I was just thinking it's a good thing the dog was the male. Can you imagine what the owner's reaction would have been if his bitch had given birth to a litter of half coyotes?"

Calley shared an amused glance with Dean. "That happened more than once when I was growing up. Of course, as kids we thought it was pretty neat to have a half coyote for a pet. One of our dogs even had a litter that looked suspiciously wolflike. The pups were pretty aggressive."

"What happened to them?" Dean asked.

Calley shrugged her shoulders. "That was one of those things my father never talked about. One day the pups were around, and the next they'd disappeared."

"So much for the romance of farm life." When their eyes touched this time, they stayed locked. "Farm kids grow up fast, don't they."

Calley continued to look deep into Dean's eyes. When she was little, death on a ranch upset her, but as she grew older, she came to understand and accept what had to be. "In the ways that count, I think they do," she said softly. "We might not know about the fads that consume city kids, but I think we grow up with a better understanding of life's greater plan. I admit I floundered for a while when I was at college. I had no idea that most of my classmates viewed college as a place to come for parties, dates, that sort of thing. Oh, yes, I did some of that, but it really didn't interest me. I guess—" Calley smiled. "I guess I escaped the early indoctrination they went through. I was too set in my ways when the temptation came."

"I'm glad you were." Dean forced himself to concentrate on the view through his binoculars, but his mind stayed with the young woman kneeling beside him. There was nothing artificial about Calley. No part of her that would choose a comfortable city existence over what she was doing now. She was, he knew, a great deal like Waina. And yet she wasn't.

"Dean!" Calley hissed. "Look at the coyote. She's stalking the deer, isn't she?"

"She's giving it a shot." Without giving himself time to think about it, Dean slid his arm around Calley's shoulder.

If they were going to see one of nature's harshest lessons, he wanted to give her something of himself to fall back on. He didn't care that she'd seen her share of deaths on the ranch. He didn't care that she didn't need him protecting her. "There must be a fawn somewhere," he whispered against her hair. "No coyote's going to take on a healthy full-grown deer."

"Scavengers. Opportunists." Calley's whisper seemed muffled. It wasn't until Dean tore his gaze from the coyote's slow glide through the brush that he realized Calley had rested her head on his shoulder. But she wasn't burying her face in his neck. She was watching the drama taking place below them.

"That sounds like a rancher's daughter," Dean said with what self-control remained. He should have learned his lesson the night of the storm. Touching Calley wasn't a wise thing to do.

"I don't hate them. They have their place in nature's plan. Dean, I think the big doe there has spotted the coyote."

Dean agreed. The doe had been feeding a few minutes ago, but now her head was up, legs spread. Her tail twitched an alarm, but she didn't back off as the determined coyote inched closer. Only one thing would keep the doe from taking flight to save her life. "Where's the fawn?"

Calley shrugged but didn't answer. As long as the fawn remained motionless, even the most powerful binoculars wouldn't locate the well-camouflaged youngster. "That's a big doe," Calley whispered instead. "Did you see the scars on her? She's been through her share of battles."

Damn! Dean didn't want Calley to see death today. But she wouldn't be out here if she needed protection from such things. "The fawn must be pretty young, or maybe it's injured," Dean speculated. "I don't know why it isn't up and running."

It didn't have to. In the end it was the doe who put an end to the distant drama. As Dean and Calley watched, the coyote continued its slow glide through the brush. Occasionally it turned its head toward the doe, but it was clear that its destination was a clump of tall grasses close to where the doe had been feeding. The doe lowered her head in order to follow the coyote's movements and backed off, her tail twitching furiously.

The three half-grown mixed-breed pups slunk along behind their mother, adding to what the doe had to keep her eyes on. When the coyote was within a dozen yards of the tall grass, the doe pawed at the ground, obviously highly agitated. Then, with a violent shake of the head, the gentle, graceful, soft-eyed creature charged the coyote. The hunter-turned-hunted whirled, teeth bared, muscled body hugging the ground as it backed off. Dean heard Calley suck in a startled breath of air, but there wasn't time for him to take his eyes off the action.

The first time she charged, the doe stopped short of the coyote, but when the doglike creature stopped running, the doe backed off a few feet and then charged again. This time the coyote turned tail completely, its body propelled by churning legs. Although the doe was intent on the adult predator, the three cubs tore off in opposite directions.

"Look. Dean, there's the fawn!" As Calley pointed, Dean saw the newborn spring to its spindly legs and stare after its mother. From its unsteady stance, Dean guessed that the fawn probably had been born that morning.

"That's one for the good guys," Dean said with a laugh. "There's nothing like a little mother instinct to even the odds."

"I'm just glad it was a coyote and not a wolf pack," Calley breathed. "Stay where you are, little fellow. Mama will be back for you."

Although the large mule doe was obviously still agitated, she soon returned to her fawn and started licking it, all the while keeping an eye on the direction in which the coyotes had fled. "That would have been one for the camera," Dean observed. "Too bad they were so far away." He gave Calley a brief squeeze and with that motion remembered that his arm had been around her the entire time. He should let her go. There was no longer anything he needed to cushion her against. But she was warming his side, stirring something familiar deep inside him. He wondered if she felt the same thing.

Slowly Calley rose to her feet. She looked down at Dean, her binoculars dangling from her fingers. Her mouth had softened; Dean wondered if she had anything but him on her mind. Finally, she licked her lips. "We have a long way to go."

"I know." That should have been his line. As they started down the slope that would take them across the burned area, Dean struggled to regain his equilibrium. There was electricity in her; they could both be burned.

There was no way he could tell himself that spending much more time alone in the wilderness with Calley wasn't dangerous. From now on he would have to be on guard against himself. There were men, he knew, who would have already explored the limits of their relationship, and a few years ago he might have done the same. But Waina had taught him so much about patience.

She was no longer part of his life, but her lessons remained. She'd said it only once, while they were waiting for their first glimpse of a polar bear on an ice-choked sea. "You must learn to wait, Dean. You grew up in a society that takes life fast. But there's another pace. A pace that has meant survival for generations of my people."

Dean was a different person now that Waina had touched his life. He no longer needed to take life fast. If something was growing between him and Calley, it would come in its own time.

The next three hours paled in comparison to the drama earlier, but Calley didn't mind. She'd never worried for the doe's safety, but her relief at seeing that the newborn wouldn't be sacrificed to feed the half-grown half-breeds played over and over in her mind. Everything, she believed, deserved a chance at life. They might not succeed, but no one should be snuffed out without first experiencing that precious quality. She wondered if Dean had been aware of how tightly he'd held her while the doe was protecting her fawn and whether that contact would take them back to the place they'd been the night of the storm.

Calley didn't regret their kiss that night, nor did she regret his touching her a few hours ago. She'd learned some cruel lessons about the substance of love through Mike, but that didn't mean she'd been so deeply wounded that she never wanted to love again. What she had learned was that the next time she would not go into anything blind.

Trail mix, a combination of nuts and raisins, and a couple of apples constituted lunch. They changed direction from north to northeast, opting for a more rolling terrain after the steep mountains they'd climbed earlier. Calley let Dean break trail. For the most part she kept her eyes on the country to her left and right, but occasionally they caught on the strong outline of his back, and her ears blocked out the sounds of birds so she could listen to his easy breathing. She was thinking about his slightly bowed legs when Dean abruptly stopped. Calley flattened her hand against his back to stop herself from running into him.

He turned toward her, eyes flashing a warning. Calley rocked back on her heels and cocked her head to one side, listening.

Nothing.

She heard nothing. And that wasn't right.

Her mouth formed the question, but Calley was too wise to speak. Dean's nostrils flared, and for a half second Calley saw something in his eyes that tore through her senses.

Fear. Dean was afraid of something out there.

Chapter Five

The forest was quiet. Too quiet. It seemed to Calley that a moment ago the air had been alive with the sound of birds, but maybe her mind had been on Dean longer than she thought it had. There was an eerie quality to the faint hum of the wind in the evergreens; Calley's spine prickled in response.

Grizzly. Nothing else could bring the wilderness to its knees.

Where? Calley mouthed. Dean shook his head. She lowered her gaze to his hands; they were knotted into white-knuckled fists. A veil now covered the emotion that had been in his eyes a minute before, but his hands still gave him away. The tranquilizing gun slung over his shoulder was not nearly powerful enough or fast acting enough to stop a grizzly at close range. Calley had known that even before she ventured into the Flathead country, but still the stark reality of their vulnerability shook her. They were in heavy brush, which meant a determined grizzly could be upon them before they knew it.

Dean pointed toward an ancient evergreen with a top seeming to touch the sky. Calley understood. While Dean waited, she scrambled into the lower branches and started to hoist herself higher. Below, she could hear Dean's breathing. A few minutes ago it was slow and regular; now it was being triggered by an emotion he might be able to control but not conquer. The sound was almost a twin of the one he made during his nightmares. She had to fight against fear herself; his emotion was almost strong enough to suck her into it with him.

Calley didn't stop climbing until she was close to a hundred feet into the tree. She settled herself on a branch, wrapped her arms around the trunk and leaned to one side for a better view of their surroundings. When Dean joined her, she brought her binoculars to her eyes and scanned what she could of the thick underbrush. The forest was still too quiet, their breathing muffling the sound of the wind.

"There! I saw it move."

Calley followed the line of Dean's finger. For the better part of a minute she saw nothing out of the ordinary; then, unexpectedly, a six-foot-high bush some distance from them shook as if in the grip of an angry giant.

"I don't think it's seen us," Calley whispered. "My God, look at the size. That one's magnificent." She gripped the tree tightly, eyes unblinking on the furred mountain slowly coming out from under the bush. The bear's muzzle was a few inches off the ground, which saved Calley from having to see its teeth. She wondered how deeply her arms would be buried in the carpet of fur around its neck if she were able to touch it. She started to speak again when the grizzly emitted a short growl and lumbered toward their tree.

"It smells us." Dean had wrapped his legs around a limb and was pulling the tranquilizing gun from around his back. "We were so close. I hate having to go after grizzly in brush or trees."

Calley glanced at Dean. He looked in control as he sighted down at the bear sniffing around their perch, but the breath of relief she heard told her he was holding his nerves in check with an effort. Her own heart had been pounding while they made their way up the tree, but now she felt relatively safe. Grizzlies were good climbers, but she and Dean were high enough up that the branches wouldn't support the bear's weight. Even if the bear decided to climb after them, Dean would be able to stop it with a drugged dart. She didn't want him to have to do that. Now she could see the radio transmitter attached to the grizzly's neck. When the bear rose on its hind legs to claw at the base of the tree, she spotted the swollen breasts. This was the female they'd tagged earlier. There was no scientific reason for tranquilizing it again.

"I wonder where her cubs are." Although it made no difference now, Calley continued to keep her voice low.

"I wonder how close we are to their den."

Calley rolled her eyes skyward. "I didn't think about that. If they're near, maybe she'll never let us down."

"Maybe."

Dean's distracted reply caught Calley's attention. This wasn't the first time Calley had scrambled into a tree to avoid a grizzly. The first time it happened, her palms had been wet with fear, but she'd learned that the most unnerving thing about the experience was having to put up with angry growls and claws tearing at the base of her sanctuary. Dean didn't seem capable of telling himself that. He was staring at the bear, his body language telling her that his nightmare was threatening to consume him.

She wanted to say something. There should be a way of helping him fight off whatever it was he was going through. But Calley knew this was something Dean had to do on his own. She might have seen his sensitive, outgoing nature, but there was another side to him. Things he had to deal with alone because, for reasons she didn't understand, he couldn't let her near.

They spent the next hour in the tree, shifting weight occasionally, never quite convinced that the grizzly wasn't going to try to climb after them. Sometimes the bear rose on her hind legs and clawed at their perch, but for the most part she ignored them as she lumbered about digging up roots. Despite her ferocious appearance, she didn't seem to have any need to prove anything to the humans who'd wandered into her territory. After a while Calley tired of peering down at the massive creature. "I should have brought my knitting," she joked. "We're going to be here forever. This is downright boring."

"Boring? Being at the mercy of a grizzly is never boring."

"I didn't mean it that way," Calley amended. "I think you know that. Dean, she isn't going to come after us. We're stuck here, and I find that boring. I'm sorry if you don't agree with me."

For the first time since they'd settled in the tree, Dean really looked at her. "Are you giving me a lecture?" he challenged.

"You're acting as if you need one." Calley didn't enjoy being at crossed swords with Dean, but she felt she had to do something to get through to him. "Sitting in a tree all afternoon is not the most exciting thing I've ever done. Don't you have somewhere to go?" she called out to the grizzly.

The bear growled and lifted her head skyward but a minute later was back at work making kindling out of a decaying log. "She's singularly unimpressed with us." Calley giggled. No matter what was going through Dean's head, she was determined to prove to him that their situation was more embarrassing than frightening.

"Just be thankful she is," Dean pointed out. He was quiet a minute. "Are you comfortable."

Calley lifted her elbow to show Dean where she'd scratched it during her hurried climb. "Not really, but I'll survive."

Dean's concerned look made Calley regret showing him the scratch. "I'm sorry," he said. "I have a salve back at camp that'll take the sting out of it."

"Actually—" Calley giggled again "—next to the way my rear end feels, I hardly notice my arm."

"Agreed." Dean changed positions on his tree limb. He smiled; the smile didn't look forced. "Sitting on bark is not the most comfortable perch in the world."

"It's almost as bad as sitting on a cow."

"A cow?" Dean's look told Calley that he thought she just might be losing touch with reality. "What do you know about sitting on cows?"

At least he'd freed himself from whatever emotion had gripped him earlier. Grateful for that, Calley explained that sitting on cows was one of those experiences usually reserved for farm children. She'd hand raised a dairy cow as part of a 4-H project, and when the Guernsey became too large to sneak into the house anymore, she'd taken to riding the patient creature. "Maude always rolled her eyes when I got on her, but she was much more tolerant than the horses. Sometimes they'd get it in their heads to buck me off, but Maude put up with an awful lot."

"Maude?" Dean frowned.

"Yeah, isn't that awful? But I'm serious. Her back was like trying to sit on a picket fence. I have no idea why I did it." Calley glanced down at the bear. "What's the most uncomfortable place you've ever been? Other than this I mean."

A shadow flashed across Dean's face, but when he spoke, his tone was light. "Probably along the Colville River in Alaska. It wasn't the cold so much as having to spend so much time there waiting for something to happen." His tone changed again, becoming something Calley didn't recognize. "I don't know why I said that," he whispered. "So much of it was good. We were studying a polar bear and her cubs. Another researcher had been tracking this one female during the fall and knew where her winter den was. We came in December and stayed there through the summer."

"We? When was that?"

"Summer before last. That was the easy part. Organizing and writing up the data we gathered took almost as long as the study itself."

Dean was trying to steer the conversation away from the direction in which it had been headed. She might regret what she was doing, but Calley needed to know what he was trying to avoid. "Who was with you, Dean?"

Dean blinked but gave no other indication that he'd been trapped. "Waina," he said softly.

"Waina?" Calley repeated. "Is she a biologist?"

"She's a member of the Haida Indian tribe."

"The woman who showed you that deserted village," Calley supplied. Why should it bother her to hear Dean mention another woman? "You spent a lot of time with her, didn't you?" she asked.

"A year. A year of my life."

"Freezing near a polar-bear den in Alaska," Calley went on. "That kind of existence brings people close together, doesn't it?"

"It was just the two of us. Every couple of weeks a pilot would fly in with supplies, but we were alone for the better part of six months. We located the bear's den and opened a hole from above so we could watch the female and her cubs. You would have enjoyed that."

Calley clung to the image of newborn bears nestled close to their hibernating mother's side. "Were you able to take pictures?" *Six months alone with Waina*.

Dean nodded. "Hundreds, probably. The cubs had already been born by the time we had access to the den, but they weighed only a couple of pounds. We were able to study them until they were old enough to come out of the den with their mother."

Calley should have been thinking about the rare experience Dean and Waina had been privileged to witness, but something he had said refused to leave her mind. Waina had been part of his life for a year. For six months they'd had no one but each other. "Did—did you leave then?"

"We stayed through the summer. We watched Taku and Auke as their mother taught them how to hunt and fish. She never got used to having us around, but I'd like to believe that her cubs accepted us as part of their world." Dean ran his fingers through his hair. "I haven't thought about this for a while. I don't like thinking about the past. But despite the cold and monotony, it was a peaceful time. It wasn't much different from what it's like here. I think that's when I came to understand the ebb and flow of life in Alaska. Taku and Auke were born to it. Waina taught me so much about not expecting more than what one needs for survival."

"She sounds like a special woman." Calley almost didn't get the words out.

"She is. She left her village to go to college. She's even been down here a couple of times, but unlike a lot of the young people in her village, she never wanted anything but to go back home. Calley?"

Calley waited. The moment was pregnant with something she couldn't define.

"I haven't talked about Waina since I left Alaska."

"I thought so," Calley said gently. She wondered if the emotion the grizzly had brought out in him had made Dean vulnerable today. "You loved her, didn't you?"

Dean didn't answer her. Instead, a slow, half-sad smile touched the corners of his mouth. "Even before they came out of the den, we could tell the difference between the two cubs. Auke, the male, was more aggressive, but Taku knew how to handle him. She'd run bellowing to her mother if Auke got too rough, but most of the time she trailed after him like a hero-worshipping younger sister. Occasionally Auke would even let her have some of his food. He probably thought he was being generous. I don't think he ever caught on that she was conning him."

"Taku was a true female," Calley said with forced lightness. "Everyone knows that women know how to con men."

"Maybe you'd like to try your skills on ugly mug down there? We're going to be in trouble if we don't get back to camp before dark."

Calley acknowledged that Dean had said all he was going to about his time with Waina. "You're the boss. Why don't you tell her the food's better over the next hill? You know, for a couple of so-called experts we're really up a tree this time."

Dean groaned. "Spare me." He didn't speak for another five minutes. When he did, once again he asked Calley if she was uncomfortable. She tried to reassure him that she'd survive, but she couldn't help making comparisons. How had he kept the cold from biting too deeply into Waina? What, other than a respect for her people's way of life, had she taught him? If it were Waina in the tree now, would Dean be talking about what went through his mind when he looked down at their captor?

When at length the female grizzly abandoned them and slowly made her way up the rise that would take her out of sight, relief seeped into Calley. True, she was more than ready to leave her high perch. But in addition to that, she'd had enough of thoughts of Dean's months with Waina.

Fifteen minutes later they climbed down out of the tree. Dean took a moment to reposition his gun and pack, but he lost no time setting a pace that angled them away from where they'd last seen the grizzly. He didn't speak for another fifteen minutes, and then it was only to ask Calley if he was walking too fast for her.

Calley understood Dean's urgency. At least she thought she did. Unless they kept a fast pace, it would be dark before they reached camp. When night fell they wouldn't be able to keep track of their progress with the compass Dean was using.

"I'm not sure I'm going to want to put all of this in the diary," Dean said as they scrambled down the last hill leading to camp. His light tone was forced. "I'll never hear the end of it if certain people read about this particular adventure."

"We really didn't have any choice but to get where she couldn't reach us. You don't think others are going to think any the less of you, do you?" Calley asked. She could see sweat glistening on the back of Dean's neck, but he was handling himself as easily as he had when they first left camp.

"That isn't my concern. It just isn't something I want to talk about if I don't have to. It turned out all right. That's all that matters." Dean sighed. "It's a good thing her cubs weren't around. I don't doubt for a moment that they'd be able to climb high enough to wrestle us for a perch."

"They're probably pretty young." Calley plunked herself down on the first log she came to in camp and started yanking at the leather laces holding her boots. "Oh! My feet are killing me. I had no idea I was using them to grip all the time we were in the tree."

Dean knelt beside her and pushed her weary hands aside. He removed her boots, and with the gun still strapped to his back, began rubbing her feet. "It's been a long day." His thumb pressed against her instep, the pressure finding and unlocking tense muscles. "What say we call and have dinner delivered."

"Fabulous idea. Pizza." Calley sighed. Her eyes closed as she concentrated on what Dean was doing. The man in the tree with her had been a stranger. This was the one she knew.

"And beer. We can't have pizza without beer."

"We can't?" Calley asked dreamily. There was something to be said for civilization. Heat controlled by the turn of a dial. Real sheets. Sleeping in a nightgown instead of flannel pajamas. Dinner at a place where waiters slipped in quietly and refilled water glasses.

Dean wasn't rubbing her feet anymore. His strong hands were slowly making their way up the outer sides of her legs. She felt his fingers on her calves, running over her knees, finding the thigh muscles. Calley willed herself not to tense. This wasn't the touch of a masseuse. This was how a man touched a woman who could have meaning for him.

And she wanted that tonight. She'd learned of what Dean had been and experienced before she met him. She couldn't do anything about the past, but she could make him part of her world today. Or she could try.

Why she wanted that wasn't important. It didn't matter. His hands were around her waist, his breath warm on the tanned V below her throat. She opened her eyes to find his face inches away. So much of the man was hidden beneath his beard, and yet his eyes were giving away his emotions.

She could surrender herself to those eyes.

"Dean?"

"Don't speak. I won't hurt you. I want—" Dean's lips finished the sentence for him.

Calley surrendered completely and unquestioningly. Maybe her willing response had something to do with their isolation and the imprisonment they'd shared earlier in the tree, and maybe it had to do with unfinished business carried over from the night of the storm. Calley closed her eyes, needing to soak in all she could of the man leaning over her. His hands remained around her and although her hands had found their way to his shoulders, there was very little body contact other than the kiss itself.

Despite being pinned beneath him, Calley felt free and weightless. When he parted his lips, she did the same. His tongue first touched the soft inside of her lips and then explored farther. Calley's body responded instantly. Forgotten were her aching legs, her scratched arm, her empty stomach. She was full with wanting him, with wanting to know how much man was inside that mountain-man body. She'd see him with his shirt off, but she'd never seen his legs when they weren't encased in denim.

"Ah, Calley." Dean sighed. "You don't belong here. You're so feminine. You deserve satin sheets."

Calley found her voice, but she answered him without opening her eyes. "Satin sheets? Hardly."

"Have you ever wanted that?"

"Never. And you're wrong. I belong here." His lips were so close. She could sense them inches away, tantalizing her.

"I know you do." Dean removed his right hand from her hip. Before Calley could feel the loss, he was touching her throat, tracing the tanned V as far as he could. "It's incredible. I've only known two women who truly belonged in the wilderness."

And Waina was the first. Calley slammed a door on that thought. "About that pizza," she said around her need to give him further access to her. "How long will it take to have it delivered?"

"A long time."

"Good." What she was expected to say after that, she had no idea. Dean's fingers had found the soft swell above her breast. Calley fought for control of her breathing, but her next breath came as a long, painful gasp. *He knows,* she thought. *He knows how much I want him.*

Dean's own breath mirrored hers. She could sense the battle within him, but she was beyond setting any brakes. Her breasts would fit perfectly within the cradle of his hands. Although she knew that as profoundly as she knew her own name, wanting him to take possession of her was making her a little desperate. She moved her hips restlessly, seeking control of the emotions surging through her. She arched her back, giving him easier access to her breasts, telling him too much.

He responded the way she prayed he would. His hand slipped completely under her bra, and her nipple was hard against his palm, giving him further proof of where he'd brought her. "I've wanted—" he started. Instead of finishing, he once again married his lips to hers. This time Calley was waiting with open mouth.

Somewhere overhead an early owl gave out its lonely call. Night cold pricked against Calley's flesh but was held at bay by the storm within. She worked her fingers under the collar of his shirt and was rewarded by the feel of warm flesh over rock-hard muscles. It wasn't fair! No one else should have claimed his muscles before her. They were for her to delight in. He had been placed here for her.

The thought was insane, but the very insanity of her selfishness allowed Calley to retain some measure of control.

She didn't have to surrender to her most primitive thoughts. She could simply think them.

Dean surfaced first. Denying his hand the exquisite softness of her breast was one of the hardest things he'd ever done, but if one of them didn't put on the brakes, the night would end with their doing something they weren't ready for. If this thing that was starting to exist between them was to last, it shouldn't be pushed. He thought he was going to be able to lean away from her without revealing too much of himself, but when he tried to breathe, it came out a groan.

"I don't think we should be doing this."

That was the sort of thing Calley hadn't heard since she was a teenager and she was the one putting an end to roving hands, but she was light years away from laughing. He was right. They weren't ready.

It was maybe the hardest thing she'd done in her entire life, but as soon as Dean had stood up, Calley found her own feet, mumbled something about needing to clean up and stumbled through the growing dark down to the river. She ignored Dean's offer to go with her. Let him worry. She needed to be alone. She knelt at its edge and splashed water on her face and arms. She winced as the cold hit her scratched arm, but pain was a powerful enough sensation to accomplish what needed to be accomplished. It brought her back to where she should have been.

Dean had been thinking about Waina today; Calley had made that happen. Waina was someone he had once loved and made love to.

Calley didn't know if Waina was beautiful by the standards her culture was accustomed to using, but Dean had said enough for her to understand where Waina's true beauty lay. A woman who lived in tune with Alaska's timelessness, who knew what it meant to be patient, to have reverence and respect for her people's way of life, had a great deal to offer a man sensitive enough to unveil those special qualities.

Waina must have been special. Otherwise a man such as Dean wouldn't have spent six months alone with her.

"Calley." She could hear Dean's voice through the night. "Calley, I don't feel safe about you being down there alone. Don't shut me out." He stepped onto the riverbank, his frame silhouetted against the sky and rising moon. Wordlessly, he stripped off his shirt and then his jeans and stepped into the river, wearing only his briefs. Calley shivered for him as he sucked in his breath, but she couldn't think of a thing to say. He was so magnificent, a superb physical specimen no woman alive would be able to ignore. He was leaving the water, coming toward her, arms wrapped around his ribs, head thrown back as if trying to avoid as much as possible of the icy water.

"I'm not shutting you out," she said when there was no ignoring his relentless presence. "I just had to think."

"About what happened up there?" He put his arm around her shoulder and pulled her close. Their twin warmth flowed together and took away the icy river's chill.

"Yes," Calley admitted. "I was thinking about us. But you're right. We aren't ready for—for what almost happened. We don't know each other well enough."

"Not yet we don't." Effortlessly, Dean turned her around until she was facing him. Without thinking, she wrapped her arms around him in an effort to keep him warm. Calley wasn't thinking about their unsure footing. His eyes were relentless daggers heading straight for her heart. "But I think it's going to happen."

"You think we're going to become lovers?" Calley couldn't remember ever being this honest with Mike, or anyone else.

"More than lovers, I hope," Dean went on. "I don't believe in casual relationships, Calley. Yes, I had my share of one-night stands when I was younger, but I wasn't very proud of those. I wasn't mature, and it showed. When I make love to a woman, it's because she's become special to me as a human being."

Just as Waina was. "Not many men feel like that" was all Calley could say.

"I'm not sure that's true." Dean pulled her closer, nestling her against his bare chest. "Men are conditioned to believe they have to brag about conquests, but I believe that the need for love, the need to belong, is universal."

Calley blinked back tears. Dean was saying something so profound that the depth of his sensitivity shocked her. For the first time since she and Mike broke up, she wanted to tell someone what she'd gone through. She wanted to tell this someone. But he was wrapped in his own thoughts.

"I wish you could have met her," he said almost conversationally. "Calley, I didn't know anyone like her still existed. She was someone with the capacity to see beyond what's artificial about our society, to accept a way of life that has meant survival for her people for centuries. Waina had a master's degree in wildlife management, but she had no desire to capitalize on that. She could have gotten a government job and made a great deal of money, but all she really wanted to do was go back to her people and use her education to help them."

"It was hard on you, wasn't it? Her leaving, I mean?"

"I miss certain things about her. But she's where she belongs. I wouldn't have it any other way." Dean shivered. "Look, why don't we get cleaned up and go back to camp. I have some tomato soup warming to go with cheese and sausage."

Calley did what Dean suggested not because she was hungry but because his explanation moved her. She needed a moment alone to think about what he'd said. She finished first and hurried back to camp. Dean had started a small campfire. She added more dried limbs to it and slipped into her tent to change into a fresh sweatshirt. After applying face cream and fluffing her hair, Calley emerged to find Dean drying himself in front of the fire.

As it had before, the sight of him took her breath away. In the red light afforded by the firelight, she could make out the long scar under his arm, but that didn't detract from his effect on her. On the contrary, knowing that he'd done battle in the wilderness increased her acceptance of what he was. A man like this would be the kind an Alaskan woman would fall in love with. Or any kind of woman.

"I should have thought of dinner," she said lamely. "I didn't mean to leave all the work for you." She took her place beside the campfire, careful to keep distance between them.

"Forget dinner." Dean shook his head wearily. He reached down for a shirt he'd had warming beside the fire and slipped it over his shoulders. Calley didn't try to break the silence while he was stepping into his jeans. Only when he sat on one of the logs they'd placed around the fire did he speak. "I told you that leaving Waina was hard. I want to be honest with you. But, Calley, both Waina and I knew it wouldn't work. We wouldn't work." He was staring into the fire, red lights seeping into his eyes. "Her commitment is in Alaska. Mine is here. I'd like to think that we both learned something from each other before we went our separate ways."

"I know that's what happened. Dean, you have a lot to share with others. Waina sounds like the kind of person who would appreciate that." She shouldn't care so much. It wasn't safe. But she did. She'd only spent a few days with Dean, but in those days he'd become part of her. "Where is she now?"

"On the Yukon Delta. She's finishing up a study of the emperor geese there. But in a couple of months she'll be going to McKinley Park. As soon as the caribou migration is over, she's been contracted to do some consultation for the park personnel on ways to protect the caribou from mosquitoes and warble flies. She says that's impossible, but I guess they want her to go there and tell them that."

"You—you know a lot about what she's doing." The words sounded as if they'd been spoken by someone else.

"We correspond," Dean said simply. "I'll always care about her."

"I don't understand why you weren't able to work things out."

"Waina and I come from different cultures. Her home is a small village. Mine is a major university."

But you share a love of wildlife. You're both dedicated to preserving the balance of nature, Calley thought. She could have pointed this out to Dean, but she didn't. Obviously this was something he and Waina had discussed before coming to the decision to lead separate lives. Calley might not cringe from facing the impact Waina had had on Dean, but she wasn't going to spend her time with him digging for intimate details. "I'm glad you're still in touch with her. I don't know many people who can do that after the romance breaks up."

"You can't?"

Calley had been staring into the fire, but now she jerked her head up. She knew where Dean wanted the conversation to head. "No, I can't," she said to ward off any further questions. "It's a dead issue in my case. You don't suppose dinner is ready, do you?"

Dean's eyes stayed on her much longer than they needed to before turning to their meal. In his look Calley read questions and resentment. He was right. He'd been honest about his past relationship. She should be able to do the same. But Mike was a painful subject, and her emotions had been subjected to enough for one night.

Calley filled the air with idle chatter while they ate, and she made a great production out of cleaning up afterward. She hoped Dean would busy himself with record keeping, but he seemed content to sit before the fire, sipping hot chocolate. Finally, there was nothing more for her to do.

Calley yawned elaborately. What she wanted to do was join Dean, feel his hands on hers, taste his lips. But she'd done nothing to deserve that. Too much separated them. "I had no idea sitting in a tree was that exhausting," she explained, stretching to emphasize her point. "I hope you don't mind, but I'm going to call it a day."

Dean continued to stare into the coals; Calley had no choice but to make good on her statement. Her tent was too big for one person; at least it was now after having Dean share it that first night. She quickly changed into her practical pajamas and crawled into the warmth of her sleeping bag, but sleep was an elusive thing. After tossing and turning for a half hour, she gave up and reached for her book and a flashlight.

For the next hour she pretended to read while listening for sounds that would tell her what Dean was doing. Even when she heard him extinguish the fire and enter his tent, she was unable to relax. His hand had been on her breast earlier. They shouldn't be going to bed as strangers.

At length, Calley set aside her book and pulled the sleeping bag over her shoulders. The sound of an owl's voice echoing off the mountains was the last sound she heard.

Dean lay on his back, staring up at the low ceiling of his tent. If anyone had asked him what he'd been thinking while he sat around the fire, he wouldn't have been able to come up with an answer that made sense. Certainly he couldn't tell Calley that he was angry at her.

But he was. He'd told her everything except the intimate details about his romance with Waina. Didn't he deserve a little something in return? True, he'd let his emotions run away with him by caressing her earlier, but their unthinking fumbling had resulted in an openness that hadn't been there before. Or so he'd thought.

He could tell her that he knew about her and Mike and force her hand, but that would be a hollow victory. What Dean wanted from Calley was freely given honesty. So she'd been in love with his predecessor on the project. There was no crime in that, nothing to be ashamed of.

But she must be ashamed, or else she would have told him.

Dean sighed and tried to find a comfortable position. For the first time since Melinda and Steve left, he wanted them back. He didn't want to spend any more time alone with Calley. Not only didn't he trust himself around her, but he now believed that their relationship was destined to dead-end. Honesty and openness were more than words in Dean's vocabulary. They were the code by which he wanted to live his life.

IT WAS DARK. A deep black greater than any other Dean had ever experienced. He pressed his hands against the ebony sheet but was unable to tear his way through it. The night had wrapped itself around him, shutting him off from every other living thing.

And yet he could hear breathing. Calley's breathing. She was drawing in her breath through tortured lungs, a scream caught in her throat. Sweat broke out on Dean's flesh; a wave of heat raced through him. Calley wasn't alone. Something, the only thing in the world he feared, was with her. Stalking her.

This time Calley's scream found life. Its high, helpless sound stabbed at Dean's heart, slicing through his own fear.

She was being attacked. Ripped apart. She was experiencing the agony he knew all too well. In a few minutes it would be over. She would be dead.

Dean was sitting bolt upright before the nightmare lost its hold on him. He sucked in deep lungfuls of night air, waiting for the storm within to subside. When he no longer was being assaulted, he dropped his head and covered his face with his hands. Would it ever go away? Would he ever control his demons?

They were getting worse. Now Calley was part of his nightmare, and that was worse than the act that led to the relentless dream. He knew that trying to go back to sleep was futile. Dean tried to lay back down, but even with his eyes open he could see the monster shape towering over the woman in the other tent.

He had to see her, touch her so he would know she was all right.

Dean slipped out of his tent and tiptoed through the alien night until his outstretched hand found the front flap of Calley's tent. He could hear her sleep-filled breathing, but until he'd felt her solid against him, he couldn't be sure. He ducked his head and entered the tent.

Calley stirred when he knelt beside her but didn't wake until he placed the back of his hand gently against her chest. She didn't jump at his touch; that warmed him. She sighed deep in her throat and turned her body toward him, drawing her knees up under her. Slowly her eyes opened.

In the morning Dean would never have done what he was doing now, but his nightmare had followed him here, and he had to know, to be sure. He bent his head and brushed his lips across her cheek. Wordlessly, Calley reached for him and drew him down beside her.

Chapter Six

She woke to the warmth of Dean's beard on the side of her neck. Calley had no idea when Dean had joined her or why, only that what had begun as a dream had turned into reality. She remembered his hand on her cheek, his whisper that was more sound than words. Through the fog of sleep tangling around her, she'd reached for him and pulled him close.

He was still here hours later. Somehow he must have found enough warmth to allow him to sleep next to her in his underwear, but now his legs were drawn up, with his arms tucked tightly against his body. Calley rolled over and inched her way out of the sleeping bag. Then she grabbed the loose side and wrapped it around Dean.

What was it he had said before they both fell asleep? Something about a dream.

But Calley didn't think it was a dream at all. She'd heard Dean in the night and knew that whatever gripped him then wasn't something he would welcome. He'd had another nightmare. Last night it had awakened him and sent him into the dark, seeking her. She wondered if she'd become part of the nightmare and if at last he'd feel like talking about it.

After building another fire, Calley took time to cover her arms and legs with lotion. She brushed her long hair until her scalp tingled, promising herself that tonight she'd heat enough water for a shampoo. Water was ready for coffee by the time Dean came out of her tent.

"I wasn't sure," he said as he joined her. "When I was waking up, I thought maybe it was a dream, but I did come into your tent, didn't I?"

Calley nodded. A crease mark remained along the side of his temple. His tousled hair and still-drooping eyes reminded her of a waking child. "I thought it was a dream, too, when I first woke up. What was it, Dean? Another nightmare?"

"Yeah." Dean busied himself with pouring coffee for both of them. "You'd think they'd go away after all this time."

"Do you want to tell me about them?"

"No." Dean was staring into the fire, flashes of red and orange dancing in his eyes. "I tried that a couple of times, but it only made them worse." He raised his eyes to meet hers. "Do you understand?"

"I hope so." She wanted to touch him, hold him, to take away some of what he had to live with. At least she should be able to do that for him. "Did you get cold?" she asked. She sounded too much like a mother. "I'm afraid I hogged most of the sleeping bag."

"It was your bag." A grin settled around Dean's mouth. "What's for breakfast, woman? Since you couldn't come up with pizza last night, what about crepes this morning?"

Calley affected an elaborate bow. "By all means, sir. Fresh strawberry crepes with cream topping. I'll be right back. Have to run to the store for the ingredients."

Dean shrugged. "In that case, I'll have pancakes. A little water and mix and we're set."

Calley went about stirring up the pancake batter while Dean returned to his tent. When he emerged, he was holding his boots with one hand and rubbing his jaw with the other. "What would you think if I shaved?" he asked.

"It depends," Calley answered slowly. "You don't happen to have a receding chin, do you?"

Dean felt along his jawline. "I don't think so. I've had this bush for so long I've forgotten."

"Then why would you want to shave it off?"

"I have no idea," Dean said with a laugh. "I guess I just wanted to see what your reaction would be."

"Then don't. I like you with a beard."

"Why?"

Calley didn't have an answer for that. At least not one that could easily be translated into words. It had to do with the beard making him even more at one with the elements. "Because we aren't going to have time today. Didn't you want to cover the mountain to the east?"

"Nag, nag, nag. Look, I need something from the truck. I'll be right back."

Calley ladled a spoonful of pancake batter onto the hot skillet and was getting ready to turn it when she heard Dean's outraged cry. She yanked the skillet off the Coleman and sprinted toward their vehicles.

He was standing in the middle of a mess. Everything that had been in the glove compartment of Calley's jeep was strewn on the ground around the vehicle. The tarp over the back of the jeep had been untied and now lay crumpled into a tangled heap. The items the men had transferred from Dean's truck to the jeep had been tossed out. The whole mess was dusted with a fine layer of dried oats.

Bear was Calley's first thought. But if a bear had been the one to ransack the jeep, the vehicle itself wouldn't be intact. Besides, they hadn't heard a bear. "Oh, no," she said, laughing. "Raccoon."

"Raccoon," Dean repeated. "A very thorough raccoon. Damn! How did he get the glove compartment open?"

"I didn't lock it," Calley explained. "He must have bumped into it."

Dean dropped to his knees. "I wonder if he took anything. So much for that box of oatmeal. Our camp robber really made a mess of that."

Calley wanted to be mad. Blankets and books and camping supplies and even camera equipment were strewn about in a twenty-foot radius around the jeep. The damage could be extensive, the cleanup chore monumental, and yet there was something so utterly absurd about this disaster that it was impossible not to laugh. "It's a good thing he didn't stick around," she said with an irrational giggle. "I'd really tan his hide."

Dean was shaking his head, trying to sort through the mail Melinda had brought that he hadn't gotten around to reading. "I'd wring his bloody little neck."

"You wouldn't really," Calley pointed out. "Not a sweet little innocent raccoon. You'd take one look at those trusting eyes and pat him on his head."

"You want to bet? Look at this bill." Dean waved it in the air. "I think that raccoon tried to eat it."

"Do you think they'd buy that as an excuse for not paying the bill?" Calley asked. She joined Dean in the midst of what had once been organized correspondence. The front cover had been torn off a wildlife publication, but that wasn't nearly as much of a mess as a graduate student's manuscript. Not only did it look as if the fifty or so neatly typed pages had been tossed into the wind, but several papers had tooth marks in them. "I hope whoever wrote this made more than one copy."

Dean took one of the pages from her. He poked his finger through the largest hole. "Now I have a perfectly good excuse for not reading it." He groaned. "I'm not looking forward to explaining this to the student in question. I think this particular raccoon had a paper fetish."

Calley retrieved an empty box that had once been filled with cornmeal. "He was a gourmet, too. I'm surprised we didn't hear him. It must have taken him hours to accomplish this."

"At least we can assume he had a good time. He must have thought he'd hit the mother lode."

It took the better part of the morning for Calley and Dean to undo the determined raccoon's handiwork. Dean blamed himself for leaving anything out where a curious raccoon could get his paws on it, but Calley refused to take the situation too seriously. She pointed out that there was no way they could have brought everything into camp, just as it wouldn't have made sense for Steve and Melinda to take anything with them. "These things happen," she said more than once. "Just think of the fun that little scamp had."

By the time they were settling down to a long-delayed breakfast, Dean was agreeing with her. "I figured we were safe because there was nothing in the jeep that would attract a bear. I just didn't think about a curious and very determined raccoon."

"I wonder if he had Boy Scout training," Calley observed. "He got through the knots holding the tarp in place slick as a whistle."

Dean grinned. He held up his coffee mug in a mock salute. "Slick as a whistle. I haven't heard that since I was a kid."

Calley furrowed her eyebrows in an attempt at anger. "Don't make fun of me, Dean Ramsey. If you do, I'll let everyone know about the four-legged scamp who made a monkey out of you."

"Scamp?" Dean mocked. "What hills did you say you were raised in? Are you sure they had TV reception in the back country?"

The easy banter continued while they cleared up after their meal. When Dean agreed that it was too late in the day for them to accomplish anything in the woods, Calley retired to her tent so that she could write to her family. She had no idea when she'd be able to mail the letters, but if she didn't get some things down on paper now, she might talk herself out of the project later on.

An hour later, Dean poked his head into the tent opening. "I don't suppose you know how to fish."

"Of course I do. I—"

"Then you're on," Dean interrupted. He stuck out his hand. "The one who catches the least fish cooks for the rest of the time we're here."

"Wait a minute," Calley protested. "I didn't bring any fishing equipment."

"I have both Steve's and mine. You aren't chicken, are you?"

Calley pushed herself up off the sleeping bag and stuck out her hand. "You're on mister. I thought you were working."

Dean shrugged before pulling her out of the tent. "I got bored. I'd better warn you, though. I'm pretty good."

"So am I" was all that Calley said. When Dean handed her a tackle box, she reached for a number 14 Adams fly, checked to make sure the pole was equipped with floating line and tied three feet of light monofilament to that. She was securing the fly to the end of the monofilament before she stole a glance in Dean's direction. He was watching her closely.

"Hmm." He drew out the word. "What kind of knot was that?"

Calley quickly draped her hand over her handiwork. "A granny," she lied.

"Yeah? You're fast."

"And good." Calley turned her back on Dean before he could see her grin. She reached the river first, easily casting her line into a riffle close to the far bank. "Find your own spot," she warned when he tried to join her. "I've claimed this one."

"That's where I was going to fish," he protested.

"I know." Calley shot him a smile. "I don't believe in cheating, but when it comes to winning bets, I go for blood."

"I should have known," Dean grumbled as he stalked off.

Two hours later Calley was back in camp with a full string of fish. She knew she was taking advantage of Dean, but he really had walked into that one. He should have known better than to assume that just because she was female she was at a disadvantage when it came to fishing.

"You cheated," Dean spluttered in mock anger. He'd walked into camp holding up a half-dozen decent-size trout, but when Calley showed him that she'd already cleaned double that amount, he quickly lost his superior grin. "Where did you learn to fish?"

Calley gave him her most superior smile. It wasn't until several minutes later that she explained. "I paid for my sophomore year's tuition with my winnings from tournament fishing," she explained after teasing him by talking about everything except the question she knew was on his mind. "I took first place in three consecutive tournaments at Kootenai, Bitterroot and Musselshell. You'd be surprised at the money to be won from fishing."

Dean groaned. "I don't suppose they were all fly-fishing tournaments?"

"As I recall, they were."

"No fair," Dean protested. "I've been had."

"That's twice today." Calley laughed. "Once by a marauding raccoon and once by a fishing pro."

Dean dropped his catch on the cooking table and squared around to face her. His eyes took on a teasing glitter. Slowly he advanced on her. Calley scrambled to her feet in mock alarm. She started to back away, but he was too fast for her. "You think you're pretty smart, don't you? Now you've had it." He wrapped his arms around her waist, pinning her arms to her side. Then he leaned over her, forcing her to arch her back in a futile attempt to escape.

Calley went weak under the gentle assault caused by his tongue and lips on her neck. She closed her eyes, secure in the knowledge that he was strong enough to support her weight. Her total focus narrowed until she was aware of nothing except the delicious sensation he was capable of arousing. Slowly he headed south with his exploration, relishing his command over her when her strangled gasp gave away her emotion.

What had started as play all too soon became passion. Dean was aware of his arousal. As long as he held her in his arms, he had almost no control over his emotions. His lips centered on the tantalizing valley he'd found with his hand last night. She could tell him to stop, and he'd obey her, but as long as she didn't put on the brakes, he would explore. Her head was thrown back, giving him easy access. That was all the encouragement he needed.

"Dean. Dean?"

Inwardly he groaned. "What?" he asked without lifting his mouth from his exploration.

"My back's killing me."

One instant longer. One last taste of silky flesh. Then Dean straightened and helped Calley regain her balance. "I think I like losing bets with you," he managed to say.

She clung to him, not because she was unsure of her footing but because they'd erased any distance between them and she didn't want distance to take over again. "When are you going to get around to cooking all those fish?"

"Later. Now—" Slowly, reverently, he ran his hands up the sides of her neck until he was holding her face in his hands. He inclined his head, relieved to see that she was waiting for him. When their lips met, he experienced an exquisite tenderness that held his inner storm at bay. She was so much more than a co-worker, but what they might yet become to each other was something he wasn't wise enough to know. What he did know was that he couldn't get enough of touching her, holding her, kissing her.

"That was quite a reward. What do I get if I lose a bet with you?" Calley asked when at last their kiss ended.

His eyes melted into hers. "Can't you guess?"

"No." The word was spoken painfully. "You said it, Dean. We aren't ready for that."

"How do you know what I was thinking?"

She didn't try to answer his question. Instead, Calley gently removed herself from his arms. She felt cold and lonely standing apart from him, but that was the only way she could regain control of herself. Her blood had become superheated; her lungs were incapable of keeping up with her need for oxygen. Touch her? His tongue in the valley between her breasts, his body looming over hers, was much more than a touch.

Shaking, Calley turned away. No matter how hard it was, she had to break free from the spell he'd cast on her. She said the only thing that came to mind. "Where have you done most of your fishing?"

Dean knew what Calley was doing. Although he wished it could be different, he understood her need to place distance between them. He spoke casually. "Many places. The best was in Kodiak, Alaska. The Salty Creek. Coho salmon."

"With Waina?"

Dean nodded. "We followed bear tracks to a shallow pool," he explained. "It was October, and the willows and alders were turning orange and red." He spoke rapidly, wanting to share as much of the experience as possible with her. "The big silvers had just arrived, and the bears knew it. I kept thinking about the bears; I could see fish everywhere. In the distance the surf was pounding. I was mesmerized by my surroundings." He took a slow step toward Calley. "I'd like to take you there someday."

"I'd like to do that," Calley admitted. "I've always wanted to go to Alaska. Do some fishing. I wish someone like Waina could go along to tell us things we can't get out of a travel book."

Dean wrapped his arm around her shoulder. He didn't try to kiss her. "Maybe I shouldn't have mentioned Waina."

"That's all right," she said from the shelter he was offering her. "I can't expect you to stop thinking about her. I understand the impact she had on your life."

"But she isn't part of what you and I are."

What are we to each other? Calley wanted to ask. But there wasn't enough of a bond between them to examine that potent question. Calley was aware that she was on the frontier of a new adventure, but if she plunged forward too quickly, it might be lost. "It looks as if we're going to be living on fish for several days."

Dean gave her a quick squeeze but allowed her to leave his side so she could finish the task of placing the fish in plastic bags. While he gutted his fish, she carried hers to the river where the cold would preserve them. "I've only had more than my fill of fish once," she explained after she'd returned and was watching him. "That's all we had to eat for a week."

"A week of nothing but fish? What happened?"

Calley laughed. "You think that raccoon made a mess of things. Have you ever seen a camp after a black bear's been through it? There wasn't enough worth salvaging to talk about."

"Where was this?"

"About fifty miles from here." Calley straddled a log before continuing her story. "Mike and I were doing research, a lot like what we're doing here. We'd chosen an area inaccessible by vehicle and were dropped in by helicopter. When that black took off with our food supplies, we had two choices. Either we could spend the next two days hiking out, or we could tough it out until the helicopter returned. That's one time I really was glad my dad had taught me how to fish."

Dean acknowledged the fact that his wasn't the only past with another person in it. "What happened? Didn't you secure your food supplies? How did the bear get to them?"

"Timing." Calley wrinkled up her nose. "We hadn't been there an hour. The helicopter had made a couple of passes, dropping off our supplies, and we were out looking for our tent when Blackie snuck in and started wolfing down everything in sight. I got back first and ran him off."

"You ran off a bear?"

Calley stiffened at the disbelief in Dean's voice. "It wasn't a grizzly," she explained. "You know how blacks are. If you make enough noise, they'll turn tail and run."

"Why didn't you wait for Mike? Let him do it."

Calley didn't know whether to be angry or amused. "If I'd waited for Mike, that bear would have done more than eat our food supply. I wasn't going to take a chance on his destroying the CB. I grabbed a couple of pans and started banging them together. I made a spectacle of myself, but it did the trick."

Calley was finished with her story, but Dean continued to stare at her. He was holding a thin-bladed knife in his right hand. His hand dropped to his side. In his mind he saw a slightly built woman standing her ground against three hundred pounds of shiny black hair, deadly claws and teeth. Intellectually he knew she was right. The chance that the black would attack her was minute. But because Dean had memories and terrors to battle, he saw the creature sinking its teeth into Calley's flesh.

"Don't ever do that again."

"Don't ever do what again? Protect my property from a camp robber?"

"A bear isn't a camp robber," Dean said through clenched teeth. "He could have killed you, Calley."

"That isn't too likely, and you know it. He started backing up the minute I showed up. I knew I could call his bluff. Dean, don't forget. I've made wild animals my life's work. I know what I'm doing."

Of course she did. Dean shook off his anger and outrage and acknowledged that Calley was right. If it had been a grizzly, she would have known how to handle that situation. He didn't have to do her thinking for her. "You're a pretty resourceful woman, aren't you?"

"I try. I'm glad you can admit that."

Dean put down his knife, wiped his hands on his pants and sat beside her. "Mike said you were the best."

"He did?"

Calley's voice sounded hollow, but Dean chose to ignore that. "He said you had an instinct when it came to animals. That you're resourceful and you don't panic."

"Coming from him, that's a compliment." Calley looked at her hands resting on the log next to his. Hers were smaller and softer, but they shared a certain strength fashioned by their common life-style. "What else did he say?"

"If you mean, did he say anything of a personal nature, no. Whatever you may think of Mike, and I take it there's a lot of bitterness there, he had the utmost respect for you professionally. He said you were someone people depended on."

"I'm surprised he sees that as a positive trait," Calley said bitterly. "Considering that's what came between us. I'm sorry." She raked her hand angrily through her hair. "I don't particularly like it when other people dissect their past relationships. I never intended to do that."

"Why not?" Slowly Dean drew her hand out of her hair, holding it between both of his. "You let me talk about Waina. Why shouldn't you be allowed to do the same thing?"

"Because you don't hate Waina."

"You don't hate Mike."

"Don't I?" Calley tried to pull her hand free, but Dean wouldn't let her. "You're right," she relented. "I don't hate him. I just don't want to talk about him."

Dean was tracing a pattern with his fingers on the back of her hand. The setting sun had cast a rosy hue over their surroundings. Calley's flesh was absorbing that color. "You'll have to someday. That's the only way you'll be able to put that to rest."

Calley straightened. She'd been watching what Dean was doing to her hand, but now she met his eyes. "You have to do the same thing, Dean. That's the only way you'll be able to end your nightmares."

Other than a quick arching of his spine, Dean gave no indication of how deeply he'd been touched by her words. "I tried that once. It didn't work."

"Then try it again."

"On you?"

Calley nodded. "I have a great deal of experience listening to people's problems." She laughed a little. "Lots of girl talk about men before Melinda figured out that she was in love with Kirk."

"Then I won't burden you with any more now." Dean released her and got to his feet. He turned back to his fish, slowly wrapping them in heavy plastic.

For a minute Calley sat where she was. She loved watching Dean work, even if all he was doing was wrapping fish. All the parts of his body worked in perfect harmony. He was big enough to be able to play football. Someday she'd ask him what sports he participated in, learn whether he followed any of the professional teams. There were a million things she wanted to know about the man who'd been part of her life for less than a week.

So many things about herself she wanted to tell him.

"Baked," she said as he was cleaning up his work surface. "With butter and onion slices."

"What are you rattling on about?"

"About how I want my fish cooked. Not that I should have to remind you, but you lost the bet. You cook from now on."

"You cheated," Dean protested. "I'm an amateur; you're a pro. You should have come clean about that."

"You didn't ask," Calley pointed out. "You're the one who was so sure a woman couldn't possibly know more about fishing than you. I can't be held accountable for your ill-advised male ego."

"Ill-advised male ego?" Dean glared. "Who hired whom, lady?"

"Irrelevant and immaterial," she pointed out. "If you're going to try to pull rank on me, I'll cry and pout."

"Can you really cry and pout?"

Calley twisted her mouth to one side. "I'm not sure," she had to admit. "I haven't tried that since I was a kid."

"Something tells me that was never part of your repertoire. I think we have enough onions to satisfy your palate. Do you think you'd possibly be able to set out the china while I attend to dinner? Just make sure you put things back where you found them. That's about the only thing that ruffles Steve's feathers."

Calley let Dean know that he was asking a great deal of her. She made a show of pulling out paper plates and mixing up nonfat dry milk to go with their meal. She'd settled herself near the campfire with needle and thread and a couple of her shirts that needed mending when Dean dropped a jacket on her lap. "While you're at it," he said. Before she could protest, he'd gone back to the meal preparation.

Calley tackled his jacket first. She brought it close to her face not because the light was poor but because the jacket held something of his essence. She ran her arm up a sleeve, allowing a slow warmth to wash over her. Had he permanently imprinted himself on the fabric? Would anyone but her notice?

When she was finished securing the loose buttons, she folded the jacket and left it on her knees while she worked on her garments. As the tantalizing aroma of onions sautéeing in butter reached her nostrils, she carried the jacket into his tent. She crawled in on hands and knees, noticing that the rumpled sleeping bag still carried his shape.

The man was everywhere.

Calley dropped her burden on the sleeping bag and backed out. His essence in the small space was more powerful than she was willing to deal with tonight. "Aren't you done yet?" she protested as she gave his work a critical look. "It isn't that hard to cook a trout."

"Complain, complain, complain. Here I've been slaving over a hot stove all day, and what thanks do I get?"

Calley ignored him. She wondered aloud when Steve and Melinda might be back and nodded agreement when Dean expressed concern that Steve might pull up stakes if he wasn't given the freedom to deal with the bear exactly the way he wanted. She sat on the most comfortable log, waiting patiently for Dean to serve her. "Not bad," she acknowledged after her first bite. "It could use a little fresh lemon."

"What do you think this is? The Ritz?" Dean glared at her over his own meal. "If you don't like it, you can always cook."

Calley shrugged elaborately. "You know about the traditional division of labor. I hunt. You cook."

"When horses fly. Aren't you supposed to be gnawing on a hide so I can have warm boots about now?"

Calley returned the glare Dean had given her, but the appeal of fish done to perfection was too much of a distraction. She could tease later. She concentrated on eating. "I didn't realize how tired I was of prepackaged, freeze-dried foods until I tasted this," she admitted. She smacked her lips. "My compliments to the chef."

"Thank you, ma'am." He was staring into the night; his eyes had a faraway look. "Have you ever tasted smoked salmon? Not the kind they try to pass off at those deli shops but the real stuff?"

"I don't think so," Calley admitted. "I'm sure I haven't tasted what you're referring to. You're talking about the way they do it in Alaska, aren't you?"

Dean nodded. Because his eyes still weren't focusing, she guessed that his thoughts weren't on the here and now. When he spoke, she knew she was right. "There's so many things I'd like to show you about Alaska. I know you'd enjoy it. What do you think of watching a dogsled race?"

"I'm sure I'd like that. I've always wanted to see the aurora borealis. I'm not so sure about nights that last twenty-four hours, though." Calley wanted her words to have the strength to take Dean away from his thoughts, but his mood was infecting her, as well. Tonight Alaska seemed a million miles away, a lifetime apart. She wondered if he was thinking about a true vacation or whether work would somehow be involved. A vacation, she hoped.

They could fly into some remote spot, burdened by nothing but photographic and fishing equipment. Dean would know where there were Dall sheep, seals, moose, fox and eagles to photograph. Although she knew better, Calley wished they could cut themselves completely off from civilization. That would give them enough time. Enough time to learn a million essential things about each other.

Calley tore herself free from the thought. "What time of year would we go?" she asked, even though it really didn't matter. "Not winter, I hope."

"What? Spring." Dean's eyes swung from the night sky. "Alaska comes to life in the spring. There are some lakes near Haines. We could put in a canoe or inflatable raft, and I'd show you a thing or two about still fishing."

"It sounds perfect. How far from Haines are these lakes? I don't want my line getting tangled up in someone else's. Are you sure we couldn't go somewhere more remote?"

"Remote?" Dean drew out the word. Because of the darkness Dean didn't think Calley could see the tension creeping through his body. Damn! Was that feeling never going to end?

"You know," Calley explained, "farther from civilization than we are now. Maybe—" She laughed. "Maybe we could chuck the CB and play like survivalists."

"That isn't very practical, Calley."

She sighed. "I know it isn't. Just indulge me my fantasy for a little while, will you? I've always wanted to try living off the land."

Damn her. The woman wasn't afraid of anything. Dean's eyes went back to the forest. There was no way she could comprehend what he was going through, sitting here surrounded by night, ears alert for alien sounds. It hadn't been this bad when Steve was here because the Indian's sense of peace about the land was infectious, but Calley was a woman. No, that wasn't it. She was someone he desperately didn't want anything bad to happen to. Certainly not what had happened to him. "It isn't as easy as it sounds. There's nothing romantic about silence so profound that it has a sound of its own," he said, testing her. "That can drive a person crazy."

Calley shrugged. "That's a pretty remote possibility. Dean?" She raked her hands through her hair in a gesture he now associated with serious thought on her part. "I've always wanted to test myself. Learn what I'm capable of. You can understand that, can't you?"

He wasn't sure. Not anymore. "Calley, what are you trying to prove?"

She looked sharply at him. "I'm not trying to prove anything. All right." She pulled on her hair. "Maybe I am. I'm finding strengths I didn't know I had. I guess I want to test the limit of that strength."

"No one expects you to."

"I don't care what other people expect. I don't know if I can make you understand this, Dean, but I want to try. It's easier being a woman than a man. Not as much is expected of a woman. But I've always believed that that's a cop-out. Complacency can backfire on a woman. If she's raised like a hothouse plant, she grows up ill equipped to handle life's problems. All right, maybe I'm overstating the case, but I don't want to go through life having never really tested myself. I want to know that when the chips are down, when there's no one to fall back on, I can stand on my own two feet."

He had to ask it. "Have you always felt that way?"

"I think so," she answered slowly. "I've always loved a challenge. That got me in a lot of scrapes when I was a kid. The bigger kids were always daring me to do something. Of course, I took them up on it."

"That can backfire on a person."

"Tell me about it." Calley laughed. "Who do you think got caught trying to break into the principal's office?"

Dean looked at her as if her intelligence was suspect. "No one tries to break into the principal's office."

"They do if someone says it can't be done," Calley explained. "Like I said, I was always game for a challenge."

"Like being dropped in some remote part of Alaska?"

"Maybe." She laughed again. "If I could survive that, I think I could handle anything."

"What do you think your chances are of coming out alive?"

"Pretty good. Does that sound egotistical?" she asked. "I'm sorry if it does, but if I don't believe in myself, who will? That's a question I think everyone has to answer. We all have to have confidence in ourselves. Believe we can handle everything that's thrown at us."

And she could. That knowledge was what kept Dean from touching her again that evening. She was sure and confident, without fear.

Damn her.

Chapter Seven

Dean and Calley were finishing breakfast the next morning when they heard the sound of a truck. Calley felt relief at the prospect of having Steve and Melinda back with them. Dean had been quiet and remote last night, and she had not been looking forward to spending the day in the company of someone who spoke only in grunts. What bothered her the most was not so much his mood as not understanding what had brought on the sudden wall that now stood between them. There'd been no hint when they started talking about a fantasy vacation, but somewhere, somehow, Dean had shut her out.

"It was marvelous!" Melinda squealed as soon as she was out of the truck. "I took sequence pictures of Steve and the park vet while they were working on the black. I'm thinking of calling *National Geographic* to see if they're interested."

"Isn't that aiming a little high? You'd be competing with photographers who've been in the business for years," Calley warned as she gave her friend a quick hug. "Are the pictures developed yet?"

Melinda admitted that they weren't. "But the story that goes with the pictures is fantastic. I just know someone's going to be interested in it. If I get paid enough, I'm holding out for a real wedding. I might even convince you to get out of your jeans and into a dress. You will be my maid of honor, won't you? Kirk couldn't argue if I paid for the traditional route, could he?"

Calley gave up. Obviously Melinda was too excited to be bothered by anyone's pessimism. Melinda probably wouldn't notice that Dean was acting like a cigar-store Indian, something Calley wished she herself could do. As soon as Steve and Melinda were settled back in camp, Steve started telling them about the trip to Yellowstone. The first day had been spent in a futile attempt to locate the injured bear, but by the next morning they'd heard from a couple of hikers who'd stumbled upon the ill-tempered creature near Whistler Geyser.

"That was one mad bear with a king-sized foot ache," Steve explained. "We figured he couldn't forage very well for himself and that he was getting desperate. He was determined to get his paws on the hikers' food. They had to take refuge in a tree to escape him. Fortunately these two hikers weren't novices. They knew the bear's behavior wasn't normal. They pacified him by letting him demolish their backpacks and then ran for the park management as soon as the black wandered off. They were making some noises about suing the park for the loss of their equipment, but I think they listened when I told them that they accepted the risk when they went into the backcountry."

"Did you get the black that same day?" Calley asked. She didn't try to hide the fact that she was both excited and disappointed. Listening to Steve's story wasn't the same as being there. "We were treed, too, but our bear was pretty bored with us," she explained. "She didn't really even try to come up after us."

Dean shot Calley a look, but she chose to ignore it. This morning she couldn't read his mind if her life depended on it. Instead, she concentrated on what Steve was telling them, that the actual spotting and tranquilizing of the bear didn't take place until the next day. Steve explained that the park management made arrangements for them to make use of a helicopter, and Steve was able to shoot the bear while leaning out of the helicopter door. "It took three tries before I hit him," Steve admitted with the lack of boastfulness Calley had come to expect from the Indian. "He was so mad at the helicopter that he didn't head for cover." Steve's voice turned serious. "I don't blame him. I would have been furious at anything man-made myself."

"Why?" Calley asked.

"Because that poor bear had a large chunk of glass from a soft-drink bottle buried in his right front paw. It was badly infected."

Calley shuddered. "But you were able to get it out, weren't you?"

Steve nodded while Melinda bobbed her head in agreement. He explained that after they'd determined what was wrong with the bear, the helicopter pilot had to go back for the vet, who'd been tied up with another emergency. Steve had been able to remove the glass, but then the vet arrived and cleaned out the wound and stitched it closed. "He used several layers of stitches and made them small so I hope the bear won't be able to pull them out before he heals. I don't know." Steve sighed. "It's a freak accident, but it's the kind of thing that's going to happen as long as bears have to share the park with humans."

"I don't suppose you were able to find anyone who wanted to hear that," Dean said sarcastically. His lips were tight as he continued. "People run all over that park, but they expect animals to live their lives as if nothing's happening."

Steve groaned. "I think I've heard this argument before. Dean, you and I can't change a park policy that's been going on for decades."

"Someone's going to have to. Otherwise there isn't going to be a Yellowstone worth going to before long."

"You don't have to tell me that," Steve reassured him. "But I think they're finally catching on. They're admitting there is a problem. Maybe there's hope for the wildlife yet."

"Yeah?" Dean sounded doubtful.

Steve went on. "Yeah. While we were there the rangers were talking about a female grizzly and her cub that had been spotted near Hayden Valley. First one in that area in at least five years. Everyone's pretty excited about the cub. They closed down the trail there. They're not going to take a chance on anyone disturbing those two. You know that kind of action wouldn't have been taken a few years ago."

"For how long?" Calley asked. Like the others, she shared a deep concern for the wildlife in the national parks.

"All summer, if necessary," Steve explained. "The park personnel admits that there are fewer than two hundred grizzlies left in Yellowstone. They're even admitting that former park management is responsible for that."

"Are they also willing to admit that only about thirty of those are cub-bearing females?" Dean asked. "The old blanket policy of killing any grizzlies that threatened man has just about wiped them out. Damn! Who was there first?"

Calley winced, not in reaction to Dean's sharp words but in sympathy for the magnificent creatures who'd been sacrificed because of the greedy needs of visitors. "It all leads back to when they closed down the old dumps," she mused aloud. "The bears had been feeding on those dumps for years. When they were closed because someone decided man was turning them into scavengers, the bears started foraging elsewhere. Like around campgrounds."

"You've done your homework, haven't you," Dean said. "Of course, the park personnel could always move the bears to remote areas."

Calley knew she was being tested. "An expensive proposition," she pointed out. "I'm sure you know that better than I do. And what if, or should I say when, the bear comes back? Are they going to ship it out again or label it dangerous and kill it?"

"What would you suggest?"

Calley was ready for Dean's question. "Two things—reopen the remote dumps and, if necessary, close down any campgrounds near a grizzly habitat."

"You'd get a lot of complaints with that plan." Dean was staring at her with a relentlessness that would have shaken her if she hadn't been convinced that the needs of the few remaining bears had to come first.

"The grizzly can't be brought back from extinction," she said simply. "Humans can be moved."

"I think you should let her be the spokesman the next time you're in Yellowstone or D.C.," Steve pointed out. "Once she gets the fire going in her eyes, they'll have to listen to her. Besides that, an attractive young woman makes a better spokesman than an ugly old man like you."

Calley laughed at herself. She ran her hand over her eyes, but the intensity was still there. "I do tend to foam at the mouth at the way the grizzlies have been mismanaged. I'm not sure I could speak without ranting. I tried to get Mike to present those arguments himself, but he said that those in charge of bear management weren't receptive. They were convinced that the methods they were using to manage grizzlies was working. Mike didn't fight hard enough. He gave up," she said softly. "It's only now that they're seeing the error of their ways."

"Are you saying the problem has been solved?" Dean asked.

"Of course not," Calley said emphatically. "What I'm saying is that finally the park management is seeing that there is a problem. I just hope it isn't too late to save the grizzlies there. Mike should have tried harder. Made them listen."

"He gave up," Dean said.

"Yes, he gave up! Don't let me get started on that," Calley begged. "I really don't want to talk about Mike or bring up some of the classic arguments we had. It's a dead issue."

Because in a few short days Dean had learned how to read most of Calley's emotions, he understood her need to put Mike out of her life. Dean was aware that there'd always been something in Mike that sought the path of least resistance. Mike presented his points logically but backed down when opposed. It might have been an admirable trait for a politician, but someone charged with the responsibility of maintaining a fragile ecosystem had to have the guts to lock horns with opposition and apathy. Much as Dean admired Mike's expertise as a biologist, he understood why he hadn't lasted in the position Dean now held. There wasn't enough iron in Mike's spine.

And Calley was a steel-tempered woman. She deserved better.

By the time the day was over, Dean hadn't changed his mind about Calley's competence. If there'd been any lingering doubt that she was capable at her job, that was dispelled under a cloudless sky. With Steve and Melinda back, the decision was made that they would break up into two groups in order to cover more territory. Although he realized that Steve and Melinda might be tired of each other's company, Dean insisted on having Calley travel with him.

It would have been easier to pair her with Steve. Dean couldn't look at her without being reminded that Calley was the one not haunted by the past. The one with rare guts. As long as she was around, Dean couldn't deny that there were things he hadn't resolved and that wouldn't release him until he'd faced them.

But Dean didn't want to spend the day without Calley. In two days they would be leaving; they might never be able to recapture what existed between them on the Flathead. He wanted to walk behind her as she plowed her way up a hill. He remembered the sensual, if unconscious, way she lifted her shirt away from her breasts when the day's heat bore down on her. He wanted to watch her do that again.

Calley had said almost nothing in the two hours since they left camp, and that bothered Dean. He searched his mind for a casual way of breaking the silence, but everything he came up with sounded artificial. He'd resigned himself to being ignored and accepted her grunt of approval when he indicated they might have a better view if they scrambled up a slope consisting of loose shale. At that point Dean insisted on breaking trail. That way he could find what solid footing existed and then turn to give her a hand if she needed it. Calley accepted his steadying hand once, but it was obvious that she wanted and needed nothing more than that from him. With a resigned sigh Dean concentrated on reaching the top some hundred feet above them.

He was digging his heel into the thinly layered rock when Calley's startled cry tore through him. At the sound he whirled around in time to see her tumbling head over heels down the hill, arms flailing in a futile attempt to stop herself.

"Calley!" he screamed. He bounced on his toes and slid down the shale after her. Before he could reach her, Calley slammed into a boulder near the base of the hill. The sound of her body hitting unrelenting rock sickened him. She sighed softly and went limp.

Dean knelt beside her, his heart hammering in his throat. Damn. He'd insisted on tackling the stupid hill and now—damn! If she was badly injured, he'd never forgive himself. "Calley," he whispered. "Calley." He touched the side of her neck, breathing only when he'd found the strong pulse there. She was alive, but he was afraid to turn her over. Had she hit the boulder with her face? Were there broken bones? How was he going to get her out of here? "Can you hear me?" he asked, aware of how insane his question must sound. Whether she could hear was the least of it, and yet he needed to hear her voice so badly that his need had become a physical pain.

Calley's body was limp. He gripped her fingers, but there was no response. If it wasn't for her pulse, he would have thought her dead. Damning himself once again, Dean bent his head close to hers, trying to catch the rhythm of her breathing. The gentle sound returned warmth to his veins. Cautiously he touched first her temple where hair and flesh came together and then made contact with her forehead.

"Calley. Can you turn over?"

"No."

The barely audible whisper was the most welcome sound he had ever heard. Dean placed his hands on her back in what he hoped was a comforting gesture. "I'm here, darling. You're going to be all right. Calley, I want to turn you over, but I'm afraid I'll hurt you. Can you feel anything? Have you hurt your neck?" Could she tell how scared he was?

"I feel rocks poking into me. This is not fun." Calley slid her right hand under her body and attempted to turn over. The effort ended in a pain-filled groan. "Bad idea," she gasped.

"What is it?" Dean knew his fingers were digging into her shoulder, but he couldn't help himself. How could she possibly joke at a time like this?

"My side hurts." Her voice was muffled. "I think I did something to it."

"Please let me try to turn you over," Dean suggested. "I'll take it easy. I promise I won't hurt you." When she didn't respond, he gently rolled her over. Calley's face was dusty, her hair snarled around her face and neck. The buttons of her shirt had pulled open, revealing a soiled bra. She was beautiful.

"Hi." Calley winked.

"Hi, yourself." Reverently Dean brushed the dirt away from her mouth. He kissed her long and deep, not caring how much of his inner emotions he was giving away. He'd been so scared. Regaining his equilibrium was going to take time. "You're a mess."

"I kind of figured that. The rocks are killing me," she said through tight lips. "There's one digging into my spine."

"Do you think you can stand up?" he asked.

"I'm not so sure, Dean," she whispered. When she continued, her voice was a little stronger. "I'm no expert at this sort of thing, but I think maybe I broke my rib."

She was so calm. Later he could marvel at her calmness, but for now he simply accepted it. At least he didn't have to worry about her going into shock. Without bothering to ask her permission, Dean unbuttoned what few buttons remained intact and pushed aside her shirt. He could see the ugly swollen welt rising over a rib on her right side. Fortunately the skin wasn't broken, but what he knew about first aid told him that if the rib was broken it might be pointing inward. "I'm going to have to hurt you," he said, hating what he was going to have to do. "I can't tell what the damage is if I don't touch you there."

"I kind of figured that, doctor." She gave him a shaky smile. "Be gentle with me."

"This is no time for a wisecrack, Calley. This is serious business," Dean reminded her. He was putting off the moment when he'd have to touch her, arguing over something that didn't matter.

"What would you like me to do? Cry?"

Yes. Cry. Fall apart. Let me know you need me. Dean wanted those things to happen because that's what past experience told him people did when they were hurt. But despite the pain in Calley's eyes, she was breathing calmly, trying to turn her head so she could observe the injury herself. He tried a joke. "You could faint."

"Sorry." She wrinkled her nose. "I was at recess when they were giving fainting lessons. Are you going to sit there all day, or shall we see what the damage is?"

"I should have a bullet for you to bite," Dean observed as his fingers made the first faint contact. Calley tensed as he continued his exploration, but other than shutting her eyes when he found the tip of the broken rib, she made no indication that she'd done more than bruised herself.

"It's broken, isn't it?" she asked when he was done.

"I'm afraid so." Damn! He didn't want her hurt. Not her. "But I don't think it's a complete break. More like a crack. I don't think it's going to cause any more trouble than it has already."

"It's caused enough," Calley pointed out. "How are we going to get back? I'm really not up to a marathon."

"I'll carry you."

Calley laughed, stopping herself when the laugh registered in her rib. "That's a tall order. I hate to have to admit this, Dean, but a hundred and twenty-five pounds gets pretty heavy after a couple of miles."

"Why don't you let me worry about that? I've taken all the first-aid courses anyone needs." Dean winced at the harsh way his statement came out. He wanted her to turn everything over to him, to let him make all the decisions. But that wasn't Calley. She wasn't a leaner. "We're going to need to immobilize that rib before we can do anything else. Are you sure that's the only place you hurt?"

"Except for needing a pillow, I'm in pretty good shape," Calley observed. "Of course, I could use a bath." She turned her head as far as possible in both directions. "We're going to need some bandages. There's a jacket in my backpack."

Dean couldn't argue with Calley's logic. Although he hated leaving her long enough to retrieve her backpack, it was obvious that she wasn't going to panic if left alone. A minute later he was back. He pulled off his T-shirt so it would serve as a cushion over the injury itself and used both of their jackets to hold the shirt in place and to restrict movement of the rib. He tried to rebutton Calley's shirt, but it barely fit over the extra layers. He was slipping back into his own shirt when she giggled.

"Oh! I shouldn't have done that," Calley admitted. Her eyes were bright with sudden tears. "Laughing hurts. I was just thinking that this is taking the concept of cleavage to ridiculous lengths. Somehow I don't feel very seductive. How far from camp are we, anyway?"

"Why don't you let me worry about that?" Dean repeated. By degrees he helped her to her feet. At one point the color left her face, but other than closing her eyes again, Calley gave no indication of what she was feeling. He knew he was causing her pain when he hoisted her onto his back, but she held on to the backpacks now draped over her neck and managed a soft "Hi ho, Silver" when he started.

The trip back to camp took close to two hours. By the time they reached the clearing, Dean was drenched in sweat, and his legs ached, but his discomfort was a vague thing pushed to the back of his mind by his concern for the woman who now felt as if she were part of him. He was aware of her femininity and temporary dependence on him, but even more consuming was his admiration for the woman he'd called "darling" a little while ago. If nothing else, Calley was courageous.

Dean dropped to his knees near his tent and waited for Calley to stand. Then he stood and gripped her shoulder to help her keep her balance. Her face was pale, her lips tight. But before he could ask her how she was, she reached up and kissed him on the tip of his nose. "Well done." She sighed. "You must be exhausted."

"What about you?"

"I haven't had to do anything but hold on," she pointed out. "You did all the work."

Even when Melinda started fussing over her, Calley continued to maintain that her rib was a minor consideration. She argued that there was no reason for them to abort their research a day early on her account. "We can just slap on an Ace bandage and I'll be fine," she argued as Melinda was removing her boots. "That's all a doctor will do, anyway."

"Will you shut up!" Dean spat out. "There's no reason for you to play superwoman. No one believes a word of what you're saying, anyway. You're going to need to be X-rayed."

Calley sighed. She was sitting on a log Steve had moved next to an evergreen. Her back was resting against the tree, her face still whiter than Dean liked. "I know that, Dean. I just feel so guilty. This has really messed things up."

"Don't." Dean wasn't going to touch her. His feet hurt, and the mug of cold water Steve had brought him was making him lethargic, but he hadn't been able to stop thinking about how much worse things could be. He pulled himself to his feet and came to stand beside Calley, who was still seated on the log. Bending down, he gently wrapped his arms around her and held her against him. Her head rested against his waist. She'd trusted him to bring her safely out of the woods. He'd never had anyone place their safety in his hands that completely before. It was a good feeling and helped to balance the scale between them. "All I want is to get you to a hospital." That wasn't entirely true. They'd lose something precious when they left the woods behind.

"I'd rather have a shower." Calley sighed. Her father had always called her bull stubborn, the original stoic. With Dean's arm around her she no longer felt a need to prove herself. And yet she wanted to tell him a little of what she was made of. "This isn't my first broken rib," she went on softly. "I had a horse when I was growing up who thought it great fun to take the bit in his teeth and take off for a tree with a low branch. Usually I'd be able to cling to his side and not get knocked off. Usually."

"What happened?" Not again. Dean didn't want to think about Calley and pain anymore.

"The tree was harder than me. So, as I recall, was the ground."

Dean had met women who wouldn't be seen dead with pine needles in their hair, dirt clinging to their torn blouses, who would never have gotten on the back of a headstrong horse or tried to scramble up a shale hill. Calley wasn't anything like them.

Seeing that now did something to him. It no longer bothered Dean to think about her getting knocked off a horse or suffering a broken rib. That was what Calley Stewart was. He didn't want that changed.

She was so precious—indeed, unique. He wanted to explore what she was more than he had in their brief time together, maybe even to tell her some things about himself. Dean resented the presence of Steve and Melinda. He wanted Calley to himself. But he couldn't have that.

No matter what his emotions, he had to load up the pickup and the jeep and get Calley back to civilization.

After resting for a few minutes, Dean joined Steve in the task of dismantling camp. Melinda stayed with Calley. As soon as the men were out of sight, Melinda helped Calley out of her soiled shirt. "You're really going to have to clean up before I let you come to my wedding," Melinda teased as she started removing the makeshift bandage. "Dean's T-shirt? The whole thing sounds pretty intimate to me."

"Don't I wish," Calley whispered. She held her breath while Melinda deftly wrapped an Ace bandage tightly around her middle. "He was in such a bad mood this morning that I wasn't sure I wanted anything to do with him. I'm surprised he paired us up."

"Are you kidding?" Melinda didn't try to hide her surprise. "You didn't see the look on his face when the two of you stumbled into camp. He was so worried it was ridiculous. I thought you were at least dead. He hates the idea of you being hurt."

Calley sighed. "I know he does. He was more worried than I was when I got hurt. That's why I can't understand his mood this morning. I mean—" She paused, testing the wisdom of saying anything more. "Sometimes things can be so right between us. Sometimes I think he knows what I'm thinking even when I don't say anything. He called me darling; I don't think that was just because he was scared for me."

"I know he feels something special for you. The signs are certainly there."

Calley shot Melinda a look of gratitude as Melinda helped her into a clean blouse. "You make it sound pretty simple. It isn't."

Melinda shook her head. "I know that. Nothing that goes on between men and women is."

Calley had reason to mull over what Melinda had said once she had been loaded into the pickup and they were on their way. She hated having to leave Bigfork but had hoped that the long trip would give her and Dean the opportunity to talk.

She was wrong. At least she was for the first hour. She had to concentrate on cushioning herself against the shock of the truck bouncing along the dirt road, but Melinda had made sure that her rib was pretty well immobilized. At length she relaxed. However, other than asking her if she was comfortable, Dean didn't seem to care.

Calley mulled that over, looking for answers she could accept. She tried to tell herself that Dean must be exhausted. That would explain his silence. She tried to tell herself that he had an aversion to injuries and was determined to steer clear of any further mention of it. But a man with a scar on his side was no stranger to pain.

Finally the silence between them became too much. Calley's head was pounding; her stomach rumbled from the missed meals. She wanted someone to pat her on the head and say the kind of things mothers say to injured children. It was, she knew, a childish emotion, but as night fell, Calley decided there was nothing that drastically wrong with indulging herself. She slid over to the middle of the seat and rested her head on Dean's shoulder.

She was thinking about hot chicken soup, a fluffed-up pillow and her mother's soft humming when Dean spoke. "We're going to be able to wrap up this study in another week or so. If the funding comes through, we could be doing the same thing in Alaska before the month is over. And there's another short project in the wind up there. My guess is we're going to be pretty busy between now and winter."

That was the first Calley had heard of moving the base of operation farther north. She'd assumed that they'd simply continue what they were doing within the continental United States. "What funding?" she asked without bothering to open her eyes.

"Through the Interior Department. I've been pushing for some funds from the Fish and Wildlife Service. Hunting interests are exerting pressure to reduce the grizzly population in Alaska in order to protect moose for hunters. The director of McKinley Park and I have been working on the Interior Department together."

Calley was exhausted. In the morning she'd have the energy to speak in opposition to hunting interests, but tonight she didn't want to think about anything more complicated than when, if ever, she'd have dinner. When Dean would kiss her again.

"I'll have to buy some clothes."

"For what?" Obviously Dean hadn't kept up with the turn of thought her mind had taken.

"For Melinda's wedding. She wants me to be her maid of honor. I don't think I own a dress."

Dean shifted his weight. When he settled back against the seat, his arm was around her. "Of course you have a dress. Every woman has a dress."

"I guess." Calley sighed. The conversation was too complicated. Concentrating on the welcome weight of Dean's arm on her shoulder was the only thing she was interested in.

Dean didn't speak for the better part of a minute. "Are you falling asleep?"

"No." She wasn't sure that was true.

"Don't."

"Why not?"

"Because there's something I want to tell you."

Calley was instantly awake, although she did nothing to let him know. "You aren't going to try to sell me a subscription to anything, are you?" she teased. She didn't want the topic to be serious.

"You're a remarkable woman. I just wanted you to know that."

Calley kept her eyes shut. She forgave him his moods, the moods he'd put her through. His words found their way deep inside her, touching her heart. "Why do you say that?" she had to ask.

"Because you're solid. Strong."

"I'm not sure that's a compliment," she said, although she would rather remain silent, tracing the effect his tone of voice was having on her emotions. Darling, he'd called her. She would remember that moment for the rest of her life.

"It's a compliment, Calley. There aren't many women who could have handled today as well as you did."

Calley sighed. The conversation was going to be serious. "I wouldn't want it any other way," she admitted. "Farm life taught me that everyone has to stand on their own two feet. I had the lesson reinforced in spades this past year. Being strong, as you call it, got me through a lot."

"I'd like to have you tell me about it sometime."

"Sometime," Calley repeated. But not now. Tonight was for listening to the beating of Dean's heart, her head moving in response to his quiet breathing. Later she'd tell him about her parents and Mike and wondering if her world was caving in around her. Later she'd ask him why he'd suddenly turned cold earlier when she thought they were reaching a new closeness.

But not tonight.

Chapter Eight

The gown wasn't Calley's first choice, but because the tight bandage would have to remain around her ribs for another week, she'd had to settle for something that would float over her body instead of cling. The pale yellow crepe was the perfect foil for her permanent tan. Because of her tan, she was able to carry off the combination of amber hair and a dress with just a whisper of color. For once Calley had actually gone to a beauty shop to have her hair done. It now caressed her cheeks before sliding gracefully down her neck. Between giggles and a few false starts, both Calley and Melinda had managed the subtle changes that makeup made on faces used to the natural look. Even Calley was impressed by what a little smoky color could do to bring out the gray in her eyes.

Now Calley was watching her best friend nervously finger the short veil that served to accent Melinda's larger than usual eyes. "Why did I agree to go through with this?" Melinda moaned for the third time. "I don't want to stand in front of everyone. What if I forget what I'm supposed to say?"

"Come off it," Calley teased. "You know you've been dying for a chance to hold center stage. If Kirk can deck himself out in an honest-to-goodness suit, the least you can do is show up without jeans."

"Yeah." Cautiously Melinda nodded her head. She ran her hands down the smooth white taffeta that skimmed over her hips and ended in layers of lace flounce at the floor-length hemline. "I feel like a princess. In fact, I might take to wearing a little makeup on a regular basis. But why did Kirk tell all the graduate students they could show up for free chow? There's going to be more than fifty people out there listening to me mess up my words."

Calley sighed. Even though she kept telling herself she had to be calm so Melinda would have someone to lean on, Melinda's nervousness was infecting her. "You aren't going to mess up anything," she tried to reassure her as she straightened the puffed sheer sleeves on Melinda's gown. "We practiced last night, didn't we? Besides, if the wind's blowing, probably no one will be able to hear you."

Melinda smiled for the first time since Calley had come over to Melinda's apartment. "The weather is cooperating. I'm so glad we're going to be able to have the wedding outside. I'll have to thank Dean for getting the powers that be to agree to let us have this show on the university grounds."

"You already thanked him last night," Calley reminded Melinda. "At least two times. All right, let's see if we have everything. You won't be gone long enough that we'll have to worry about your plants needing to be watered. Darn. I wish the two of you had time for a real honeymoon."

Melinda winked. "We've been practicing. I think we have the idea."

Calley winked back. "I get your drift. Okay, keys, something to change into after the reception, Kirk's ring?"

Melinda reminded her that she, Calley, was carrying Kirk's ring, and then the two women got into Calley's jeep for the short drive to the campus. They drew several surprised looks as they drove through town in their finery. Calley tried to point out to Melinda that she'd washed the jeep and that there was a clean blanket on the front seat, but when a couple of little girls at a street corner started clapping, Melinda got the giggles.

By the time they reached the campus parking lot, both women were relaxed and eager to get the show on the road. Because Dean had been called into service to make sure the parklike area they'd selected was properly set up, Calley hadn't seen him since the rehearsal dinner the previous night. Calley glanced at her image in the jeep's mirror one last time before getting out. Not bad. Maybe Dean would sit up and take notice. He'd been buried under paperwork since their return to the campus two weeks ago. Except for going out for dinner several times and work-oriented meetings, they hadn't been together.

Of course, the phone calls had been nice, Calley admitted. Every night promptly at 7:00 p.m., Dean had called to ask how she was feeling, catch her up on his day and see how she was coming along with compiling the data they'd collected on the Flathead. But work wouldn't be getting in the way today. It was fantasy time; romance would surround them.

What, if anything, might come from today was what made Calley hurry Melinda along. "You look fine," Calley said as Melinda tried to check her lipstick in the rearview mirror. "Seeing you in a dress is such a contrast to your usual attire that everyone will be impressed."

Melinda grabbed Calley's hand with cold fingers. "Look who's talking. You're the one who said she didn't own a dress."

"I didn't. I had to buy this one. Did I tell you I'm sending the bill to you?"

Melinda's protest and Calley's mock argument kept them from getting too nervous until they reached the quiet park-like area chosen for the outdoor wedding. Melinda and Calley slipped into the nearest building and waited until they were informed it was time to make an entrance. Melinda's hand, clutching Calley's, was still icy, but the smile that lit up her face when she caught sight of Kirk waiting for her reassured Calley that her friend wasn't going to back out at the last moment.

Calley took her place near the profusion of roses held in place by a white trellis and watched Melinda glide along the packed granite trail to where Calley, the minister and Kirk's best friend waited. Melinda's eyes were soft with wonder as she turned toward the man who was about to become her husband. As Melinda began her vows under a cloudless Montana sky, Calley made her decision. If she ever got married, it would be out-of-doors.

It wasn't until the happy couple was receiving the good wishes of their friends on the newly mowed lawn where the reception would be held that Calley looked around for Dean. It wasn't hard to spot him. Despite the beard and thick, almost shaggy hair that was his trademark, he looked very much the modern sophisticate in his dark suit. He looked, Calley decided in the instant it took for his smile to reach her, as intriguing as the first time she'd seen him.

"What if I get you some champagne?" Dean offered as he gently circled her waist with his arm. "You looked as if you were really wrapped up in what they were saying during the ceremony."

"Did I?" Calley asked dreamily. "I'm kind of relieved that it's over."

"Don't you like weddings?"

"I don't like knowing fifty people are going to see if I faint. Does that sound conceited?" She laughed. "They're watching Melinda and Kirk, not me."

Dean held her close against his side. "You're not used to being part of the show. Don't worry. You're beautiful. I really like what you did to your hair."

"Thank you," Calley whispered. "You couldn't tell I was trussed up? This fabric's pretty thin."

Dean turned her toward him. Gently, he ran his hands over her shoulders, lightly lifting the fabric of her dress. "It isn't thin enough for me," he whispered before kissing her. "I couldn't believe you were the same woman who beat me at fishing. You looked as if you could float off into the sky."

Calley melted. It was such a beautiful thing to say. His words held so much promise. Dean had kept her at arm's length while she was recovering from her accident, but he was telling her that that time was coming to an end. She wondered if he had any idea how hard the waiting had been. She tried to push back so she could look at him, but with his hands on her she lacked the strength. There were too many layers covering him today. She didn't want to feel the crisp suit. She wanted him naked from the waist up, the way he'd been that first day on the Flathead. She wanted things she didn't have words for.

"How long is this reception going to last?" Dean whispered. He hadn't given any indication that he was ever going to let her go.

"I don't know. Why?"

"Because I want to be alone with you."

"Oh." It was a stupid response, but it was the most Calley was capable of. His warmth, his sexuality, was reaching her through his suit. She felt weaker than she had when she'd broken her rib.

"You're beautiful."

"I think you said that before," she managed to say.

"I'm saying it again." Dean ran his lips across her forehead. "You look so feminine today; I can't get used to it. I'm not sure I ever want to see you in jeans again. I didn't know you had legs."

Calley could laugh. "I hate panty hose. They feel like I've glued something on my skin."

"I can take them off for you, you know."

"Dean!" Calley wasn't really shocked, just shaken because his thoughts were dovetailing with hers. They were communicating without words. Her rib had gotten in the way of so much in the past two weeks, but the doctor had told her it was healing nicely and she could experiment with removing the wrap for short periods of time. She didn't need to curtail her activities anymore. What that might mean in the terms of her relationship with Dean was going to be explored later today. That was what didn't need to be said.

Calley met Melinda's parents and Kirk's mother. She sobered when Kirk explained that his parents had divorced when he was a child and he had very little contact with his father. She tried to throw off the impact of what Kirk had said by sampling from the laden table set on a level part of the lawn, but the quiet whispering memory of her past year refused to fade.

"Personal relationships are so complicated, aren't they?" she asked Dean as they shared a glass of champagne. "When I think of how much Kirk's father has missed— He should be here today."

Dean stopped her with a kiss that reached her toes. "You can't make the world turn out the way you want it to, Calley," he whispered. "We can't live other people's lives for them."

"I know." Calley couldn't bring her eyes up to meet Dean's. She was so aware of him it was almost frightening.

It was all she could do to keep her fingers wrapped around her glass. "How I know!"

Dean tilted her chin upward until there was no hiding from the question in his eyes. "This mood of yours has to do with what you've been through recently, doesn't it?"

Calley nodded but gave him no answers. "Not now," she managed to say. "I want to be happy for Melinda."

Dean relaxed his hold on her. "Then later," he said softly.

Later. The word had never held so much potency before. Calley went through the rest of the reception in a fog. She spoke briefly with several people who were interested in what they'd been doing on the Flathead and a couple of professors who remembered when she worked for Mike, but her mind was on what she was going to tell Dean when they were alone. She was a little nervous, because she knew how much emotion was involved in the story, but she had no desire to put it off. Dean wasn't just the man she worked for; he was the only man who had a right to see her emotions.

An hour after the wedding, the group began to break up. Melinda gave Calley the name of the motel where she and Kirk would be staying and asked if Calley would make sure there were some groceries in the refrigerator for their return. After a hug and tears that acknowledged the new direction Melinda's life was taking, they were off.

"I think this is going to be one marriage that works," Dean observed as he steered Calley toward his truck. "Those two seem to understand that they can't live in each other's pockets. They love each other, but there isn't going to be any smothering."

Calley agreed. "Kirk was the one to suggest that Melinda keep her own name," she explained. "Melinda established herself in her career before they were married. He doesn't want her to lose that identity."

Dean frowned and then shrugged. "I have a problem with that," he admitted. "I think a couple should have the same name. It's a sign of commitment to each other."

"Maybe." Calley slid into the truck and straightened her skirt. "But it takes more than the same name to make a marriage."

Dean squeezed Calley's hand. "Where to, milady?"

Her place? His? It didn't matter. "You decide."

Dean drove to the house on the outskirts of town that he'd leased when he first came to the university. As he'd explained to Calley, he could afford better, but because he didn't expect to be spending much time in Missoula, he couldn't see putting much money into four walls. As he unlocked the front door he was telling her about the continued contact he'd had with the Mount McKinley Park personnel.

"If we do go to Alaska, it won't be for several more weeks," he explained. "At least that's what they're saying now. And I don't know how long we'll be there. It depends on how receptive certain people are to some of the suggestions I want to make. The director's in my camp, but he doesn't run the whole show."

Calley nodded, but she wasn't really concentrating on what he was saying. She'd told Dean that he needed to make his house less of an office/storage room and more of a home, but obviously she hadn't gotten through to him. "I suppose the tent's still in the spare bedroom."

"I was going to repack it this weekend," Dean explained. "I did mend the tear near the flap."

"Good for you." Calley ran out of things to say. They'd been rushed for time or she'd been "off limits" because of her injury every time they'd been here in the past two weeks. Suddenly, it seemed, they had all the time in the world.

"You're feeling all right now?" Dean asked. He unbuttoned his suit jacket and threw it in the direction of the couch.

"All right," she echoed. "The doctor said that as long as I didn't jump on a trampoline, the bone would stay in place."

"I'm glad." Dean yanked on his tie. He ran a finger under his collar and stretched his neck. "That's enough of that monkey suit. Sit down, Calley."

She sat on the couch next to his suit jacket. She thought about crossing her legs, but the gesture seemed artificial. Instead, she slowly ran her hands over her knees, trying to get used to the feel of having them covered by hose. "No runs." She smiled, indicating her stockings. "I didn't think I'd get through the day without ruining them."

"You can be a lady when the occasion calls for it, Calley."

Calley turned his words around in her mind, searching for the core meaning. "That all depends on what your definition of a lady is," she said.

Dean sat down beside her. He was looking at her throat, and his glance traveled downward, but still hadn't touched her. "A lady is a chameleon. She's whatever the occasion calls for. No matter what, she knows who she is."

Calley didn't know if she fit that definition. She did know she was much more comfortable at the Flathead than at a wedding, but she was able to enjoy both experiences. "Do you think that's possible?" she asked. "I wonder if anyone is always in control."

"Maybe not in control," Dean amended. "But a lady, or an adult, if that's the better term, knows what his and her strengths and weaknesses are. What makes them vulnerable."

Calley smiled. Despite what Dean was doing to her senses, she was moved by what he'd said. "I notice you didn't say that adults should be able to eliminate their weaknesses or try to live without vulnerability."

A shadow touched Dean's face and stayed. "Admitting vulnerability is the same as admitting we're human. No one can live totally hardened. Those who try are doomed to failure."

Reverently, Calley ran her hand over Dean's cheek. Although she touched beard, she believed his skin felt the gesture as well. When she walked through the door, she'd been a little frightened, because tonight was going to be different from any other she'd spent with Dean, but now hesitancy was turning into a gentle joy. "Macho man doesn't exist?"

"Macho man is a lie. Any man who believes that about himself doesn't know himself."

Oh, Dean, how wise you are. How wonderfully wise. "You're very perceptive," she whispered. Speech was becoming almost impossible. If it wasn't for the shadow still lingering around Dean's eyes, she wouldn't have tried.

"Philosophical." He laughed, but the sound was an effort. "Fortunately, trying to be philosophical doesn't happen to me very often. That tends to bore people. It was a nice wedding, wasn't it? That's the first one I've been to for a long time."

"I'm glad they could have it outside." Calley searched her mind but came up with nothing that would continue the conversation. Instead, she leaned back against the couch and closed her eyes. They had all night together. Maybe she should be nervous; she wasn't. She kicked off the unaccustomed high heels and wriggled her toes, sighing.

Dean's hand was on her knee. As he explored the silky feeling of filmy hose, Calley's thoughts went with him. It felt so good to have him touching her, reminding her that she was indeed a woman. Maybe, she thought disjointedly, she should wear a dress more often.

A minute later she learned that Dean was intent on removing that dress. She didn't open her eyes or object when his hand moved from her knee to the flesh left exposed by the low-cut bodice. Calley's mind followed the trail of his fingers across her collarbone, down the line of her bra strap, over the soft mound hinted at under the soft crepe. She acknowledged a timeless restlessness deep inside her as his fingers dipped as far as they could under her bra.

They were going to become lovers. She'd known that since they were at the Flathead; at least she'd fantasized about the possibility. The only real question had been when.

Tonight? It was what she wanted.

"Dean?" The question was spoken by a voice she didn't understand. She wasn't sure she needed to say anything.

Dean took a deep breath. "If you're going to tell me no, say it now. It's the only thing I've thought about since I saw you standing next to Melinda. I want you to spend the night with me."

How honest he was. He was right. They were adults, not children. She could tell him she wanted to spend the night, too. "I wasn't going to say no," she responded.

"Then what?"

She hadn't known what she wanted to say. She wasn't sure she could sort things out enough to form any words. There was fear and nervousness and anticipation and the dream of experiencing something she'd never had before, not even with Mike. But how was she going to tell Dean all those things? "Nothing," she said with a sigh.

"There was something. Don't be afraid to tell me anything, Calley. I want us to always be honest with each other." His hand was keeping her breast warm and giving her heart a reason to beat.

Calley breathed through nostrils that no longer were capable of bringing in all the air she needed. "I want this to be good for you."

Dean kissed her. A long, searching kiss. "That's what I'm supposed to say."

"I don't care." Calley couldn't open her eyes. She wanted to concentrate on the sound of his voice, the feel of his lips, the warmth of his hand. "I—you're a good man, Dean. I didn't think I'd ever find anyone like you." Was she saying too much, stripping herself naked emotionally? "I want to be what's right for you."

"You are, Calley. You are." His words came out on the end of a long breath. "When I saw you that first day I knew you were someone I'd been looking for. I want to make love to you this afternoon. I hope it's what you want, too."

It is. But telling Dean that she needed to be made love to was something Calley had never done before. She didn't know how to piece the words together or express so much of herself. "We're doing a lot of talking."

"You're right." Dean removed his hand from the velvet pocket he'd found and pulled Calley away from the couch. He didn't speak until he'd unzipped her dress down to the waist. "I didn't bring you here to talk."

While Calley stood with her feet spread to support her quickly yielding body, he helped her step out of the filmy garment and picked it up so he could drop it on top of his jacket. The air was cool on Calley's bare shoulders. She could concentrate on the strong bearded face inches from hers and take strength from his lingering kiss.

Calley pressed her body against his, unmindful of the layer of cloth still around her ribs. Soon he would unfasten the bandage and encircle her waist with his large, competent hands. Until that happened, she could sense his warmth on her breasts, feel his hardened legs tight against her softer ones.

He fit along her length. There wasn't a part of her that couldn't find a home. Calley worked her fingers into Dean's beard and held on to him, lost in wonder at all the directions a kiss could take. It might be no more than lips against lips, mouths opened, but in the greater scheme of things, this kiss was being registered on Calley's breasts, stomach and thighs.

She wanted him. Needed him. There was no denying, or wanting to deny, that fundamental fact.

"In the bedroom," Dean whispered. He lifted her in his arms and carried her through the late-afternoon shadows into the darkened room. Calley pressed herself against him, her eyes slits through which she could make out only him.

When he put her down, Calley stood for a moment, regaining her equilibrium. Then, before he could do it for her, she lifted the slip over her head and tossed it on the foot of the bed. She trembled when his hands covered her upper arms, but that turned to a soft giggle as he searched for the end of the elastic bandage. "I don't think this is part of the usual scenario."

Dean's laugh was as relaxed as she hoped it would be. The sound stripped her of any lingering tension. "It does add a certain dimension to things, doesn't it? There," he said with a sigh when the bandage was removed. He touched her side. "The bruise is almost gone. You aren't going to fall apart now that that thing's off, are you?"

"No, I'm not going to fall apart. However—"

"However, what?" he asked worriedly.

"It itches."

"Hmm." Dean held her at arm's length as he considered the ramifications of what she'd told him. "Maybe I can help." He placed his hands over her sides and started a slow, sensual rubbing motion. "No wonder," he went on. "The bandage was so tight that it left marks on your flesh."

Calley looked down but Dean's hands were in the way, and she was unable to see that part of her body. It didn't matter because she wasn't interested in what she looked like. Calley's hands had been on Dean's shoulder; now she was exploring the matt of hair covering his chest, finding his nipples and holding them between thumb and forefinger. She dipped her head, taking hair between her teeth, pushing through the forest with her tongue until she had reached his flesh.

Dean gripped her more firmly; his breath came quicker. He was so fast to respond. For an instant Calley panicked. What if his self-control was a tenuous thing?

As soon as the thought surfaced, she was able to push it away. No. They had been alone in the forest for days at a time. That was all the proof she needed that he was able to exercise restraint.

Restraint lasted until they'd helped each other out of their clothes and were locked in each other's arms on the bed. Calley thought she was in control, believed she could direct the ebb and flow of their lovemaking until the moment his moist tongue found her hardened nipple. The wave of desire that tore through her then was unlike any she'd ever experienced before. It wasn't that Dean was too bold; it wasn't that she'd been sleeping alone too long.

It was that she wanted him so much.

Dean's hands and mouth and tongue found nerve endings Calley had never acknowledged before. She gloried in what he was teaching her about herself. Her own exploration of Dean's body was bold beyond her most erotic dreams. It seemed as if she'd been waiting a lifetime to make love to this man, to let this man learn everything there was to learn about her body and its capacity to respond.

She was willing, oh, so willing, to let him caress her in the most intimate ways possible, to enter her, to bring her to the brink of a vast chasm and, finally, to send her flying out into space.

"Are you all right?" Dean asked when there was nothing left of her except satisfaction.

"All right?" She didn't want to talk. She wanted to wrap her body around him and spend the rest of her life like that.

"Your rib?"

"Were you worried about that? Oh, Dean, I'm not going to break." Was there anything about him she didn't love this afternoon?

Dean rose up on one elbow. With his forefinger he traced a slow line from her forehead to between her breasts. He stopped with his hand resting on her stomach. "Would you tell me if you were? You don't always have to be strong, you know."

"I know that, Dean," she reassured him. She marveled at her ability to lie still with his hand intimately on her, wondered how soon she would start to respond to him again. "That's the way I am. I'm not trying to prove anything. Honest."

Dean sighed, a little raggedly, it seemed to her. "I hope not. Everyone needs someone else. Don't ever be afraid to admit that."

Calley wanted to drift off, but she didn't. Dean was, she believed, trying to tell her something important. Because it wasn't easy for him, she tried to help. "I know a great deal about needing someone," she admitted. "Unfortunately, I didn't get that support when I needed it."

"Do you want to talk about it?"

Strangely, she did. She was able to acknowledge that making love to Dean had made her want to be emotionally close to him, but maybe there was more to what she was experiencing than simply bathing in the aftermath of lovemaking. Something involving her heart.

She told him what no one except Mike and Melinda knew. "My parents were divorced last year. I've never felt so alone."

Dean was quiet for a long time. "What happened to Mike?"

The question about Mike's role in the experience came faster than she wanted, but she didn't try to hide from what Dean was asking. "He wasn't there when I needed him."

"The bastard."

Calley had been staring at the ceiling, wondering why she no longer felt bitter. Now she turned toward Dean. "Maybe," she acknowledged. "But I don't blame Mike for what he is. Not anymore."

"That's magnanimous of you. I wouldn't be so forgiving."

"Don't," Calley warned. "I don't want to argue with you about Mike."

"I'm not arguing." Dean's hand was still on Calley's midsection, effectively keeping her from anger. "I'm just saying that when two people are in love and one of them is in a crisis, the other has to help. It isn't much of a relationship if that can't be taken for granted."

"I know that." Calley sighed deeply. Her voice shook a little as she went on. "That's what I wanted. It's what I expected from Mike. And he tried, I guess. But you know how much he hates confrontations. He was uncomfortable with the arguments between my parents. He said he hated seeing me being torn between them."

"To hell with his feelings. That's not what mattered."

Calley rolled toward Dean. She needed more than his hand on her. She wanted to feel his body wrapped around her. She felt no sense of surprise when he pulled her close.

"He went to the ranch with me when I first heard that my parents had separated. But he didn't stay long. He said he had to get back to work, but I understood what was really going on inside him. He called a few times, and I called him more than I told myself I was going to, but—"

"After a while you gave up expecting something from him, didn't you?" Dean was gently rubbing what he could reach of her back, his body close and yet quiet, not distracting her from what had to be said.

"After a while I guess I just didn't care anymore," Calley admitted. "It took all the emotional strength I had in me to try to help my parents. It was as if I didn't exist as a separate human being anymore. I was an extension of my parents, nothing more." Calley wondered at her ability to put her emotions into words. "I forgot what I felt for Mike, what he looked like—everything. And when I had to leave the project, it didn't bother me that I wasn't going to be seeing him again."

Dean brushed his lips across Calley's eyelids. "I never understood why you left. The divorce took that much out of you?"

"No." There was no reason to be embarrassed. She could tell Dean what had happened after the divorce. "We almost lost the ranch. My folks weren't concerned with keeping the ranch going. They—they were going through so much pain of their own. We had some unexpected losses, a hard winter, poor cattle prices. We couldn't pay our bills."

"We? You had a job, other responsibilities. The ranch shouldn't have been your problem, Calley."

"You don't understand," she moaned. "Having a ranch isn't like any other kind of job. It's a mistress. A master. Sweat and blood and too much love. Dean, my parents finally put their differences behind them and banded together to save the ranch. They got divorced, but they worked together until we were back in the black. That's how much that damn land means to us."

"Are they still living there?" Dean asked.

Calley laughed; there was no joy in the sound. "They split the acreage down the middle. Now Mom has a foreman to help her with her half. Dad's new wife is working with him."

"And you?" Dean whispered. "Where did that leave you?"

Again Calley laughed her bitter laugh. "Without a job. That's why I came back to the university. But—" She sighed. "I'm stronger now. I learned I have more backbone than I'd given myself credit for."

Dean didn't want to have to say a word again, but it was either that or maybe never fully understanding. "Mike wasn't here when you returned. Did you hope he would be?"

"No. No," she said, softer the second time. "When I told him we might have to file for bankruptcy, Mike said that was probably the easiest way to solve things. He'll never understand that turning our place over to a bank would be like giving up a child. Dean? I needed him to be stronger than I was then. He wasn't, and that killed everything I felt for him."

Because the bastard didn't have enough backbone. Because Mike had always taken the path of least resistance. Dean could admit that about his longtime friend without hating him, but then Dean hadn't been the one who'd been in love with Mike. "I don't ever want anyone to hurt you like that again," he told her.

"I don't want it, either. I—I don't need Superman," she whispered. "But Mike taught me something. He hid from confrontations. I couldn't accept that. I can't understand anyone who doesn't face everything life dishes out."

Dean had nothing to say.

Chapter Nine

"If I wanted just any joker off the street, I would have advertised in the classified section. I want you up here, Dean. This so-called conference is a thrown-together con job by a couple of hunting groups. They've managed to sweet-talk some legislators into coming to Anchorage for it, but if you and I don't show up, there isn't going to be enough weight on the side of wildlife management."

Dean shifted the phone from his right ear to his left. "I didn't say I didn't want to come. It's just that this is damn short notice. I wasn't going to start thinking about Alaska for another couple of weeks."

"You're telling me. Look—as I see it, it's a long-shot gamble by the hunters, but who knows what kind of garbage they're going to be able to plant in the heads of certain legislators if we don't present our side of the issue." The man at the other end of the long-distance call sighed deeply. "We haven't seen each other since you and Waina broke up. That isn't going to cause a problem, is it?"

"Not if it doesn't with you," Dean pointed out. His friendship with Hawk had always been based on the deepest honesty. "You want me up there this weekend? How long is this shindig going to take?"

"I wish I knew. The conference is scheduled to last only the weekend, but I'm hoping to take at least a couple of our public servants into the park. I'm going to try to convince them that they can't make any decisions about territory they've never seen. If that pans out, I'd like to have you along to back me up."

"I don't know about that," Dean hesitated. "Besides, since when did you need backing up? Once you get wound up, no one can get a word in edgewise. You'll do just fine on your own."

"You aren't trying to weasel out of this, are you?" the superintendent of Mount McKinley National Park asked.

"Don't try to turn the screws with me, old friend. I'll be up there. And I want to bring someone with me."

"Male or female?"

Dean laughed. Hawk had never believed in sidestepping an issue whether personal or professional. "Female. She's part of the project I'm working on here. She's never been to Alaska, but she wants to go."

"And that's the only reason you want her up here? She wouldn't happen to be young and good-looking, would she?"

"Why don't you let me worry about that," Dean pointed out. "And while we're on the subject of women, you wouldn't happen to have gotten married, would you? You aren't getting any younger, you know."

"Now you sound like my sister. All right. Get your tail up here in two days, and I'll take you and your lady friend on a tour of the neighborhood before we settle down to business." Hawk gave Dean a list of things he needed that he wasn't able to obtain in the remote areas where he spent most of his time, brushed off Dean's complaints that there wouldn't be room for Dean's or Calley's luggage along with Hawk's junk and hung up after telling Dean that he'd already made plane reservations for him but would change that to accommodate Dean's friend.

Dean leaned back in his seldom-used chair. He'd been back at the university for several weeks now, long enough for the novelty to have worn off. There was no denying that getting back out in the field was exactly what he needed. Calley had said she wanted to see the state where he'd done much of his work. Hawk's request meant juggling schedules, but Dean was already mentally packing for a trip north. Calley would want to go; he didn't have any doubts about that.

Although Dean wasn't the kind of man who usually planned elaborate surprises, he was looking forward to seeing Calley's expression when, instead of eating at her place, he took her to a restaurant. They'd have a leisurely dinner, talk over their day and look into each other's eyes. And then, when what he really wanted to do was take her back to his place and make love to her, he'd ask if she had any plans for the weekend or if she might find time for a quick trip to Alaska.

"ALASKA? This weekend? Dean, you're crazy!"

"That's entirely possible," Dean admitted. Candlelight was dancing in Calley's pale hair. Her face was muted by shadows. Although she was in slacks and a sweater, she'd put on a little makeup for the occasion. With her sitting across from him, Dean had hardly been able to concentrate on selecting something to eat. They'd been sitting here talking for at least ten minutes; he hadn't let go of her hand in that time. Quickly he filled Calley in on the conversation with Hawk, at least most of it.

Calley sighed. She met his eyes, for a moment no emotion riding in them. Then Dean saw what he'd been waiting for. A smile tugged at the corner of her lips. "Alaska..." She sighed again. "Just like that."

"Just like that. We don't have anything that pressing going on right now. We can juggle things around."

"Alaska? Now? You're sure?"

Dean squeezed her fingers. He hoped she'd never lose her enthusiasm for life. "Would you like to talk to Hawk? If you don't believe me, maybe he can convince you."

"I believe you, Dean." Calley blinked. When again she met Dean's eyes, her own were shining. "Where will we be staying?"

Dean explained that Hawk had arranged for hotel rooms in Anchorage for all of them to stay in during the conference. But once that was over, they, and any public officials they could drag along with them, would be taken on a tour of the park. "I told him you'd never been there before. If we can get out of here on Thursday, Hawk promised to give us the busman's tour of the lakes and farm country around the city before the conference."

Calley lifted Dean's right hand and brought it close to her mouth. She brushed it with her soft lips. "It sounds perfect. Can't we leave tonight?"

"Tonight I have planned."

After a dinner neither of them had much interest in, Dean took her back to his place, where their intentions of deciding what to pack took a back seat to the emotion that had taken hold of them while at the restaurant. It was, Dean made note of, the fourth time they'd made love since the day of Melinda's wedding. It was also, he was certain, the best time.

After lingering lovemaking that left him stripped of any strength, Dean lay awake with Calley sleeping on his chest. He played with her hair, listened to her breathe, thought about the gentle inroads she'd made in his life. From the day he'd met Waina, he'd known they came from different worlds. It wasn't like that with Calley. She was passionate about the same things that concerned him; she never tried to hide from reality. There was strength and substance in the woman. He could, he admitted, place his life in her hands if it came to that. There were times while they were at the Flathead when he'd hated her strength, and that might happen again, but it was that same strength that was bonding him to her now.

Despite dangers that Calley couldn't guess and he didn't want to face, sharing the next few days together was what they needed. It might answer the one essential question. He'd given her everything he had to give physically. Was he capable of doing the same with his emotions? "I'm not everything you think I am, darling," he whispered. "I wonder if you can live with that. I wonder if what you feel for me will survive?"

A little before dawn Calley awakened. She was curled, naked, next to Dean's warm body. As her thinking processes returned, she tried to mentally place herself and Dean in Alaska. Yes, she was eager to see as much as possible of the state. But it was more than that. Alaska had claimed Dean for more than a year; it was there that he'd fallen in love and seen that love die. Calley was aware of the pocket of himself that Dean kept from her. She thought Waina might be the reason for the wall between them, but she couldn't be sure. It frightened her to think about confronting that wall, but it had to happen if they were ever going to be more than lovers.

Lovers. Calley's mind caught on the word. She loved the reality of being Dean's lover. In four short days she'd gone from an unrelenting restlessness to having her every physical desire satisfied. Dean touched places within her that had never been touched before, struck emotional chords she'd never known existed. He'd taken her so far in four days. How much further he might be capable of taking her both frightened and excited her.

"Are you going to sleep all day?" she whispered. She let out just enough breath for it to reach his ear.

Dean sighed. He turned over, reaching for her. "You're here."

"Of course I'm here. Where did you think I'd be?"

He didn't answer that. "Don't leave."

"I won't leave you, Dean." Calley shivered when she heard her words. She was exposing so damn much of herself. Maybe more than was safe.

But it was safe this morning. Dean took her with grace and consideration, strength and energy. He took control of all of her; she loved him for what he was doing. When his weight was over her, she reached for him and brought him down to her. She ran her hands over his smooth, muscled back and arched her spine to receive him. No matter what the future might bring, this time with Dean was perfect. She wanted commitment, but until she knew him and her heart completely, she would take these moments.

They showered together. Calley relished the pleasure she received when he covered her breasts with his palms and lowered his head to brush his lips over the valley between them. In the past a small part of her had always flinched from the total vulnerability that came from exposing herself to a man, but she wanted Dean to touch every inch of her. She was his this morning; he had to understand that.

"Are we going to be sharing the same room in Anchorage?" she asked while he was drying her with long, sensual strokes that left her weak.

"Do you want to?"

You must know I do. She answered in the only way that didn't need words. The towel dropped to the floor as she pressed her body against his. He lifted her off her feet, wedding them together. Calley buried her head against Dean's chest, drinking in his masculine scent. Her legs were wrapped around his hips. Would she ever get enough of him?

Later that day, as Calley tried to work, she thought back on the way she'd acted in his bathroom with a kind of wonder. Calley had never considered herself a sensual woman, but Dean had unlocked that side of her nature. Or maybe he'd created it. She'd have to ask him about that someday as a way of letting him know how much her present joy hinged on what he was to her. If something happened to shatter the perfection they'd begun to create, she wasn't sure she'd survive intact.

Dean called twice to remind her of things she needed to pack. He dropped by her office late in the afternoon with a book on Alaska he thought she might want to read and wound up accepting her invitation to dinner. They spent Wednesday night at her place.

Early Thursday morning Steve drove them to the airport, and they left for Anchorage aboard a commercial flight. Calley sat next to the window, taking her eyes off the view only when Dean spoke to her. She was prepared for the majestic snow-capped mountains the plane passed over, but the size of Anchorage spreading out toward the mountain slopes took her breath away. "I had no idea it was so big," she exclaimed. "It's a real city."

"Yes, it's a city." Dean chuckled. He leaned across her for a glimpse of the tent camp turned metropolis that they were approaching. "Hopefully we won't have to spend too much time here."

Calley nodded. She recognized the beautiful Chugach Mountains and Cook Inlet, with arms of the inlet cradling the city on both the northwestern and southern sides. It was easy to believe that half the state's population was centered in Anchorage. "It's hard to believe there was an earthquake here," she admitted. "Are there many signs of it left?"

"Hardly any," Dean explained. "You're looking at the state's commercial heart."

A few minutes later their plane touched down. Dean waited until most of the passengers had debarked before helping Calley into the aisle. "You aren't going to embarrass me by gawking like a tourist, are you?" he asked in a stage whisper.

Calley gave him a mock glare. "My instamatic's in my pocket. Where's the sled dogs? Melinda will have my head if I don't have pictures of them."

"Then you're going to have to go around without your head," Dean pointed out. "It's the wrong time of year for snow sports."

Hawk was waiting inside the airport. Although Dean had told Calley little about the man, he was exactly what she expected of someone who had the responsibility of supervising a national park. He was taller than anyone else in the room, but it was more than his height that singled him out. Hawk carried himself with a confidence that seemed to radiate from him; the others in the crowded room kept their distance.

All except Dean. Pulling Calley along with him, Dean reached Hawk and thrust his hand into the Alaskan native's work-tempered paw. "You're getting fat on bear meat," Dean said, punching at Hawk's rock-hard middle. "It must be those long winters and soft living."

"Soft living? I should expect that from a man who thinks roughing it is not having running hot water." Hawk turned toward Calley. "I take it you're here to keep an eye on this man. He needs all the help he can get."

Calley looked up at Hawk. She liked what she saw in the man's eyes. There was intelligence and compassion and a certain timelessness lurking within the deep-set black eyes. Although he was dressed conventionally, she guessed that he wouldn't be at Anchorage International Airport, surrounded by brightly costumed tourists, if there was any way he could avoid it. "I've been looking forward to meeting you," she admitted. She stuck out her hand, liking the firm but not intimate way he took it.

"You might not say that after you've seen me in action," Hawk explained as he led the way toward the crowded baggage area. "I'm not going to mince words around those so-called sportsmen. They're going to find out they've bit off more than they can chew when they try to take me on."

Dean laughed and shared a wink with Calley. "Think of all the money that hunting would add to the Alaskan economy. You'd probably get your salary doubled. Surely you aren't going to deny hunters the opportunity to dump a bundle in the state."

"You damn well better believe I'm going to deny them anything." Hawk snorted before grinning at Calley. "I hope you came up here ready for a fight. Dean tells me you've been gnashing your teeth since you found out what this little meeting's about."

"I have been," she reassured the big man. "Any congressman who votes to enlarge hunting privileges in this state should be recalled."

Hawk wrapped his arm around Calley's shoulder and gave her a squeeze. "You know how to pick them, Dean. This one's on our side."

After collecting their luggage, Hawk drove them to the downtown hotel where the weekend meeting was going to be held. Calley saw just enough of Anchorage to realize that what she'd heard of the residents' love of plants and flowers was true. Every home seemed to have a garden, and the public buildings all displayed elaborate flower beds. Hawk left them alone long enough to unpack, but he was back a half hour later, pacing the spacious living area. "What say we blow this place?" he suggested as soon as Calley came out of the bedroom dressed in her trusty blue jeans and warm sweater. "You aren't one of those women who spend their free time shopping, are you?"

Calley patted her jeans. "Do I look like a clotheshorse? Dean said you'd made some rash promise that had to do with a tour of the area outside the city."

"Now you're talking," Hawk said with a grin. He pulled Dean to his feet and propelled him through the door. "Remember the time we saw those eagles gorging themselves near Haines? That was one time we really messed up by not having cameras. No one would believe us," Hawk said as the trio reentered the rental car. As Calley listened in fascination, the men told her about traveling up the Chilkat River northwest of Haines for a view of eagles feeding on salmon carcasses. Hawk explained that groundwater seepage kept a section of the river thawed even in the middle of winter. The area served as home for some two thousand bald eagles that built seven-feet-deep nests. "There were at least a hundred of them perched in trees or stalking the riverbank the day we were there," Hawk explained. "When those creatures dive after a fish, it's a sight to take one's breath away."

It didn't take Calley long to realize that being born and raised in Alaska hadn't blunted Hawk's love of the wilderness. In answer to her question, he explained that his parents had named him Robert after a bush pilot who brought supplies to their village, but the name Hawk was stuck on him at an early age. Hawk tried to tell Calley that it was his keen eyesight and survival instincts that led to the nickname, but Dean interrupted to set Calley straight. It turned out that Hawk had been a skinny youngster with a larger than usual nose. "I've seen some old pictures of him," Dean supplied. "He was all beak back then. He's just lucky they didn't call him Buzzard."

"Enough," Hawk interrupted. "Where to, Calley? Your wish is my command."

Calley thought for a moment. "I wouldn't mind a quick tour of the city, but after that I'd like to see the farmland Dean told me about. I kept looking for it while we were coming in, but I didn't see that much flatland."

What stuck Calley about Anchorage wasn't so much its international flavor as the profusion of flowers throughout. Her earlier glimpse was just a taste of what existed. "Despite rumors to the contrary, the whole state isn't one big glacier," Hawk said. "You wouldn't believe the summer homes around the valley lakes. I have a friend who owns a sailboat. As soon as he puts away his snowmobile, out comes the bathing suit. Now his kids are pushing for something with a little more power so they can water-ski."

Calley shivered. Although the day was warm enough that she didn't need a jacket, all it took was a glance at the snowcapped mountains to make her admit that waterskiing and sailing weren't sports she associated with Alaska.

She almost changed her mind when Hawk took them into the Matanuska Valley. Nestled between mountain ranges was dairy land, wheat fields and acres of vegetable gardens. This time it was Dean who filled in the blanks. He explained that years ago over two hundred families had settled in the valley and turned to farming. Although only a fraction of them stuck it out, the area remained a fertile pocket. "She'd like to see the Old Believers, Dean," Hawk said. "Too bad there isn't time to take her to the Kenai Peninsula."

Before Calley had a chance to ask Hawk what he was talking about, Dean pulled her next to him in the back seat. "The Old Believers are a sect of Russian Orthodox Christians," he explained. "They cling to traditional ways of farming. The women wear long dresses and head scarves. The men are all bearded, and the children have daily religious training. Whether you share their beliefs or not, you can't help but be moved by their life-style."

"Oh," Calley whispered. One more aspect of Dean's personality was being revealed to her. Since they'd gotten into the car, he'd let Hawk do most of the talking, saying just enough for her to realize that he was enjoying himself completely. Now he was telling her that he was capable of doing more than just observing the world; the world was constantly shaping him. Calley nestled against him, more interested in the man than in her surroundings.

From the valley it was a short drive into the mountains where the road no longer resembled a modern highway. While Dean and Hawk reminisced about fishing in icy streams and hiking to Matanuska Glacier, Calley was content to gaze at the mountains. Hawk pointed out sheltered hillsides where purple-blue lupine grew and indicated where in winter they would find frozen waterfalls. At Calley's prompting, they drove to Matanuska Glacier, a twenty-seven-mile-long ice river that stretched back in time to the Ice Age.

She had no words for her first look at a glacier—a monster tongue sawing its way down a cut in the mountains. It seemed to Calley that they had left earth and entered another galaxy.

"Out of the car, woman," Dean ordered. "There's no way I'm going to bring you all the way to Alaska without getting you out onto a glacier."

Calley wasn't sure her boots were made for walking on sheer ice, but with Dean and Hawk on either side of her, she managed to walk the better part of a mile. What struck her most about the frozen, slippery surface was its utter lifelessness. It had been sculpted by wind and melt and glowed with a silvery-blue aura that seemed capable of drawing her into its depths.

The afternoon was warm. Hawk warned her that the glacier took on a totally different character when touched by the sun. Twice she heard distant sounds, as if a rifle were being shot, as the ice cracked. Under her feet the ice creaked and groaned. The wind murmured a giant shiver through the ice beneath her feet.

"It's awesome," Calley breathed once they were back in the car. "It makes me appreciate modern transportation. It's hard to believe we could practically drive up to a glacier."

"Remember the time the three of us flew into McCarthy?" Hawk asked Dean. "You couldn't get over the fact that there were children living clear out there being taught by their parents. That the place was too small to support a single schoolteacher. That was before you'd seen some of the really remote Indian villages." Hawk glanced at Calley. "Dean wants everyone to think he's an expert. You should have seen him rubbernecking the first time he was here."

Four hours after leaving Anchorage, Hawk reluctantly admitted they should return to the hotel if they were going to be prepared for the meeting tomorrow. The two men disappeared into a bar in the hotel while Calley went upstairs to change into slacks. She felt a little self-conscious about entering the bar alone, but when she spotted Dean in the dim light, she was no longer aware that anyone else was there. She was hundreds of miles from home, in a city where she knew no one. It didn't matter. The man smiling at her was the only one in the world who existed for her.

Calley controlled her smile and took a deep breath. For once in her life she was going to make an entrance. She held her head high, walking with slow steps around the small tables, vaguely aware that several men were watching her. *No wonder,* she decided without conceit. Dean's eyes were telling her that she was desirable; that was how she felt.

"I'm still trying to talk Dean into taking the time to join me in McKinley after this nonsense is over," Hawk said after Dean ordered white wine for her. "You want to see my turf, don't you? Take the Cook's tour? I can get you closer to the Dall sheep than you'd ever get on your own." Hawk turned toward Dean. "You haven't been up there since..." His voice trailed off.

"No, I haven't." There was a quiet warning in Dean's words. "I don't think we're going to have time, after all, Hawk."

"Yeah?" Hawk was looking at Dean with an intensity Calley couldn't ignore. "Then when are you going to have time, Dean?"

Dean's hand tightened around the beer mug he was holding. His voice came from somewhere deep in his chest. "Why don't you let me worry about that. Who all is going to be at this meeting, anyway? It seems like that's what we should be talking about."

Calley didn't try to enter the conversation as Hawk gave Dean a thumbnail sketch of the people they would be meeting. Something had happened a moment ago that had been like a knife slicing through a deep friendship. Obviously Hawk thought he could bring something up. Just as clearly, Dean was shutting himself off from whatever that was. As far as Calley could tell, Dean had been in favor of going into the national park when they were in Montana. Now, it seemed, he was doing everything possible to avoid the place. Calley remembered Dean's sudden silence when the pilot pointed out Mount McKinley rising stark and silent out of the clouds. There had been something out there that was now eating away at him.

Even when they left the bar for a simple dinner Calley was unable to ignore the tension that had become part of Dean. It was almost as if he'd forgotten that she was there. He was so intent on making sure that Hawk said only the right things that he couldn't concentrate on her. She wondered if she could get up from the dinner table without Dean noticing. That hurt not because Calley felt she should be the center of attention but because she didn't want the barrier Dean had placed between himself and his old friend to extend to her, as well.

As soon as they were finished eating, Hawk excused himself by saying he wanted to go over his notes before morning. Calley lingered over coffee, watching Dean's stony profile in the dim light. "Why don't you want to go to McKinley?" she finally asked.

"I didn't say that." Dean wasn't looking at her.

"Yes, you did," Calley pressed. "Not in so many words, maybe, but you're tight as a spring. I'm feeling it now, and I felt it when we saw the mountain from the plane window. I thought you wanted to come to Alaska."

"I thought I did, too. I did," Dean amended. He ran his hand over his forehead, pressing it tightly against his eyes. "It took a long time for you to tell me about your parents."

"And that has something to do with what you're going through?" Calley prompted. She touched his hand, but he still didn't look at her.

"Don't push it, Calley." Dean moved back his chair and rose quickly to his feet. "We have to go."

Damn him. Calley leaned back in her chair, eyes blazing with an anger she had no words for. "You go," she said tightly. "I haven't finished my coffee."

Dean left her. Calley didn't think he was going to, but in less time than it took her to blink, she was staring at his retreating back.

It was wrong for us to come here, Calley thought as she wrapped her hands around the cup of coffee she no longer wanted. Something was here, something Dean wanted out of his life. She could, she knew, run after Dean and insist that he let her be part of his thoughts, but she didn't. She understood that there were times when a man needed to be alone.

But that didn't mean that being alone and left ignorant was good for her. Calley had come here because she wanted to be with Dean. Somehow she would have to find the key that would release what was bottled up inside him. Five minutes after Dean left, she, too, headed toward the elevator that would take her to their floor. But it wasn't Dean's room she headed toward.

She stood outside Hawk's room, hesitating a moment, and then knocked. "I was expecting Dean," Hawk said when he opened it.

"I won't stay long," Calley promised. She stepped into the room and slowly turned back toward the tall man. "How long have you known Dean?"

Hawk frowned. "Years." He sat on the edge of his bed and waited for Calley to settle herself in one of the chairs in the room. "How long have you known him?"

"A few weeks." Was that all it was? It seemed to Calley that Dean had been part of her emotions forever. "What was he like? I don't understand what's happening."

"Don't you know?" Hawk leaned forward. His dark eyes never left Calley.

"I'm not sure. I thought I did." She ran her hand over her forehead with the same weary gesture Dean had used. "A few minutes ago I tried to ask him what was bothering him, but he walked out on me."

"He didn't tell you?"

"No. I was hoping you would."

Hawk pushed himself to his feet. His long legs took him to a window overlooking the city and the distant mountains. "Don't ask this of me, Calley. I'm not going to rat on Dean."

She should have expected this from Dean's friend. "I'm not asking you to rat on him," she pressed. "I just want to know if—if I'm going to regret asking him to open up to me."

Hawk turned back around. "I can't answer that for you, Calley. I don't know what's going on inside Dean's head. I think I do, but I can't be sure."

"What do you think it is?"

Hawk shook his head. "I'm not the one you should be asking."

"I know." Calley sighed. She'd been wrong to put Hawk on the spot. Only Dean could answer her questions, and only when he was ready. "There's one thing you can tell me," she said as she got to her feet. "You said there were three of you when you flew into McCarthy. Who was the other one?"

"My sister. Waina."

Chapter Ten

Calley felt nothing; either that or she was feeling too much to be able to assimilate it all. The clues had been there from the moment she knew Hawk existed, but somehow she'd made herself ignore them.

"Your sister was the woman Dean was going to marry." The words were spoken without emotion.

"Dean didn't tell you?" Hawk shook his head angrily. "Who knows what's going on in that man's head. Sit down, Calley. I'm going to tell you some things about Dean and my sister. If he doesn't want you to know these things, he can take that up with me later."

Calley sat. Dean had made love to her. His actions, words and emotions told her that she was important to him in ways that went far beyond the physical. She could learn about his past without pain. "I think I know most of it," she said softly. "He has talked about her. There was a cultural difference between them."

Hawk was studying her closely. He folded his arms over his chest and leaned against the windowsill. "It's funny, isn't it? I'm Haida, too, but that hasn't prevented Dean and me from being close. In fact, despite the fact that we don't see each other often, I consider Dean one of my closest friends. But there are some things about our upbringing that you have to understand." Hawk paused a moment and then told her about two children born to an Indian couple in a remote village. The older child, the son, was sent to boarding school in Anchorage during his early years, but by the time Waina was ready for school, the parents had seen the error of their ways.

"I was turning into a white man," Hawk explained. "When I came home for vacation, I'd changed in ways my parents didn't approve of. I'd become worldly. There were things I wanted to experience that I couldn't in a remote village without electricity. I knew I'd never be able to come back to the village and raise a family the way my parents had planned. I didn't think I was turning my back on my heritage, but they did. It wasn't enough that I was determined to dedicate my life to preserving Alaska. They wanted me to live in a cabin, raise lots of babies and spend my days hunting, fishing and gathering firewood. I knew I'd go crazy if I tried to fit that mold."

"Waina wasn't sent away to school?" Calley asked. Hawk was a handsome man by any standards. His dark features and coal-black hair, coupled with his powerful build, would have drawn attention anywhere. It wasn't hard to imagine Waina with the same kind of handsome good looks. "She's a trained wildlife researcher. How did that happen?"

Hawk pushed himself away from the window and sat back down on the bed. He looked penned in by his surroundings. "Waina was taught through correspondence courses until she was ready for high school. Many of Waina's playmates never really learned how to read, but she's an educated woman. At least my parents didn't try to deny her brains. She was sent to live with relatives so she could go to school in Haines. It wasn't the small village she was used to, but it was far different from Anchorage, and she lived with people who were carrying on a lot of the old traditions."

Calley nodded. "In other words, Waina didn't get out into the world until she had a strong concept of what it meant to be Haida."

"Exactly," Hawk said, and Calley thought she detected a sadness in his eyes at his words. "Sometimes I feel like shaking my sister because she's so stubborn, but she has a strong sense of what she is. I don't. I'm the superintendent of a national park, but I'm not sure I know what I am inside." Hawk tapped himself on the chest. "Trying to bridge two cultures has affected my sister and me in different ways."

Calley took a deep breath. She had only one question left for Hawk. "And that's the only reason Waina and Dean broke up? Because there's that much difference between what they are?"

Hawk neither shook nor nodded his head. "There's more to it than that, Calley. But that has to come from Dean, not me."

Calley rose to her feet. She hadn't really expected a pat explanation for a complex human relationship. As she started for the door, she realized what made Dean and Hawk close friends. Hawk might look as if he should be on a whaling boat, but there was much more to the man than a native trying to survive a hostile land. Hawk, like Dean, cared about what took place in the hearts and minds of those they knew. They'd sensed that about each other; that formed the frame for their friendship.

"Thank you," she said. "I just hope Dean will be as honest with me as you were."

"I hope so, too, Calley. I believe the man loves you, but there's a lot tied up inside him."

Hawk believed Dean loved her. It was those simple and yet complex words that gave Calley the courage to enter the room she was sharing with Dean. She wasn't fully inside before she sensed, rather than knew, that he wasn't there. Calley turned on the light and kicked off her shoes. A glance at the desk told her that Dean hadn't touched the material he intended to present in the morning. There was no note for her.

Calley took a long shower before dressing in the silky floor-length garment she'd received as a birthday present three years ago and had never worn. The soft, pastel yellow fabric did almost nothing to hide her curves; that was precisely why Calley had brought it. Dean would eventually return to their room. She wanted to be ready for him.

She tried to pass the time by sorting through the volumes on endangered species, but because her ears were tuned to the sound of a door being unlocked, she was unable to concentrate. Neither Dean nor Hawk had said anything about whether she would be allowed to be present at the meetings, but unless someone barred her, she planned to attend. She'd never seen Dean defending his position where grizzlies were concerned. She wanted to hear the passion she knew he'd bring to the topic.

An hour after her shower, Calley heard the sound she was waiting for. She tensed, both ready and nervous about seeing him again. Dean stepped through the door; the look he gave her told her nothing. "I didn't know if you'd be here," he said.

"Where else would I go?"

"I don't know." Silently Dean ate up the distance separating them. He stood over her, his hands inclined toward her. "I'm sorry."

That was all she had to hear. His words made the waiting worth it. "You don't ever have to be sorry for what you are," she whispered as she rose to meet him. He smelled of smoke, and there was liquor on his breath, but nothing in his manner indicated that he'd had too much to drink. She pictured him alone in the dark bar, alone with his thoughts.

She didn't want Dean to be alone ever again. He'd done so much for her. It was time to give as much as she had taken. "I've been talking to Hawk."

A deep shudder disturbed the pattern of Dean's breathing. "I thought you might have. What did he tell you?"

"Nothing I shouldn't have been able to piece together on my own. He said that if I wanted to know more about you, not Waina, that I should come to you." Calley tried to focus on what she was saying and not on the fact that Dean wasn't touching her, hadn't kissed her, but that was impossible. Wanting Dean in her arms and in her bed had become almost a physical pain. "He's a remarkable man, Dean. There aren't many like him."

"I know." Dean looked down at her. His lips were so close that she felt as if she might fall apart with wanting him. "Do you want me here? I acted like a fool earlier."

Calley fingered the folds of her nightgown. "Do I look as if I want you here?" she asked.

"Yeah." Dean's arms went around her. Calley leaned into him, burying her freshly shampooed hair against his chest. "I think you do."

"Then—" Calley didn't try to say the rest. She tilted her head upward, wanting only one thing. Dean's kiss was sweeter than any she'd experienced in her lifetime.

Calley was helping Dean out of his shirt before she spoke again. "I wish I understood you better," she said softly. "There's this wall I keep banging into. I'm not even sure you know it's there."

Dean knew, all right. In the past hour he'd gone over a thousand times what he eventually had to tell her. The words were simple enough, and the telling wouldn't take long, but tonight Dean wanted to make love to the most beautiful woman he'd ever known, not tell her that he wasn't as much of a man as he wanted to be for her.

"Where did you get that nightgown?" he asked instead. "Do you know what it's doing to me?" He touched the dark outline of her firm nipples through the single layer of transparent fabric.

Calley laughed. "Why do you think I brought it?" she whispered.

When Dean was wearing nothing from the waist up, he wrapped Calley against him. He'd done such a damn stupid number on himself while sipping on the beer he couldn't taste. He'd tried to face having to come back to the hotel room to find her gone. He'd told himself he deserved that. But she'd been waiting for him; she had readied herself for him. She wouldn't have done that if she didn't— Was it possible that Calley Stewart loved him?

"I don't deserve you," Dean admitted. His lips found her offered throat and tasted a sweetness that registered throughout him.

"I don't deserve you, Dean." She was looking up at him with the same naked desire he felt.

How wrong she was. Calley was everything he'd ever wanted in a woman. She was as strong and independent and proud of herself as Waina had been. But Waina hadn't been able to give him all of her heart. He didn't think it was that way for Calley.

"Don't say that, Calley," Dean whispered as he started inching the silk gown upward. "Don't ever think that of yourself. You have so much to give."

Slowly Dean stripped Calley of the tantalizing garment. When she stood naked and trembling slightly before him, he showed her with actions and not words that she was totally desirable. He ran his hands down the soft flesh of her arms, placed her hands around his waist and, still standing, bent over and took her left breast between his lips. He ran his tongue around the nipple until it jutted out in arousal. He would have liked to test the limits of his ability to excite her, but his need for her was too great to allow a lengthy foreplay. As he lowered her onto the bed and joined her, he wondered if the time would ever come when he didn't feel a sense or urgency about their lovemaking.

Calley was stretched out on the bed, turned slightly toward him, giving him access to her entire body. Breathing deeply but too rapidly, Dean accepted her gift. Her breasts were made for being covered by his hands and mouth. She gasped in delight when he ran his tongue from her breasts down to her belly. Calley was no placid lover. She found his chest and ribs and hipbones, at last shyly running her fingers over his arousal. With that gesture, Dean lost whatever rational thought remained. He wanted to explore much much more of her, but the heat pounding through his veins couldn't be denied. Gently, Dean lifted himself over her. He found her mouth and fastened on it, surrendered his separate self to her. His climax came quickly; it was joined by hers.

"I could get drunk on you" was the first thing Dean said after rolling off her. His hand lingered on the exquisite softness of her inner thigh. He shook off the promise of sleep clinging to him. "I don't think I'll ever get enough of this."

"Really?"

"Yes, really." He opened his eyes, but in the darkened room there was no reading the expression on her face. If his world was to end tomorrow, he wouldn't leave this bed. He thought she would be relishing her mastery over him, but her simple question told him otherwise. He kissed her lovingly on the cheek. "Don't you believe that?"

"I—I don't know," Calley turned onto her side and drew her legs upward. She pressed her body against him and gripped his shoulder with desperate fingers. "I don't understand my emotions around you," she whispered. "Sometimes—sometimes I think I'm giving you too much of myself. I don't know what's left of me anymore."

She was scaring him. "Don't say that, Calley. Please don't ever think that."

She released him but didn't draw away. She was a long time answering. When she did, the words were forced. "Dean? I'm going to tell you something. I don't know if it's right or the time, but I have to say it, anyway."

Dean closed his eyes and drew in a deep breath. Scared? He was terrified. "Tell me."

He sensed her staring at him. "I think I love you."

The word entered Dean, spread throughout him, lit up his life and made him young. She loved him. She was afraid to tell him that, because being in love made a person vulnerable, but she loved him just the same. It was his turn to speak, but he had to choose his words carefully. He laid his hand across her cheek, mirroring the gesture parents use to comfort their children. "Why were you afraid to tell me that?"

"Can't you guess?" Her laugh was harsh but directed at herself. "I don't know how you feel about me. Maybe I'm telling you something you don't want to have to deal with."

She thought he might not want her to love him. That was incredible and ridiculous. He couldn't believe that she didn't know what she was doing to him. "I think—" He paused for a moment and then went on. "I think I've been waiting to hear that since the first time I kissed you." He shook his head at the absurdity of what he'd said. Love didn't come that quickly. "I'm glad it's dark in here. I'm going to say some things that aren't going to be easy." Dean sought her lips, relieved to find them as warm and giving as they'd been before. "The night you walked into camp? I took one look at you and knew something special was going to happen between us. I didn't know what that was, and because I'm not a dreamer, I tried not to let myself think about what that something might be. But Calley, when I'm around you, and even when I'm not, it's as if meeting you has opened up a whole new dimension to my life. You make it all worthwhile."

"I do?" The tremor in her voice told Dean that she, too, was grateful for the darkness.

"I feel alive around you. I—" Once again Dean sought time by kissing her. "I wouldn't feel that way if I didn't love you."

"Oh." Calley sighed. "Oh, Dean."

"What?" he pressed. He felt both freed and trapped by what he'd just revealed. Free because loving Calley opened up a whole dimension to their relationship and trapped because now she had a right to his deepest secrets. "Is that all you're going to say?"

Calley rose up on her elbow. He didn't breathe when her fingers started trailing over his chest. "I think maybe we've said enough for one night," she whispered. "I feel drained."

"You should," he said in an attempt to lighten things. "You've just made love to a man who might very well be insatiable."

"That wasn't the kind of drained I had in mind," Calley said before following up her words with action.

They held hands in the morning as they left their room. When they joined Hawk for breakfast, he glanced at them only briefly before shaking his head. "I take it you slept well?" he baited them.

"Why don't you mind your own business?" Dean snapped with mock irritation. Soon the conversation turned to the business at hand, but even though Dean now felt secure in the feelings they'd shared and revealed to each other last night, he knew the greatest hurdle was still ahead.

For the first time since it had happened, he honestly wanted to tell someone, as long as that someone was Calley. It was worth the cold sweat and pounding pulse he knew would come with the words. His hesitancy came only because the time wasn't right. What he would tell Calley might change what she felt for him, but he had to, wanted to, take the risk. Otherwise they would never be able to go beyond expressing an emotion that might be no more permanent than morning mist on a lake.

Dean quickly seconded Hawk's observation that having Calley at the meeting might be a positive factor in defusing what could be an explosive situation. "That hunting organization doesn't want us here in the first place. In fact, they tried to get the meeting date changed when I told them I was coming. They said my presence wasn't really needed. Fortunately for us, this is the only time the congressmen are all able to be here. The hunters might not pull out the heavy artillery with Calley around."

Calley laughed at that idea. She didn't believe the presence of a female would suddenly turn everyone into perfect gentlemen. On the other hand, she had no hesitancy about personally locking horns with someone who tried to contend that killing grizzlies in any way served the good of mankind.

The meeting was being held in a spacious convention room within the hotel. In attendance were a half-dozen representatives of a group that called themselves Sportsmen United and three politicians representing the Department of the Interior. A large round table had been provided in what Calley took to be an attempt to make everyone feel like equals. She wondered if this had been Hawk's idea.

After a casual, good-natured get-acquainted session, the meeting got down to business. Basically, the sportsmen were presenting an argument for expanding the hunting areas around the Wrangell Mountains. Their contention was that there was enough sanctuary for grizzlies within the national parks. Hawk snorted derisively several times but said nothing until the moderator provided by the local chamber of commerce introduced him. With an economy of words, Hawk pointed out that grizzlies were all but extinct from the lower forty-eight states and that expanded hunting grounds in Alaska would mean a giant backward step following recent improvements made by the National Park Service. When he was finished, he introduced Dean as the bear researcher who knew more about grizzlies than any man alive.

To Calley's surprise, Dean didn't reinforce what Hawk had said about the necessity for giving grizzlies enough space to roam. Instead, what he said was designed to strike at the emotions of the men who held the future of bears in their hands.

"Stepping into bear country can, I believe, be one of the most powerful experiences of one's life," Dean began. "Most people tend to think in such terms as 'petrified by fear' when they imagine sharing the same turf with something that weighs over eight hundred pounds. Yes, I've felt that very real fear, but it's much more than that. We're debating something we're going to lose for all time if we don't appreciate that a grizzly is one of the last remaining ties to a vanishing way of life. When I'm in grizzly country, my senses are extraordinarily sharp. There is a superawareness about myself and everything around me. There's a continuum in grizzly country that exists from the beginning of time. I can't imagine being able to duplicate that emotion any other way." Dean leaned forward, resting his hands on the table. "That's when I feel the most alive. It's a sensory charge that can't be described, only experienced."

Dean exchanged a look with Calley before continuing. "A grizzly is history. A wilderness area is an ancient, immensely complex system capable of producing and supporting life. Perhaps the answer to the mystery of the origin of life lies in the grizzly and his turf. Gentlemen, a grizzly isn't only a wilderness animal. He is the wilderness. Destroy that and you've destroyed a little of yourselves, as well."

Calley felt chilled. Dean's words had an impact she could no more deny than she could resist. The men listening to him would have to be emotional cripples not to understand the point he was making. Dean couldn't have made the matter any clearer. Just as a spaceship was proof of how far man had gone, a grizzly was living proof that yesterday still existed. Dean was asking them not to destroy yesterday, the wilderness.

Although the politicians cloaked their questions and observations in bureaucratic terms, Calley felt heartened. Most of their questions were directed at Dean and Hawk. Just as the meeting was breaking up, three of the congressmen asked if Hawk could take them on a tour of Mount McKinley National Park the next day.

"I think we have them in our pockets," Hawk said later as the three met in his room. "Did you see the look on the sportsmen's faces when I said I'd have a plane ready at dawn? I'm sure it was what you said, Dean. That business about a grizzly being synonymous with the wilderness really got to them."

"That's why I said it," Dean admitted. He and Calley were sitting on Hawk's bed. He was resting his back against the headboard, while Calley leaned against him. He was slowly rubbing her shoulders and neck, his warm breath making it difficult for her to concentrate on the conversation.

"What are you going to show them?" Calley asked. "They aren't going to be able to learn a lot in one day."

Hawk frowned. "I've been worrying about that. I've taken groups like this through the park before, but I'm never sure they're getting enough of the picture. What do you think, Dean? Toklat? They should be able to see a grizzly there."

Behind her Dean turned into a pillar of stone. She wanted to look around so she could see what was in his eyes, but his body language was telling her he wasn't ready for that. "They should" was all he said.

"Will you come with us?"

Until Hawk asked his question, Calley had assumed that she and Dean would be part of the expedition into the park, but now she wasn't sure. Dean was so tense that his fingers were digging into her shoulders. She flinched from the pressure but sensed that now wasn't the time to distract him from his thoughts. There were still mysteries and shadows to Dean. Now she knew that the answers lay in the place called Toklat.

"I'd like to come along," she said, consciously taking the decision out of Dean's hands. She might be backing him into a corner, but they'd made certain commitments to each other last night. She believed she could force him to face himself without it destroying the relationship they'd begun.

"What about you, Dean?" Hawk repeated his question.

"You're a bastard. You know that, don't you?" Dean growled.

"Yeah." Hawk's eyes narrowed. "So I'm a bastard. Are you coming?"

"I'm coming."

Dean didn't speak for the next five minutes. Calley filled the silence by asking Hawk about Toklat, the river called "dirty water" by the Tanana Indians. She could reach out and touch the tension in Dean but chose to ignore it. When and if he was ready to open up to her, she would listen.

"It's too bad you won't have time to hike any great distance along the river," Hawk was saying. "The river itself isn't much to look at, because the meltwater is filled with glacial silt, but it's a natural roadway for many animals. If we're lucky, the Dall sheep will be down where we can see them. Bring your camera."

"And the bears," Dean said tersely as he pushed Calley aside so he could slide off the bed. "Don't forget the damn bears."

"There's not a chance of either of us forgetting that, Dean," Hawk said to Dean's retreating back. He continued after Dean had left the room. "It isn't getting any easier for him, Calley. The man has tied himself up in knots over this one."

"Over what?" Calley protested. "All I know is he doesn't want to go to Toklat. What happened there?"

"The three of us had flown in there—Dean, Waina, me. Ask him, Calley. That's what he's going to have to tell you."

Calley picked up her shoes and said goodbye to Hawk. There'd been a barrier between her and Dean last night; talking and loving each other had knocked down that barrier. Now it was back in place. Feeling as if she was caught in a relentless time warp, Calley opened the door to their room.

This time Dean was waiting for her. "Sit down, Calley," he said. "I have something to tell you."

"I kind of figured you did," she said in an attempt to keep things light. "I hope we can get everything out in the open this time. I can't keep up with your moodiness."

"You're responsible for it, even though I can't expect you to understand," Dean said in a conversational tone that didn't fool her for a moment.

"Is it something I'm going to want to understand?" she asked. Dean was sitting on the bed. She took the nearest chair, not wanting to touch him but wanting to be close enough to reach him in any other way he needed.

"I'm not sure. Calley, I was at Toklat a little over a year ago."

"You were with Hawk and Waina," she said in an effort to help him.

Dean nodded. "How much did Hawk tell you?"

"That's all he told me," she supplied. She tried folding her hands in her lap, but that didn't feel right. Finally she let them trail over the sides of the chair. "He said the three of you had flown into McKinley."

"We flew in because there was a large concentration of grizzlies fishing the east fork. Things weren't going well between Waina and me. I guess I was hoping that we still might be able to work things out. We worked together so well professionally. I wanted her to see that."

"I see," Calley said, although she didn't care whether she did or not.

Dean went on. "We set up camp there after warning hikers to stay out of the area. We planned on staying the better part of the week observing and photographing the bears. I think we wound up counting a dozen of them."

Calley whistled. She'd seen Dean's pictures of a group of browns fishing in McNeil River in southwestern Alaska. Although there was a certain playfulness in the way both mature bears and cubs dipped their paws in the fast-moving water in an attempt to snag salmon, knowing that some of the bears weighed as much as fifteen hundred pounds and could rear to a height of nine feet made her hold the photographs in awe. "So many," she commented.

"That's one of their favorite spots," Dean explained. His tone was conversational enough, but Calley noted that he was gripping his knees with white-knuckled fingers. "The fish population was high at that time last year. It attracted bears for miles around. They were pretty aggressive. That's why we closed down the hiking trails."

Calley's mind locked on what it felt like to be surrounded by bears, to never know when one of them might emerge from the lower slopes of the mountains. "What happened there?" she asked, although she was beginning to believe she knew what he had to tell her.

"That's where I got the scar."

It took every bit of reserve Calley had to keep from launching herself at Dean. He was battling a thousand demons; she could see that in his eyes. But if she stopped him now, they would only have to come back to this point at another time. "How?" she asked.

Dean stared at his hands. When he lifted his eyes, his knuckles were still white. "I was ambushed. Caught off guard. That's not supposed to happen to someone who makes a living following them, but it happened." He took a deep breath. "It was almost dark. I didn't see them until they were on me."

"They?" Calley didn't dare close her eyes long enough to blink. Otherwise, the image Dean's words were painting might overwhelm her. Dean, the man whom she loved, had been attacked by more than one grizzly bear.

"Two of them," he said in an icy voice that frightened her. "A couple of immature males, we later decided. I don't know how big they were, but big enough for me to believe they could drag me into hell."

Once again Calley fought down the need to wrap her arms and body around Dean. Not yet. He wasn't finished. "Didn't you have a weapon?"

"Yeah, I had a weapon; not that it did me any good. I didn't have a chance to use my rifle before they were on me. I should have sensed them, Calley. It was too quiet. Nothing moved. I had enough warning, but earlier that day Waina said she wasn't going to leave Alaska. I wasn't thinking about the right things."

Dean had been thinking, all right, Calley realized. He just hadn't had his mind on survival. "Where was Hawk?"

"In camp with his sister." Dean's lids slid down over his eyes. "I've started, so please let me finish. It was almost dark. I'd been near the river but was leaving it to return to camp. I shouldn't have been moving so slowly, but I was thinking—well, I was trying to reconcile myself to leaving Waina behind in Alaska. The first I knew I was in trouble was when I smelled them."

Calley shuddered. She wished Dean would open his eyes so he would know he wasn't alone.

"They charged me. A grizzly can be silent when he wants to. By the time I saw them, it was too late for me to use my rifle. Besides, there were two of them. I didn't have much of a chance."

"You're alive," Calley whispered.

"I didn't think I was going to make it. Calley? They stayed with me for hours. Hawk thinks it was at least three."

"Oh, God!" Calley couldn't stop herself. She launched herself out of the chair and onto the bed. She tried to pull Dean against her, but he remained frozen, staring out at something she couldn't see. At least he let her take his cold hands in her own.

"I knew my only chance was if I played dead. Have you ever tried to make yourself go limp when a bear is ripping the jacket off your back? When he picks you up in his jaws and drags you toward the mountains? When Hawk scared them off by shooting at them, I thought I was hallucinating. I don't remember much of that part."

Calley felt the shudder rip through Dean's body. She didn't think his reaction would have been this intense if he'd spoken about it before. But for reasons she didn't understand, he'd buried the experience deep inside him and let it fester. Now it was almost more than he could handle. "I wish you'd told me earlier."

"I couldn't." Dean turned toward her, but Calley couldn't be sure he was really seeing her. "I've thought about telling you a hundred times, but I never knew how to get started. Calley, this is hard to say, but—I didn't know it was possible to be that scared."

"You lived through it," she said gently. This was the one experience that would always separate them. She couldn't possibly imagine the hell he'd been in. Just the same, she wondered if what she was feeling would reach him. "That's what counts. You're alive."

"I have nightmares."

"I know that." Even though it was an artificial gesture, she smiled at him. "I might have been able to help if I'd known what the nightmares were about."

"I told myself you didn't want to hear this, but now I know I was looking for excuses."

"I know you were," Calley agreed. She was relieved to see a little expression reentering his face. His eyes were no longer closed. They were still too large, but at least he was focusing. "Hawk and Waina knew what you'd gone through. They were the ones who found you. Weren't you able to talk to them?"

Dean shook his head. "Afterward, they flew me to a hospital in Anchorage. Hawk couldn't leave the park for long, and Waina— She flew with me, but I told her I didn't want her to stay."

"Oh, Dean! I can't believe the two of you couldn't put your problems behind you at least until you were out of the hospital."

Dean's laugh was derisive. "That's what she tried to tell me, but I just wanted to be alone. I didn't want her to know that I couldn't shut my eyes without seeing those two bears, remembering how helpless I felt."

"You wanted her to leave thinking that you were something more than human." Calley didn't care whether her disgust showed. Dean had done everything in his power to deny emotions that anyone would understand. As a result, he hadn't come to grips with the attack and its aftermath on him. "They say that if you fall off a bike you're supposed to pick yourself up and get back on. You didn't go back to Toklat."

"I didn't get out of the hospital for a month," Dean said without moving his clenched jaw. "By then I had other responsibilities. I couldn't."

"I'm not going to argue that point with you." Calley ran her fingers under the buttons of Dean's shirt. His heart was beating just beyond her reach. "But you're going to have to now."

"I know."

"You won't be alone," Calley said softly. "Hawk and I will be there."

"I know," Dean repeated. "Those two won't be waiting for me. It'll be different this time." He wasn't sure he believed a word of what he'd just said.

Calley was watching him too closely. "You don't have to go if you don't want to. It isn't going to change how I feel about you."

"I'm going," Dean said through tight lips. "It's too late to back down now. What time is it? I'm hungry."

Calley turned over Dean's wrist so she could look at his watch. It was four in the afternoon. They'd gone through the meeting without a break. "I'll buy you lunch," she offered.

Dean nodded agreement, but when Calley started to slide off the bed, he pulled her back against him. "We could wait for dinner," he whispered.

"What would you like to do while we wait?"

Dean covered her offered lips with his own, but even as he felt himself sinking into her arms, he was aware of the mental warning bell that refused to be silent. Calley Stewart read him so well. Too well. She knew when he wanted to make love and when he needed to talk. He wondered if she knew how he'd handle himself at Toklat if they came across a grizzly?

He also wondered how she could continue to love him if he failed this test.

Chapter Eleven

Nothing could possibly have prepared Calley for her first view of Mount McKinley. Although Hawk had warned her that the highest peak on the North American continent rose over twenty thousand feet, seeing it emerge triumphant from the other mountains as they flew near, took her breath away.

She was aware of cameras clicking as the politicians took pictures, but even when Dean leaned across her for a look, she didn't take her eyes off the formidable mass. "Denali," Dean said. "Home of the Sun."

"A good name," Calley admitted. "Look at the glaciers, Dean. When I think that they've been there for centuries— It dominates everything. I can't believe people actually climb it."

"To tell the truth, neither can I." Dean wrapped his arm around her. "Hawk and I talk about climbing it, but fortunately we've never had time."

Calley laughed but continued to watch as the plane skirted the mountain, giving a view of barren peaks that seemed to be challenging her and mocking her frail strength. Hawk explained that he would have preferred to pass over later in the day. "Around midday the sunlight glistens on the snow and the glaciers. It's too bright for some cameras to capture. But twilight is when the mountain really shows off. The mountain is covered by delicate pastel shades that change every few minutes. That's when I stop thinking about how majestic it is and admit that its beauty is timeless."

Calley glanced at Hawk. She was surprised to hear him speak of the mountain with reverance, but as low-lying clouds drifted around the mountain, cloaking it in a soft white mantle, she saw that Denali was capable of reaching the deepest senses. She shivered slightly. "No wonder they made this area into a national park. That mountain is something no one can ignore."

The small plane touched down at park headquarters. After spending a few minutes transferring cameras and people, Hawk got behind the wheel of the park minivan and started on the road that led to the Toklat River area. Although the mountain hadn't been visible from the headquarters, it wasn't long before Calley was catching glimpses of it, this time from ground level. Calley was content with what she could see from a window. It was one of those days of rare perfection for the park. Although it was cool and the wind was blowing, there was none of the rain Hawk had warned them against, and the wind was keeping the clouds from settling around the mountains.

"How many people have died climbing that thing?" one of the politicians asked as he was loading his second roll of film into his camera.

Hawk shrugged. "I'd have to look that up. It isn't that inexperienced people attempt to climb it; it's just that storms are always a factor. It can take up to three weeks to make the climb. I'm sorry we couldn't do this a few weeks later. You might have been able to see the caribou migration."

Calley had been sitting with Dean in the seat directly behind Hawk. She leaned forward. "Do you think we'll see any caribou?"

"Could be. They range all over the park. This time of the year both males and females have antlers, so it's quite a show. What you should visit, though, is the mainland across from Barter Island. That's the true calving ground. You know, if you were smart, you'd get that boss of yours to take a year off to give you a decent introduction to Alaska."

"Sure," Dean said, laughing. "I get as much free time as you do. I'm afraid that for now Calley is going to have to be content with a weekend."

Calley took Dean's hand, cradling it in her lap. She'd expected him to be tense and uptight, but he seemed to be enjoying himself. He'd added to what Hawk was telling the visitors about the frustrations and pleasures of managing a wilderness area encompassing thousands of square miles. He'd brought the reality of never-ending night into focus by describing the simple message "No More Dark" etched in the ice on the side of a small school. As they traveled on the only road through the park, Dean pointed out where moose, wolves, red fox, golden eagles and grizzlies were occasionally spotted without having to leave a car.

Calley wished she understood the change in Dean's behavior. Surely it hadn't been easy for him to close his mind to the reality of returning to the site where he'd nearly lost his life. Obviously he loved this country. Maybe the answer was as simple as that.

"I wish we could stay longer," Calley admitted as they passed a slower-moving car on the paved single-lane road. "I'd like to be here after the tourists have left."

"No, you wouldn't," Dean pointed out. "Not unless you're into months of subzero weather."

"I'm not asking for a weather report," Calley shot back, although her eyes refused to be serious. "I'm indulging in a little fantasy right now."

"How about it, Dean?" Hawk spoke up. He kept his voice low so it wouldn't carry to the other passengers. "We could get rid of these three characters and take Calley for serious exploring tomorrow. What's another day or two here?"

"Are the two of you ganging up on me?" Dean asked. "Some of us happen to have work waiting for us."

"Work!" Hawk snorted. "Work can wait. You're not going to deny Calley the opportunity to spend some extra time in my presence. I can take her places she's never been before."

"Spare me," Dean said with a laugh. "We'll see. Let me call the university tonight."

Calley tried to hide her excitement, but a delighted laugh escaped nonetheless. "I packed an extra pair of jeans. And I haven't used up all my film."

"Between you and Melinda there isn't enough film left in the stores for the rest of the world," Dean pointed out. "I'm not making any promises. We have plane reservations back to Montana for tomorrow."

"Tomorrow be hanged," Hawk snorted. A moment later he pulled the minivan over to the side of the road and allowed his passengers to get out to try for a better picture of a golden eagle whose weight bent the top of a scraggly tree. Calley and Dean scrambled out together, but when one of the congressmen called Dean over, Hawk signaled for Calley to join him.

"There's something you should know," the park supervisor whispered. "While we were at headquarters, I checked on some reports we'd been getting about a grizzly and her cub near Toklat. She's torn up at least two camping sites in the past week. She's still at it. Apparently, last night she took off after a hiker less than a mile from the ranger station there. The hiker threw off his backpack, and while she was tearing that apart, he did the four-minute mile."

Calley tensed. "Should we be taking these men to Toklat?"

"We won't be getting far from the road," Hawk explained. "Because of the flat, open terrain there, any grizzlies they see will be through binoculars. But, Calley, I'm going to have to move this old female grizzly." Hawk was staring down at her, his eyes deeper than she'd ever seen them.

Calley swallowed, as what Hawk was saying sunk in. He didn't want Dean and her here an extra day only so they could play tourist; there was work for them to do. "She's near where Dean was attacked, isn't she," Calley said with deadly finality.

"She could be. Calley, Dean isn't a coward. He didn't panic on you when the two of you were treed. He told me about that. I don't think he knew what else he was telling me. He doesn't know how strong he is inside. I do. I think you do, too. I hope we can show him."

"By forcing him to capture a rogue grizzly?" Calley fought the shiver spiking through her spine. "He wouldn't do that to me. He deserves the same treatment."

"I know it." Hawk dragged his weathered hand through wind-tossed hair. "The push has to come from inside Dean. But, Calley, he's never going to be free until he's faced his demons."

Calley wanted to tell Hawk that Dean wasn't any less a man because he had to live with the memories of a nightmarish attack. She loved him for what he was. He was capable of touching her in ways she'd never been touched before. But much as she hated admitting it, Hawk was right. Although Dean was all she'd ever want him to be, he wasn't content with what he saw in himself.

But what if he failed the test? What if he couldn't stand near Toklat River and sight down a tranquilizing gun at a grizzly? Would he be able to live with himself?

"Tell him. Ask him when the time is right," she said reluctantly. "But the decision has to be his. I'll back him no matter what he says."

"I knew you would." Hawk put his arm around Calley's shoulder. "Did I tell you how damn lucky that man is to have found you?"

"I'm the lucky one," Calley whispered.

Once everyone was back in the minivan, Hawk continued on the road, which became a graveled surface once they reached Savage River. They slowed to a crawl on the winding, narrow road with its many sharp curves. Hawk pointed out that between here and Toklat the road wound through the foothills of the Alaska Range. The foothills here were covered with vegetation, but soon the road would take them through areas of both swampy tiaga and treeless tundra.

Hawk pulled off before the road crossed the bridge. He locked eyes with Dean for a minute before turning to his guests. "If you don't have your boots on, I'd suggest you do that now. We don't want any twisted or broken ankles. With any luck you're going to see what all the controversy is about. The river is still pretty high. We won't be able to cross it, and that will limit how far we can go. We're going to be making our way through the river channels. There's a wide valley filled with gravel created by the river. We'll be sharing a route the bears take."

One of the politicians voiced concern about being unarmed when leaving the vehicle but Hawk reassured them that the land was open enough that there was little danger of a bear sneaking up on them. "The grizzlies' den is in the brushy willows along the banks, but this time of day any that are in the area will be out and about. We'll let you know if we find fresh signs. Keep your binoculars on the mountain slopes. You might see some Dall sheep."

Calley waited for Dean to either get up or move aside so she could get out of the minivan. He was staring straight ahead, all emotion sucked from his face.

"You don't have to go if you don't want to," Calley whispered.

"Yeah, I do. It happened five miles from here. This doesn't look like hell, does it?"

Calley shivered as Dean's deathlike voice reached her. She held out her hand to help him to his feet, but he ignored it. "Don't patronize me, Calley. I don't need a keeper."

Calley bit back a retort. She wanted to shake him and make him realize that she'd never been down this road before and might make mistakes, but this wasn't the time for anger. If Calley loved him as much as she said she did, she'd weather his emotions. "What do you want me to do?" she asked softly.

"I don't know. I don't know what I want from myself." He turned away from her and exited from the van.

Hawk explained that the politicians were to stick close to him and then struck off downstream, the men following close behind. Calley and a silent Dean brought up the rear. Hawk explained that it was along the lower branch of the Toklat that Charles Sheldon, the man responsible for the park's existence, spent a winter studying the wildlife of the area and becoming convinced that the land should be set aside as a sanctuary for that wildlife.

"It's spectacular," one of the men said to no one in particular. Mountains rose on either side of the river, the lower green slopes contrasting with the reddish rocks above. The man's open smile faded a little when Hawk pointed at a small craterlike hole made by a bear digging for ground squirrels.

Dean took Calley's hand, holding it but not speaking to her. His eyes were constantly sweeping over the open terrain. Fifteen minutes into the hike he whistled low and pointed toward a mountain slope. Calley lifted her binoculars and brought them into focus. The white dots she'd mistaken as tricks of the eye turned into a small group of heavy-horned Dall sheep dozing under the sun. "They look like aristocrats," she whispered. "They're smaller than I thought they'd be, but they're so white. I count, what, three young ones."

"They look pretty sure of themselves," one of the men observed. "Don't they have to be on the lookout for bears?"

Dean managed a short laugh. "Not as long as they stay high in the mountains. Their true natural enemies are wolves, but wolves don't get that high, either."

"Then what do the grizzlies eat?" the man asked. "Other than us, that is."

When Calley realized that Dean wasn't going to answer, she explained that the usual diet of grizzlies consisted of everything from rodents and fish to roots and berries. "They'll go after larger creatures, but not if there's an adequate food supply. And they don't make a habit of dining on congressmen."

"That's a relief," the man said. "I wonder if it's true that animals can smell fear. If it is, I'm putting out signals that can be picked up for miles."

The two-mile hike to where the valley bent southward was uneventful. Calley was impressed by the view of the Divide Mountains to her right and green rolling hills covered with dwarf birch and willow to her left, but Dean's silent tension had seeped into her, making it impossible for her to concentrate on everything Hawk was telling them.

She was torn between wanting to spot a grizzly so that the visitors would be able to see the magnificent creatures and her concern about how well Dean would handle it. She'd sensed his tension when they were tagging the grizzly at the Flathead and later when they were treed, but until he'd told her everything, she'd attributed his emotion to caution. If only it were that simple.

"You're quiet," the short, nearly bald man the others called Robert finally said to Dean. "I suppose this is pretty old hat to you."

"It never becomes old hat," Dean answered shortly. He'd released Calley's hand as they made their way over a soggy, sandy area, but now he reached for her again. He glanced at her but didn't smile.

"I don't guess it does," the man mused aloud. His eyes locked on the entwined hands, and he pointed. "I'm glad to see that. When I saw the two of you for the first time yesterday, I thought at least one of you was a fool if there wasn't any chemistry there."

Calley blushed, but she thought that her cheeks, already reddened by the wind, wouldn't give away her emotion. "Are you married?" she asked, turning the conversation in a safer direction.

Robert explained that he'd been married to the same woman for going on twenty-five years. "We have a new grandchild that I haven't seen yet."

Calley freed her hand only to wrap her arm around Dean's waist. It wasn't hard to picture herself twenty-five years down the road still in love with the same man. "He's a lucky man," she whispered as Robert left them.

"He is, isn't he?" Dean agreed. He pulled her around so Calley could look up at him. "A good marriage takes a lot of work." With his free hand Dean brushed the hair off

Calley's forehead. "Being honest and open with each other are essential."

Calley was losing touch with her surroundings. She hadn't expected Dean to have that much control over her with the others around, but now that it was happening, she accepted it willingly. "I hope we can always be honest with each other," she whispered.

"What would you say if I told you I'd give anything not to be here today?"

"I'd say that admitting it is half the battle."

"I'm not sure I'm going to win this battle, Calley. I can't shake off the memories." Dean pressed her close to him, the power in his arms a silent reinforcement for his words.

"It doesn't matter. It just means you're human," Calley whispered from her welcomed prison. "I love you, Dean. That's what matters."

Dean shuddered but didn't release her. "I wish it were that easy. But unless I can face certain things about myself, I'm not going to be any good for you."

"Will you stop that!" Calley didn't care whether the others heard. She'd listened to Dean say the same thing yesterday. She'd tried everything within her power to convince him that not being able to talk about being attacked by a pair of grizzlies didn't make him any less of a man in her mind, but he wasn't listening. He was hung up on attaining some stupid goal he'd set for himself. "I'm scared to death of speaking before a group. Does that make me less a woman in your eyes?"

"It's not the same thing, and you know it."

She did know that. The analogy was a poor one, but it was the best she could come up with. "Tell me how I can help you? What do you want me to do?"

"Nothing. That's the hell of it. I'm the only one who can do this."

He was right, of course, but that still didn't make it any easier. She wanted them to be able to share everything, the entire range of human emotions. Being shut away from him in this way was tearing her apart. "I'm sorry I don't understand what you went through," she said. "Maybe if I had I'd know what you're asking of yourself."

Dean held on to her with a desperation that frightened her. "I don't want you to ever go through that. You're too precious to me."

Calley's heart latched on to Dean's words, but that didn't keep her from feeling empty when he turned from her to respond to something one of the others was asking. She wanted to take him away from here, but she couldn't do that. She wanted him to be able to gaze at the scenery without being sucked back in time, but she couldn't block out his nightmare.

"It's damn hard for him, isn't it?" Hawk asked as they started back.

"Hard isn't the half of it." Calley's senses were alert for evidence of a grizzly's presence. Unless her honed instincts had failed her, they weren't sharing the river area with anything larger than a fox. "But he's doing it." She groaned. "I thought he'd find peace if he came here."

"That's the easy part. It's mentally facing those two young males again that's tying him in knots."

"What does he want?" Calley groaned again. "A repeat performance?"

"Maybe. Maybe facing a bear out here is what it's going to take."

Calley was silent for a long minute. Finally she faced Dean's friend with stony eyes. "That's what you want to have happen, isn't it?" she accused. "You've been thinking about that female and her cub since you asked Dean to come to Alaska."

"Maybe."

"Maybe nothing." Calley gripped Hawk's wrist, not caring whether her nails dug into him. "You've been planning this."

"Yeah, I've been planning it." Hawk sighed heavily. "Look, Calley, I'm the one who carried Dean out of there. Do you think it's been easy for me? But I've been back to the Toklat a lot of times since the accident. I learned that facing something square on is a hell of a lot easier than sitting hundreds of miles away, letting that night continue to eat at me."

Calley released Hawk and hurried after Dean. She was both angry at Hawk and understood what he had done, but Hawk wasn't in love with Dean. She was proud of what Dean had accomplished with his life. She didn't care about the one small flaw he saw in himself.

"What were you and Hawk talking about?" Dean asked when she rejoined him.

"Not much," Calley sidestepped. "It's so peaceful out here. But even in summer I can feel winter waiting to descend. It's in the wind. It doesn't take much of a storm to make the river overflow its banks, does it?"

The group had retraced a mile of their hike when Dean stopped so quickly that Calley almost ran into him. He pointed ahead of them on the opposite side of the river. "There they are" was all he said.

To the untrained eye the distant brown lumps could have been mistaken for rocks, but Calley had seen too many grizzlies to be fooled. She stared at them through her binoculars. "There's three of them," she whispered to the men now gathered around her. "Just before the bend in the river. They're either drinking or fishing."

The distant bears seemed to be as interested in sniffing the air as they were in satisfying their need for food and water.

When the largest of the trio rose on his hind legs with his nose extended in the air, the politicians let out a collective gasp. "He's taller than I am," Robert whispered. "Look at the size of that creature."

"That's at least eight feet of bear," Calley explained. "They don't know we're here because the wind's blowing in the wrong direction. Maybe they're picking up the scent of some sheep. Something has their attention."

"Can't they see us?" one of the others asked nervously.

Hawk shook his head. "Their eyesight is pretty weak," he explained. "As long as the wind doesn't shift and we keep our voices down so the river masks us, they'll think they're alone."

"And if the wind shifts?"

"They'd still have to cross the river, and it's pretty deep and swift right along there. Here they see enough humans so that most grizzlies leave them alone. However, I would suggest we sit down and wait for them to leave." Hawk shot Calley a quick glance. She followed his gaze as he turned toward Dean.

Dean hadn't set down the binoculars since the bears were spotted. Calley was aware of the tension radiating out from him, but she couldn't detect an increase in his breathing rate. "Two females and an immature male," Dean said almost conversationally. "They're well fed."

"They should be," Hawk supplied. "Spring came early this year. They've gained back most of what they lost during the winter." Hawk told the politicians a little about the winter behavior of bears, and Dean added that the average weight of a grizzly born in January was less than a pound. Calley felt heartened because Dean was able to contribute to the conversation, but she was aware that he had yet to take his eyes off the creatures.

A half hour passed before the grizzlies abandoned the river and ambled up a slope until the group finally lost sight of them. The three congressmen were hesitant to continue back toward the road until Calley struck out to lead the way. Dean was in the middle of the group, his attention still on the spot where the bears had last been seen.

"I'm delighted this happened," Robert admitted. "There really is no way we can understand a bear's place in the scheme of things until we see them in their natural habitat."

"Do you believe they have a place there?" Hawk asked.

"I think Dean said it best yesterday," Robert went on. "The reasons for saving the grizzly are intellectual, esthetic and compassionate. The world will continue to exist without them, but if that happens, I believe we will have lost something of ourselves, as well."

Tears welled up in Calley's eyes. For a man who spent his days and nights in smoked-filled rooms, Robert had a realistic grip on the world beyond those walls. "Is that the decision you're taking back to Washington, D.C.?" she asked.

"You've hit the nail on the head, young lady. And unless I don't know my colleagues as well as I think I do, I'm not the only one who feels that way."

Calley grinned openly at both Hawk and Dean, but the park superintendent was the only one who returned her smile. Throwing caution to the wind, Calley linked her arm through Dean's as they walked the short distance back to the minivan. Hawk was taking a poll of the politicians to see if they wanted to continue to the end of the park road when the CB radio in the van sputtered to life. Hawk scrambled into the van. When he reemerged a few minutes later, his face was grim.

"Gentlemen, I'm afraid an emergency has come up. If you're interested in a hike of less than a mile, I can give you a graphic demonstration of the awesome power of a grizzly."

Calley heard the explosion of breath coming from Dean but didn't look at him until he spoke. "Bear attack?" was all he asked.

"She took apart a camp some fool pitched near a sandbar along the lower Toklat. Apparently the people were out hiking when it happened, but they're fit to be tied."

"She?" Dean repeated. "How do you know it's a female?"

Hawk met Dean's question square on. "Because we've had trouble with a female and her cub here since spring."

Dean snorted. His eyes blazed with an anger that frightened Calley. "You knew that before we came in here. I'm not a fool, Hawk. What is this? Reality therapy?"

"Maybe," Hawk challenged.

Calley was aware that the three other men were taking in every word of the conversation, but she didn't have time for them. Dean's reaction to the challenge Hawk was presenting was all that mattered. "What are you going to do?" she asked Hawk when Dean remained silent.

"I'm not sure," Hawk replied. "I know I'm not going to put her down no matter what those fool hikers want. But we've got to get her away from people before she kills someone."

"North Peak," Dean said tersely. "You've flown rogues there before."

Hawk nodded. "I'm shorthanded, Dean."

"Damn," Dean hissed. "Damn you." He hoisted himself into the van without looking at Calley.

After a hesitation that lasted no more than five seconds, Calley joined Dean inside. She sat beside him but made no move to touch him. Because she loved him, she understood that this was one time he needed to be alone with his thoughts. The politicians stayed outside with Hawk, asking questions about what they might find when they reached the ravaged camp. At length, Hawk poked his head into the van. "Are you coming?"

Dean was still staring straight ahead. Calley glanced at him, feeling the massive barrier around him. Slowly she rose to her feet. "I'm coming," she said as she left Dean. As she emerged from the van, she knew she was leaving her heart behind.

"What'd he say?" Hawk whispered.

"Nothing." Calley stared at the ground and they looked at the bend in the river that would take them to where Hawk was needed. "This has to be his decision."

"You're damn right."

Calley whirled at the anger in Dean's voice. He was emerging from the minivan, the tranquilizing rifle the van was equipped with cradled in his arms. "You weren't going to forget this, were you, Hawk?" He tossed the rifle at Hawk.

"Knock it off, Dean," Hawk shot back. "I have a potential killer to deal with. I can't wet-nurse you."

"It's about time you figured that out. You want your damn bear? Let's get moving." Without waiting to see if the others would fall in line, Dean struck off in the opposite direction from where they'd gone earlier. Behind his back Hawk made a gesture to indicate he'd like nothing better than to hit Dean over the head, but when he glanced at Calley, she caught a glimmer of admiration in his eyes.

Calley stayed behind Dean and Hawk so that she could keep an eye on the other men, who might behave unpredictably in an emergency situation. She had no idea what Dean would do when and if they spotted the rogue. She could only go with the gut feeling that his training would win out over fear. If they were able to deal successfully with the grizzly, and that's what she prayed would happen, she and Dean could get on with their lives.

But if Dean reacted in a way that he couldn't take pride in, she wasn't sure there'd be enough pieces of him left to pick up.

When Dean and Hawk pulled a little ahead of the others, Robert asked her what was wrong with Dean. She could have manufactured an excuse, but she didn't. "He almost lost his life here last year," she said simply. "Grizzlies got to him."

"Good God," Robert whispered. "It takes guts to do what he's doing."

"He hasn't done it yet," Calley pointed out.

"But he's here. That has to tell you something."

What it told Calley was that Dean wasn't giving up without one last fight, that maybe he was going after the grizzly because he felt he had something to prove to her as well as to himself. You don't have to do this, she wanted to tell him. It won't change how I feel.

But maybe it would, because failure would change Dean.

One of the other politicians made the observation that introducing a controversial bill in Congress was a piece of cake compared to what they were doing, but other than that one joke the men remained silent. Calley knew that the chance the large group would be attacked was next to nothing. Not only were they traveling along a wide river flat, which gave them an excellent view of their surroundings, but the chances were that the creature they were seeking had already left the area.

It wasn't hard to locate the ransacked campsite. Even before they came close enough to be able to identify what the fleeing campers had left behind, they could see litter strewn out over several hundred square feet. As Dean bent over the thick severed pole that had once held a canvas tent in place,

Robert whistled. "Would you look at that? She put her teeth clear through some cans. There isn't enough left of that tent to make a good rag."

"That's the other side of the story, gentlemen," Hawk observed. "Now you have a pretty good idea of what a grizzly thinks of humans."

To Calley's relief Robert laughed. "I've come across some special-interest groups in my career who would like nothing better than to do this with something of mine. At least your rogue lets you know where you stand with her."

"That she does," Hawk agreed as he picked up a metal bucket that looked as if it had been run over by a truck. He kicked at a scattered deck of cards. "I guess she wasn't interested in games."

"What was she interested in?" one of the other men asked.

"Food," Hawk explained, pointing at a shredded cereal box. Calley knew that wasn't the whole story. True, food probably had attracted the grizzly initially, but the complete destruction strewn around was the work of a creature with a chip on her shoulder. Instinctively, Calley moved closer to Dean.

"Did you see the droppings?" he asked.

Calley nodded. "They're less than a day old."

"We'd better get these men back on their plane."

Calley wrapped her arm around Dean's waist. "And then what?"

"Then we come back after her."

"We?" she repeated.

Dean sighed. He pulled her close, his eyes on the horizon. "That's what you wanted to hear, isn't it?"

"Don't dump this one on me, Dean," Calley warned. "Either this is something you have to do, or it isn't. I can't make that decision for you."

"Maybe not. But if it wasn't for you, I wouldn't have to make the decision."

There was no way Calley could hide from what Dean was telling her. She was the catalyst that had brought him back to the Toklat River. Hawk wouldn't have been able to accomplish it alone. For reasons that were too complex for her to vocalize, Dean was facing his nightmare as much for her as for himself.

"I want to be part of this," she insisted.

"I don't want you to."

"I know that," she forged on. "But you heard Hawk. He's shorthanded. I know what I'm doing almost as well as you do."

Dean turned her to face him so that she had no choice but to look up at him. "What if I asked you not to come back here?"

Calley drank deeply of the crystal clear air. Things were coming to a head between them, but she was who she was. She couldn't change her nature and be someone either she or Dean could be proud of. "If you love me, Dean, you won't ask that of me. Here, with you, is where I belong."

Chapter Twelve

In a one-minute telephone message, Dean told Steve that he was to hire an air taxi and be at McKinley Park before dark. "Hawk doesn't have the experience for this hunt," he explained. "He'll handle getting a helicopter so that we can transfer the grizzly once she's down, but I don't want anyone but a pro out there with us."

Dean turned from the phone and faced Hawk and Calley. "Sorry to be pulling rank on you, Hawk, but you're a bureaucrat. You're going to have your hands full keeping the press away."

Hawk glared at Dean but said nothing. Calley acknowledged a shiver born of both fear and excitement. Grizzlies were unpredictable enough; one who openly hated man couldn't be trusted. "We're going to need guns," she pointed out.

Dean explained that Steve would be bringing a couple of guns with him and then asked Hawk the question Calley knew he'd have to. Were there any high-caliber rifles available?

"Yeah," Hawk said reluctantly. "And two-hundred-grain bullets. Don't use them if you don't have to."

"I don't intend to," Dean said shortly. "But neither do I intend to endanger anyone's life. Let's take a look at that map of yours. I want to know where and when she's been spotted."

Calley joined the men in Hawk's office. She tried to concentrate as they pieced together the bear's movements, but she was restless. She felt better knowing that Steve would be around, but Dean was the only one who could accurately pinpoint where they would be most likely to come across the grizzly and her cub. Unconsciously Calley rubbed her hands over her jeans in an attempt to remove the perspiration there. What was it her mother had asked when Calley made the decision to return to work at the university? Something about a wildlife researcher being no kind of a job for an unmarried woman. "How are you going to find a husband in the middle of nowhere?" her mother asked.

Because at the time she was hurting with the twin pains of losing Mike and facing her parents' divorce, Calley had replied that marriage was the last thing she was interested in. That was before she met Dean.

"You better get some rest," Dean said as he was folding the map and placing it in his pocket. "We're going to be out of here as soon as it gets light."

"Are you dismissing me?" Hawk had excused himself to talk to one of the rangers about another problem, which left Dean and Calley alone in the office.

"I'm just saying that tomorrow is going to be a long day. I want you sharp."

"And I want the same of you," Calley countered. "Dean, we're not going to do each other any good if we're at each other's throats."

Dean rested his weight against Hawk's desk. He folded his arms across his chest and looked down at where she was sitting. "This isn't what I wanted to happen up here, Calley," he said softly. "I wanted to show you a place I've grown to love despite everything that's happened, not to risk your life."

Calley had to steel herself against surrendering too quickly to Dean's tone. "Maybe we'll have that time yet," she whispered. "But this has to be done first."

"I know." Dean clenched his teeth, but Calley didn't know who, if anyone, he was angry at. "Maybe—" He drew out the word. "Maybe in the back of my mind I hoped this would happen. I can't go on hiding forever."

Calley pulled herself to her feet. She stood before Dean, not touching him, wondering if her love was reaching him. "You aren't hiding," she said. "You wouldn't be doing what you do with your life if you were."

"That's what I told myself." Dean sighed. "I told myself that working on the Flathead was proof that being attacked hadn't changed me that much. But I don't handle field work as well as I did before the attack. And being on the Toklat today..." He left the sentence unfinished.

Without waiting for a sign that Dean was ready to have her touch him, Calley took the chance. She rose on tiptoe and kissed him. "One step at a time," she whispered. "That's how we'll take it."

Wordlessly Dean folded Calley into his arms. He drank in her fragrance, instantly remembering how perfectly her body molded itself to his. He knew he'd been impossible to put up with today, and yet she was still here, reaching for him when he couldn't admit even to himself how much he needed that. A tidal wave of desire washed over him. There was no way he could hide the emotion from Calley. "I want to make love to you," he whispered. "Now."

"Oh, Dean. I needed to hear you say that." Calley didn't lift her head from his chest. Her voice was muffled when she spoke. "I wish we could spend the rest of our lives like this."

"It could get awkward," Dean pointed out. "Hawk said there's a cabin we can use tonight. If that's what you want."

"You know that's what I want. I—I'm shaking. I'm sorry."

What she was apologizing for, Dean had no idea. She had every right to make her wishes known if she wanted to make love. After all, hadn't he just given free rein to his own thoughts? "I love you, Calley. No matter what happens tomorrow, I love you." He didn't add that he wasn't sure his love would be returned after the day was over.

It was after midnight before Calley and Dean finally had time to think about sleep. They had to collect the supplies they would need, finalize plans with the helicopter pilot and decide on exactly where the grizzly and her cub would be transplanted if they succeeded in capturing them. Steve arrived and had to be brought up-to-date on the situation. Phone calls from a wildlife-preservation organization, which had somehow heard about the operation, had to be dealt with, and the upset hikers with the destroyed campsite had to be pacified.

"I think I'd rather face a rogue than those tenderfeet," Steve observed as he was getting ready to head toward the cabin Hawk had provided for him. "I can't believe those people had no idea there were bears in the area. Leaving food inside the tent was an open invitation to trouble."

Dean was still muttering about the ignorance of some people when he closed the cabin door behind him, but when he turned toward Calley, she was the only thing on his mind. "You aren't going to get the rest you need," she said.

"Neither are you," he pointed out before demonstrating what would take the place of sleep. He wanted this night in Alaska to be special, but because he couldn't avoid the thought that it might be their last, he took her with a desperation that couldn't be denied. Dean undressed her quickly, barely taking time to pull a blanket over them before pulling her to him. He wanted to tell her that she was the best thing to ever come into his life, but when she responded to his urgent caresses with an urgency of her own, there wasn't time for words.

When they awoke in the middle of the night and repeated the act of lovemaking, this time at an almost languid pace, once again neither of them spoke. Dean had spent himself and was hovering in that void between wakefulness and sleep when he felt hot moisture on his chest. Calley, with her head cradled on his chest, was crying.

He buried his fingers in her long tangled hair, knowing his touch wasn't enough but not knowing what else to do to reach her. *Don't cry, Calley,* he thought. *Don't keep yourself shut off from me. I'll always be here for you, if you want me.*

Before dawn when they responded to the sound of the alarm, Dean didn't mention either their lovemaking or Calley's tears. In a world where all emotions were safe, he would have asked for an explanation, but he'd learned that certain things could be given life only when their time had come. Calley's crying scared him. And because he believed he knew what caused the tears, it was something he couldn't speak about.

After taking quick showers in the rustic bathroom, Calley and Dean dressed and then stepped out into darkness that was tinged with the first blush of morning. They walked over to the jeep Hawk had provided. Steve was waiting for them. "Have you had breakfast?" Steve asked, his voice hushed.

Dean shook his head. Food was the farthest thing from his mind; but he should have thought of Calley's needs. "What would you like?" he asked her.

"Nothing" was her terse reply.

With Dean driving, the trio left park headquarters. They acknowledged Hawk's presence at the door to his office but waved without stopping to speak. Everything that needed to be said had been said last night.

The drive to the Toklat bridge didn't take long, and they were unpacked before it was light enough to see clearly. All three of them carried both tranquilizer rifles and the weapons with which Hawk had supplied them. Jammed in their pockets was extra ammunition, and strapped to their sides were the communication systems that would keep them hooked up with each other and Hawk. They all carried binoculars. The plans had already been made. Calley and Dean were to travel along opposite sides of the lower Toklat, while Steve would cover the East Branch, where the rogue grizzly had also been seen a few weeks ago. They were to communicate with each other every half hour and had agreed to shoot off three quick shots if any of them were in trouble.

"We're taking no chances," Dean said in a repeat of his instructions of the previous night. "Most of the country around here is pretty open, but under no circumstances are any of us to go into the brush."

Steve nodded. "How old is her cub? Has anyone gotten a good look at it?"

Dean explained that the cub's age had been estimated at six months, since it appeared to weigh around fifty pounds. "We're taking a chance at finding the right female. The bear population is pretty high here."

"She'll be the one coming over to shake our hand," Steve quipped. "We'd better get going. It's going to be a long day."

Dean and Calley traveled together until they reached the ruined campsite they'd checked the day before. Dean had been intensely aware of his surroundings since leaving the jeep. Knowing he would have to let Calley take off on her own only increased his sensitivity and unease. He understood that the pain gnawing at his side existed only in his head, but knowing and conquering it were two different things. "I don't like this," he said honestly. "I don't want you out there alone."

"You'll be alone, too," she pointed out. Calley shrugged her shoulders to redistribute the weight of her rifles. "Are you sure you're going to be all right?"

Her question shouldn't anger him, for her concern was as natural as his. But there was no stopping his quick retort. "I wouldn't be out here if I wasn't all right."

"Maybe. And maybe you don't know what's going on inside you." Calley gave his hand a quick squeeze and released it. Then she made an impersonal note of the time before starting off.

Dean crossed the river by picking his way across the shallow sandbar and jumping several narrow channels. By the time he was on firm footing, he could no longer see Calley. The thought that the river might keep him from reaching her should she need him buried itself deep inside him. It was still so damn much easier for her. She didn't have to worry about drowning in memories or wonder if she could truly count on herself. His mind was doing things that he hated.

For close to three hours Calley made her slow, cautious way, keeping the river always in sight. She'd spotted several white dots that turned out to be Dall sheep and came across a fox den in the bushy willows growing along the riverbank. Although she remembered to communicate with the men at regular intervals, time seemed suspended. Calley's thoughts were with the man whom she could no longer see or touch. She believed that somehow he was beside her, sharing a quick glimpse at two distant magnificent rams squaring off at each other, their massive horns lowered for fight. Dean would understand her delight at finding proof that a family of foxes had made a home here. It seemed unreal that she was out here looking for a creature capable of killing her. It was too peaceful, the distant ice-capped mountains too awesomely protective. The Toklat River was a place for lovers, not danger.

When the silence came, Calley was slow to recognize it. She'd been intent on the beating of her heart when the knowledge finally seeped through her; her heart was the only sound.

Instantly Calley reached for her walkie-talkie. As a result of her last communication with Dean, she guessed he was no more than a half mile away, although the sprawling river made the distance seem much more. "There's something here," she said with a calmness she didn't feel.

"What?" came the quick reply.

"I don't know. I can't see anything." She didn't have to explain the silence.

"I'm on my way."

"Be careful," Calley warned. "She might be near the river."

Calley had no idea why she'd identified the unseen presence as a female, only that the conviction couldn't be shaken off. Dean had said he was on his way. There'd been nothing in his tone that said he was fighting private demons; she could depend on him.

There. Movement over by the river.

Calley sucked in a deep breath, speaking into the walkie-talkie at the same time. "I see a cub. I think it's trying to fish."

"Where's the mother?" Dean's voice came in short hisses, the sounds made by a man running.

"I don't know." Calley's voice remained calm. The cub hadn't lifted its head or made any indication that it knew it was being watched. "There's no one direction to the wind," she continued. "I'm not going to be able to depend on staying downwind."

"Stay out in the open, Calley! Watch your back."

Calley didn't need to be told that, but neither did she waste time arguing the point with Dean. Slowly she moved in a circle, eyes straining for any movement. Dean would understand that she had more important things to do than talk to him. Besides, his energy had to go into reaching her.

A cough that sounded like a guttural moan coming from the bowels of the earth snaked through Calley's nerves. She couldn't see the mother bear but it was out here with her. Maybe ready to charge. Calley brought the walkie-talkie into position again but cut off the words before they were out of her mouth. There was nothing Dean or Steve could do.

Once again she made her slow circle, the tranquilizing gun now held in her hands instead of on her back. She knew why she'd reached for that weapon instead of the one capable of killing. Even if this was the rogue, Calley had never killed a bear. She wasn't going to start now.

The grizzly was on the hillside above her, staring down at her with tiny eyes. Slowly it reared up on its hind legs, its front legs hanging limp but ready. Calley was between the mother and her cub. She had no doubt that this was the one they'd come after.

"Hurry, Dean," she whispered. It didn't matter whether the grizzly heard her or not; Calley simply couldn't raise her voice beyond a strangled hiss. She wanted to look at the river, to see if she could spot Dean, but she didn't dare take her eyes off the grizzly.

Shaking, Calley sighted down the rifle, zeroed in on the massive silver-tipped chest and fired. At that same instant the bear dropped back down onto all fours. The tranquilizing dart shot harmlessly over the bruin's head.

"No!" Calley didn't know she'd cried out until the word slashed a path through the silent air. The bear was advancing on her, large paws splaying outward with every step. As Calley threw down the useless rifle and grabbed for the other one, it seemed to her that the bear, the world itself, was slowing down. Although she knew that the bear had broken into a trot, every movement was so clearly defined in her mind that it was as if she had all the time in the world to watch hundreds of pounds of fury coming at her.

Dean, crossing the river, was waist deep in icy water when Calley's strangled cry reached him. Although there were several hundred yards between them, he could read her mind. The high-powered rifle was in her hands, the barrel pointed at the charging bear. She could empty the rifle into the bear; its life in exchange for hers.

But Calley wasn't a killer. Either that or she was frozen with fear, Dean realized. Even faced with the choice between her life and the grizzly's, she wasn't squeezing the trigger. Unless Dean wanted to lose the only thing he really loved in life, he would have to kill the bear himself.

The decision was made in a heartbeat. During that minisecond Dean had no existence beyond what was happening. He felt no inner pain, had no memory of a bruin dragging him into the wilderness. There was no fear, no terror. There was only Calley and the love he had for her. Dean felt the heavy rifle in his hands. He swung it up, focused and fired. At the same instant he leaned forward, losing his balance in the swift-flowing river.

The bullet slashed a path through the grizzly's fur but did nothing more than nick the skin. Roaring in fury, the grizzly skidded to a halt and snapped at her side.

Dean managed to regain his footing without dropping either rifle in the river. He could see Calley trying to bring the tranquilizing gun back into play and cussed her humanity, but there wasn't time for anger. He had to kill the bear before it killed Calley.

Or—

The thought stopped Dean and then took over. Dean was no more than thirty feet from the cub now. The female could be diverted from Calley if— Without consciously being aware of the act, Dean swung the rifle around and fired near the cub. The bullet deliberately pounded into the earth inches from the cub's nose.

A startled squall from the cub was all that it took to tear the female's attention from Calley. With a responding growl, the sow dug in. She charged for her cub, and beyond it, at Dean. The quickness of her response caught Dean off guard. There wasn't time to think, only time to act.

He dropped the hunting rifle and reached frantically for the tranquilizing gun. Dean was shooting almost before he had the grizzly in his sight. The dart buried itself in the huge creature's chest just as she reached her cub. For an instant the two creatures touched noses; then the rogue swung toward Dean. She started bouncing up and down on her front paws; short grunting noises shattered the air.

Then, slowly, gracefully, the bear lowered her head as if weary of life. Her legs splayed outward. A moment later the ground shuddered as she rolled heavily onto her side.

Dean glanced down. Icy water was seeping up his pant leg. The expensive rifle Hawk had entrusted to him was floating down the river. The cub was pushing at its mother with a pink-tipped nose.

Calley was walking toward him.

"Are you going to stand there and freeze?" she asked in a small voice.

"Are you all right?"

"Yes," Calley managed to reply. She held out a hand to help him out of the river, but once he was on firm ground, she collapsed against him. A spasm tore through her; he clutched her tightly, running a hand through her hair as a parent might comfort a frightened child.

"You're shaking," he whispered.

"So are you." Calley tried to draw back, but she lacked the strength.

"I'm cold," he said laughing. "Calley? We have work to do."

"I know." Still holding on to him, she reached for her walkie-talkie to interrupt the staccato questions coming from Steve. After reassuring him that they were all right, Calley switched the walkie-talkie to park headquarters and handed it to Dean. It took him less than a minute to inform Hawk and the helicopter pilot of their location.

"They'll be here in a few minutes." Dean sighed. "It's all over, isn't it?"

"But the work," Calley pointed out. However, she knew that wasn't what he was thinking about. "Do you have any idea how proud I am of you?" Although they were making their way back to where the dozing bear and loudly complaining cub were, she hadn't let go of him.

Dean pressed the palm of his hand against his forehead. "I didn't think about myself. I don't remember jumping into the river or what I was thinking about when I shot at the cub."

Calley stopped. "Were you trying to hit it?"

"No." He gave her the answer she wanted to hear. "I think I was trying to distract the mother. If she'd kept after you—" Dean shuddered and gripped Calley, pulling her closer.

Calley surrendered herself to Dean's arms. They still had work to do before the helicopter and Steve arrived, but that would have to wait. First they needed to reassure each other that everything had turned out all right—that neither of them had been injured or killed. Calley wanted to know more about the emotions Dean had felt at the moment he'd heard she was in danger, but that could wait, too. It was enough to know he'd come to her and not run away.

"That poor baby," Calley said at length. She turned away from Dean long enough to watch the confused cub, which was still trying to get his mother to her feet. "We have to take them to where they'll be safe."

"Where everyone will be safe," Dean pointed out. He held Calley away from him but still hadn't released her. "I don't think I'll ever get enough of holding you."

"It's a reaction to what happened," Calley said with a heartfelt whisper. She knew she didn't have to add that she was feeling the same emotions. It didn't make sense, but even when she was the target of the grizzly's wrath, her mind had been on Dean. He'd gone through so much already, she had thought. The grizzly couldn't turn on him. It couldn't.

She suppressed another shudder before turning to the task of caring for the bears. The cub scrambled off when they came near, but when they started checking the location of the dart to judge the dosage in the huge creature, the cub slunk back. It would be an easy matter to capture it when it came time to load the animals. Calley knelt on the barren ground around the river and held out her hand. "Come on, little fella. I'm not going to hurt you," she tried to reassure it.

"I don't think it's going to work," Dean pointed out. "This isn't a puppy you're talking to."

"I guess not." Calley sighed. "Born wild. Always wild. I wish those politicians were here. I think they'd see the dignity in that."

Steve reached them before the helicopter arrived. By his red face Calley guessed that the Indian had run the entire way. He asked a minimum of questions, but his eyes settled first on Calley's and then on Dean's face. "Are you going to tell me?" he asked finally.

"Tell you what?" Dean asked.

"You know what! How'd it go?"

"Fine. No problem."

"Yeah?" Steve said skeptically. "Then how come Calley looks like she's been stuck in a deep freeze?"

Dean studied Calley for a minute. He placed his hands over her cheeks and gently rubbed color back into them. "I thought you were lady cool," he chided gently. "You aren't going to cave in on me now, are you?"

In reply Calley covered Dean's hands with hers and held them in front of him. They weren't as steady as they used to be. "What's this?" she asked. "Coffee nerves?"

Steve sighed loudly. "The two of you are going to tell me the whole story as soon as we get Sleeping Beauty here to her new home. When's that helicopter getting here?"

In response to Steve's question, the river's solitude was broken by the low but growing hum of a powerful engine. A minute later a large helicopter appeared over the mountains and dipped lower to hover over the trio and their sleeping quarry. The pilot dropped a cable with a hook and carrying net at the bottom of it. It required a major effort on the part of Dean, Steve and Calley to roll the sleeping grizzly onto the net and secure it around her. Next the pilot dropped a rope, which Steve secured around his middle before signaling the pilot to lift him into the helicopter.

Calley and Dean stood back as the powerful engine revved and slowly climbed upward. The limp grizzly hung suspended over them, moving higher and higher until at length she was little more than an indistinguishable mass. Below her the cub bellowed his confusion.

"Come on, little fellow," Calley crooned. "We'll get you back to your mom as soon as we can."

Before the bewildered youngster could scamper away, Dean picked up the blanket the helicopter pilot had dropped and threw it around the now squalling and fighting cub. Once the blanket was around the youngster's head, he stopped struggling and allowed Dean to lift him into his arms.

"You missed your calling," Calley observed once Dean was sitting cross-legged on the ground with the cub cradled between his knees. "You should have been a professional baby-sitter."

"As long as the babies are smaller than this one," Dean pointed out. "I just hope this kid grows up with a more mellow temperament than his old lady."

Calley plopped down next to Dean. She reached out to rub her hand over the cub's head. "I couldn't kill her," she said to no one in particular. "I know. I should have been thinking of my survival first, but when I thought of this little guy becoming an orphan..."

"So you endangered your own life. That wasn't the smartest decision you've ever made."

Calley refused to take offense. She hadn't taken time earlier to notice the day, but it really was perfect. There wasn't a cloud in the sky. The temperature was in the seventies. They were surrounded by Dall sheep and eagles and maybe were being watched by a fox or a wolf. "It turned out all right," she said, not trying to keep her feeling of contentment out of her voice. She was intuitive enough to realize that tonight's sleep wouldn't be peaceful, but for the moment she wanted nothing more than to enjoy being with Dean.

"It did, didn't it?"

Calley took note of the wonderment in his voice. "Why didn't you try to kill her?" she asked.

"I did," Dean explained. "But I lost my footing and missed."

"You could have tried again."

Dean frowned, but the gesture didn't last long. "I didn't think you'd forgive me if I did."

"When did you have time to think?" Calley rested her head against his shoulder. He felt stronger to her than he ever had before.

"I didn't. It was just something I knew." Because Dean had his arms full with the cub, he was unable to put his arm around Calley. Instead, he ran his lips over the side of her face. "I know you pretty well, Calley Stewart. That smelly old sow's life is important to you. I figured there was a chance I could divert her from you. It worked."

"And if it hadn't?"

Dean tensed. "Don't make me think about that, Calley," he said sharply.

"You have to," she whispered.

For the better part of a minute there was no sound except that made by the river and birds flying overhead. "If that grizzly had killed you, it would have killed me, too."

"Were you scared?" Calley asked her question, holding her breath. What she felt for Dean at the moment left no room for anything as unnecessary as breathing.

"There wasn't time for that emotion. Calley, you were what mattered. Nothing else."

It was the answer she had to hear. "I think you learned something about yourself," she whispered. "You're stronger than you thought you were. As strong as I knew you were."

"You never thought I might turn and run?" Dean was staring down at the blanket-covered lump in his arms.

"Never," she replied with the conviction of her heart. "But I also knew it was something you had to discover for yourself. Oh, Dean! So much has happened today." She wasn't talking only about capturing and transporting a rogue grizzly.

There was little that needed to be said in the time the two spent waiting for the helicopter to return. Dean ventured a guess that Hawk would splutter and complain about the lost rifle but that he wouldn't care as long as Dean and Calley were safe. "We'll keep Hawk in suspense until we get back," he said. "They can tell him a little from the helicopter, but if he wants the details, he's going to have to wait."

Calley didn't mind waiting. Time hung suspended as the Alaskan sun warmed their backs and dried Dean's pants. Her mind drifted off from time to time but kept coming back to one glorious fact. She and Dean were together. Loving each other. Dean had met and passed his supreme test. Now he knew what she did already. He was a man who could stand up and be counted when the circumstances dictated.

And yet Calley held back from telling Dean that. Certain things didn't need words to bring them into focus. It was enough that they'd shared today.

"Montana's going to seem tame after this," Dean said when they heard the first faint hum of the helicopter returning. "What are you going to do for excitement now?"

Calley pretended to be debating the question. "Didn't you and Hawk say you've about run out of excuses for not climbing Mount McKinley? What are you doing next week?"

"Next week I'm taking you to Hawaii. Warm sand. Surfing. Tourists all over the place."

"Spare me." Calley laughed and got to her feet. "If you go to Hawaii, you're going alone."

"Isn't that just like a woman." Dean tucked the blanket more closely around the cub before handing it to Calley.

"I've already taken her to one of the most glamorous spots on earth, but is she satisfied? No way. We may have to discuss this at length later."

Calley balanced the weight of the squirming cub in her arms and turned her attention to the helicopter landing a short distance from her. Dean gathered up their equipment and stepped into the open helicopter door as Calley lowered her head against the wind caused by the whirling blades. She handed the cub back to Dean and climbed aboard. As the helicopter started lifting, Calley took a last look at the place where so much had transpired. Her eyes sought out the spot where she'd been standing when the grizzly challenged her.

"I'd like to come back here someday," she said so softly that the helicopter engine almost swallowed up the words. She reached for the bundled cub and insisted on holding it during the trip to where its still-drugged mother lay waiting.

When the pilot indicated that they were ready to descend, Calley leaned over and looked down. She could make out the huge brown mound and the solid man standing guard over it. "I wonder if she'll find her way back to Toklat," Calley mused aloud. "Too bad we can't explain to her that she'd save herself and everyone else a lot of trouble if she just stays put."

"If she comes back, we'll haul her out again."

Slowly Calley nodded. Dean was right. Some people piloted helicopters. Some passed laws in the nation's capital. Others, like Steve and Dean and herself, had taken on the mantle of responsibility that would ensure the continued existence of one of earth's largest mammals. "Hold on, kid," Calley admonished the cub when it tried to jump out of her arms. "We'll have you with your mother in a few minutes. Ungrateful brat!" she gasped as the cub dug a paw into her right thigh. "I'm trying to save your hide. Can't you get that through your thick skull?"

The cub was still testing its strength when Steve helped her out of the helicopter. She could have handed the cub over to Steve, but this was something she wanted to do herself.

Calley walked over to the inert mound lying on the Alaskan tundra and slowly dropped to her knees. Only then did she pull the blanket away from the cub's eyes. For perhaps three seconds the cub lay passive in her arms.

"You're home, baby," Calley whispered. "Wake up your mama."

With a loud squall the cub catapulted itself toward its mother. It sniffed anxiously at the unmoving head and then swatted the grizzly on her nose. "Serves her right," Calley said with a laugh as she turned back toward the waiting helicopter. "I hope you turn out to be a juvenile delinquent. Give the old lady a few gray hairs."

Calley accepted Dean's assistance back into the helicopter and sat with her body wedged against his during the trip back to headquarters. Although the men were talking animatedly about the day's excitement, she was content to simply sit and listen. It was enough to hear the mixture of admiration and lingering concern in Dean's voice as he relayed the details of what had happened.

The story had to be told over again once Hawk had hauled them out of the helicopter. Over coffee in Hawk's office, Dean restated his belief that the grizzly wouldn't cause any more trouble as long as she was kept away from large concentrations of tourists. Hawk pretended to be dismayed when Dean told him that the park was out one rifle, but that didn't prevent him from insisting that Calley and Dean stay one more night before flying out.

"You still haven't seen the park. Not really," Dean observed as they were walking back to their cabin. "I'm going to have to get your boss to give you more time off."

"As long as you serve as my guide." Calley slipped her arm through Dean's. It seemed as if they'd left the cabin only a matter of minutes ago, but already the sun was setting behind the high mountains. "I wish we didn't have to go back," she said with a sigh.

"You really like it here?"

Calley waited until they were in the cabin with the door closed behind them. "I love it here. So much has been left the way nature intended it to be. You don't suppose—"

"You don't suppose what?"

"Nothing." Calley shook her head. It was too early in their relationship for her to be thinking about forever with Dean, and yet the thought was there. What she'd almost said was did he think Alaska was a place to come for a honeymoon. "Hawk said we should have dinner with him. That's going to leave us less than an hour to get cleaned up."

"Calley?" Dean touched her arm, the gesture enough to turn her toward him. "Would you mind if we didn't eat with him?"

Of course she didn't. Food was the last thing on her mind. "What will he think?" she had to ask.

"I think he'd figure it out." Dean touched the side of her neck with fingers that had suddenly gone cold. "I need you next to me, Calley. Every time I think about what could have happened—"

"It didn't happen," she reassured him. She didn't know which of them was trembling. "It turned out all right."

"I know." Dean's whispered breath caressed her cheeks. "But I still need you next to me."

Calley closed her eyes, but that didn't stop her body from swaying. He couldn't name the emotion coursing through her body, only that she was accepting it, loving it. "Please make love to me, Dean. That's what I need."

Reverently Dean covered her mouth with his. "Do you have any idea what you're doing to me, Calley Stewart? How much you mean to me?"

"Show me," she said.

Chapter Thirteen

"No one goes to Alaska for a honeymoon."

Melinda's words followed Calley out to the car on a trail of rice. Calley bent her head to escape the white shower, waiting impatiently as Dean opened the door and helped her in. She smoothed the white satin she'd been married in around her and pushed the short veil back from her face. "Except us," Calley continued the conversation once she was safely inside. "Besides, I don't think we can honestly call it a honeymoon since we're going to be there on business."

"You just got married and you're going on a trip. That qualifies for a honeymoon." Melinda squeezed her friend's arm in reinforcement. "You can't tell me you aren't going to find time for a little recreation."

Dean was behind the wheel. He leaned across Calley to speak to Melinda. "You have a point there. We might not get out of the first motel."

Calley blushed; fortunately Dean started the jeep before she had to face a knowing look from Melinda. She turned and waved at the friends who'd attended their wedding and then slid close to Dean. The day was perfect. Despite an earlier threat of rain, only a few puffs of white clouds were in the sky during the ceremony, held in the same magic garden spot where Melinda and Kirk had been married. Dean was unbelievably handsome in his dark blue suit. Calley could still hear echoes of his softly spoken words of commitment. "Melinda said to tell you it's about time we tied the knot. She said we've been acting like newlyweds ever since we got back from McKinley."

"Hmm." Dean carefully removed Calley's veil and smoothed her hair with his hand. His eyes told her that she was beautiful. "That's pretty much what Steve told me. I had no idea people were that interested in us."

"They're just glad to see us together." Calley closed her eyes, content beyond her wildest dreams. The sun caressed her cheeks, reinforcing her belief that she'd been married in the one perfect place. "Drive on, sir. I'm ready to blow this town."

"Don't you want to know where we're going to spend the night?"

Calley smiled but didn't open her eyes. "This is your show," she pointed out. "I'm just along for the ride."

Dean put the jeep in gear and pulled out of the parking lot as their friends waved them off. Calley stirred herself long enough to respond, but once they were alone, she settled back against Dean again. "You're putting me on the spot, aren't you?" he teased. "Are you going to hold it against me if there are any snafus?"

"Of course," Calley said with a laugh. "I expect perfection from start to finish. I assume you've booked us into a luxury hotel on the Admiralty Islands."

Dean whistled in mock distress. "Would you settle for a furnished cabin?"

"I suppose, but you have to keep in mind that I'm accustomed to a certain life-style. I'm not sure how long I can handle such primitive arrangements."

"I could always send you back home."

"You're not getting rid of me that easily."

In response to her statement, Dean pulled her even closer. "I have no intention of getting rid of you, Calley. But you do understand that we're going to have to make business a priority. I'd like nothing better than to spend weeks serving as your guide, but since a lumber company is paying our bills—"

"I know," Calley reassured him. "It doesn't bother me. Honest. Are there really as many brown bears on the island as I keep hearing?"

Dean nodded. He explained that the estimate of one brown, or grizzly, as they were sometimes called, per square mile on the Admiralty Islands was an accurate estimate. Both Calley and Dean were concerned that the demand for logs would jeopardize the island the Indians called the Fortress of Bears. There was no way men and their saws could come on to the island without it having an impact on the wildlife there, but that impact could be minimized.

Their first destination, after dropping by their off-campus house to change their clothes, was the airport. They boarded a charter plane to Alaska and touched down in Juneau. A rental car was ready for them there. "You really are trying to impress me," Calley observed as Dean filled the trunk with their luggage. "No foul-ups so far."

"Actually," Dean admitted, "this car is courtesy of the loggers we'll be seeing tomorrow. However, we do have tonight to ourselves."

After leaving the airport, Dean drove to downtown Juneau, where he gave Calley a tour of the main street with its historic buildings surrounded by forested mountain slopes. They checked in at the Alaskan Hotel and Bar, for Dean thought Calley would like to spend the night in a place that was on the national register of historic sites. Calley was delighted with the rustic bar and historically decorated rooms.

They walked a short block to the Red Dog Saloon, and after entering through swinging doors, they stepped onto a sawdust floor. "Your finest for my bride," Dean told the bartender. He pushed back an imaginary ten-gallon hat. "How's this for luxury?" he asked her once their frosty beer mugs had been delivered.

Calley could barely keep her eyes off the relics from the gold-rush era that decorated the saloon. "It's perfect," she said with a sigh. "I couldn't ask for more."

"I could," Dean said softly. He leaned across the small table so that his voice wouldn't carry. "After dinner we're going back to the hotel."

Calley shivered under his unspoken suggestion. He was right. Perfection was a night together in a room that took them back over a century. They lingered over their beers before walking through the now quiet town to a restaurant specializing in baked salmon. Although their conversation centered around their meeting tomorrow, Calley was all too aware of a heightened tension between them. Tonight was going to be different. Tonight was the first time they'd sleep together as man and wife.

Arm in arm they made their slow way through the peaceful town back to the hotel. "I wish we could be here for a week," Dean said. "There's so much I want to show you. The old Russian church, the graves of the men who first found gold here, the governor's mansion."

Calley giggled, resting her head on Dean's shoulder as they walked. "We wouldn't want to disturb the governor."

"Good point," Dean observed. "I guess there's nothing left to do but get some sleep."

Sleep, it turned out, was the one thing they almost didn't get around to. While Dean moved around the room, getting organized for the early morning flight to the Admiralty Islands, Calley indulged in fantasy. She sat on the high bed, fingering the hardwood headboard. The man intent on his task wasn't a modern researcher. He was a miner just in from the Alaskan gold fields. She was one of a handful of dance-hall girls brought in to entertain the men. "I don't have all night, mister," she observed. "I'm expected in the cancan line in an hour. You're not the only sourdough to walk through the door, you know."

Dean straightened up. "Whatever are you talking about?"

"I'm talking about there being other miners with more gold in their pokes than you've shown me. If I'm going to have time to get into my strapless red dress, we're going to have to get this show on the road."

"You're crazy." Dean turned from his task, his eyes slowly running from Calley's face to her toes. "This is the 1980s."

Calley crossed her legs, swinging them in an imitation of frontier dance-hall queens. "This is 1887, and we're on the Klondike."

"Hmm. That's quite an imagination you have there, lady."

Suddenly Calley no longer needed a fantasy. She was supremely content with the flesh-and-blood man standing before her. She hopped down from the bed and crossed the barnwood floor to where he stood. Behind him a single oil lamp had thrown the room into red shadows. Calley reached for his shirt, feeling both shy and bold. "Mrs. Dean Ramsey. It has a nice sound," she whispered.

"What do you have in mind, Mrs. Ramsey?" Dean whispered back. He was watching her trembling hands as they pulled his shirt out of his waistband.

"I want to feel like your wife."

"That I can do." Dean took her cool hands in his, brought them to his face to warm them with his breath and then gently kissed her fingertips. "Don't be afraid, Calley. What we're doing is right."

"I know it is," she whispered. "I don't know why I'm nervous."

"I think I know what to do about that." Dean placed her arms around his waist before starting on the buttons of her blouse. He undressed her slowly, reverently, making Calley believe that she was the most desirable woman in the world. Even before he unfastened her bra, her nipples had come to life. "You're beautiful, Calley. You'll always be beautiful to me."

"Always?" Calley repeated. "I'm going to get old."

"We'll grow old together." Dean's hands slid from her breasts to her waist, pulling her toward him. "We'll have a lifetime to experience together."

"You mean that?" Calley wanted to believe him without question, but she still wanted to hear the reassuring words.

"You're right for me, Calley. And I'm right for you. Not many people can say that."

"I know." Calley buried her head against Dean's chest. His hands on her back were both comforting and exciting. "Our getting married was right. I feel it in my bones."

"In your bones?" Dean's fingers were pinpricks of flame on her back.

"All right." Calley sighed, the sound a far cry from being weary. "In my heart. In—everywhere."

Dean chuckled deep in his throat. "Admit it, Calley. You like having me make love to you."

"Of course I admit it. You happen to be a very sexy man, Mr. Ramsey."

"And you're a sexy woman, Mrs. Ramsey." Dean had started to remove her jeans but he stopped halfway through the task. "No regrets?" he asked.

"No regrets," she answered without having to think. "I want to grow old with you, Dean."

He helped her out of her jeans and underpants. Dean stood with his hands at his sides, taking in the sight of his naked bride. "Let's take that one step at a time. One day at a time."

"One night at a time," Calley amended. She held her breath as Dean helped her up onto the bed and immediately reached for him. He was right. They had a lifetime together ahead of them. Every step of the journey was to be cherished. Calley lay back on the bed, no longer trembling as he began to make love to her. Only one thought reached her. She'd been born so that she could be touched by this man.

Outside, Alaska clung to the last month of summer. Soon fog and driving rain would isolate the state's residents from the rest of the world, but for Calley and Dean, the isolation had come already. They needed, wanted, nothing more than each other.

Even when the sound of the predawn alarm tore them from each other's arms, they remained emotionally bonded together. They squabbled good-naturedly over rights to the bathroom mirror and debated at length over what constituted the perfect breakfast. When they boarded the small plane provided by the lumber company, they were holding hands. Once they were airborne, the pilot pointed out a ferry making its way down the channel that separated Juneau from thousands of acres of national parkland, but Calley gave the large modern conveyance little more than a glance. She was aware of glacier-capped mountains, a carpet of trees and hundreds of tiny nameless creeks braiding their way through the island, but Dean was the only reality she needed.

Even a day chock-full of exploration and discussion failed to change Calley's mood. If she'd been an arrogant woman, she might have believed that the awesome wilderness they were exploring had been placed here for her alone. As it was, she felt blessed to be able to share the day with the man she loved.

After meeting the two businessmen responsible for regulating logging on the island, the foursome transferred to a large kayak manned by a Tlingit Indian. The Indian served as their guide through a paradise of coastal rain forest that was inhabited by beaver, river otter, Canada geese, bald eagles, black-tailed deer and, of course, bears. Calley was sure she spotted a sea lion in the rookeries. From their guide they learned that the Tlingit way of life was still closely tied to the land. Their culture was shaped by shores, forests and streams.

"I think we should have done this earlier," one of the businessmen told Dean. "This is the first time I've seen the island through the eyes of someone whose roots are here."

"It's so easy to disturb the relationship between wildlife and the ecology," Dean pointed out. "That's my primary concern."

The group continued their discussion that evening at one of the forest-service cabins. Although the discussion occasionally became heated, by the time Calley dragged Dean off to their cabin, she felt confident that the company men were sensitive to the need to retain the island's primitive quality.

"I'm just glad the tour is going to last two days. It takes one day to get used to the raw beauty here and another one to get a sense of how rare that beauty is."

"Well put, Mrs. Ramsey," Dean agreed as he joined her on the thin mattress that was going to see them through their second night as husband and wife. "When we're through, there's one more place I want to take you."

"Oh?" Calley reached for him. "Will we be alone?"

"I'm afraid not. But I think you'll find out it's worth it. However, since we won't be alone tomorrow night, I suggest we make the most of tonight." Within minutes he was showing her what he had in mind.

Calley prepared breakfast for the men the next morning. Over coffee the men congratulated Dean and Calley on their marriage. "I wouldn't be able to get my wife up here in a million years," the older of the two logging executives explained. "Anyplace without running hot water might as well be on another planet as far as she's concerned."

Calley had to laugh. "I consider running hot water a luxury."

Dean gave her a mysterious glance. "A luxury you may soon experience, Mrs. Ramsey" was all he would say.

Ten long hours later Dean was directing their guide to a remote corner of the island. They'd returned the businessmen to the spot where their plane would pick them up, and now Dean and the Tlingit guide were swapping tales about a man named Stan Price. Calley gathered that Price had lived near a remote creek off the Seymour Canal on the Admiralty Islands for more years than anyone knew.

It was dark by the time they climbed out of the kayak in the middle of the island wilderness and headed toward a small cabin barely visible through the trees. Only the sounds of night creatures disturbed the vast silence. Calley turned to wave at their guide, but he was already making his way down the creek that served as the only roadway through that part of the island. "Are you sure he knows we're coming?" Calley asked. She sensed that Price's cabin was the only man-made structure for miles around.

"I sent word to Stan when I knew we would be on the island," Dean explained. "Unless the mail was late, he'll have coffee on."

The aroma of strong coffee reached Calley's nostrils as soon as the cabin door opened. Shyly she stepped inside and faced her host. Stan Price was at least eighty years old, his body bent with age. When he spoke, his voice was rusty from disuse. "It's about time," he told Dean. "I just about gave up on you." Stan stuck out a weathered hand toward Calley. "You're a pretty one. Don't let this wild man get away with anything."

Calley laughed, liking the old man already. Anyone who actually lived in this remote wilderness commanded her utmost respect. "Dean wouldn't tell me anything about you. I hope you'll fill me in."

It was obvious that Stan was delighted to have company. Over coffee so strong that Calley had trouble swallowing it, Stan explained that he'd come here as a prospector over fifty years ago and never got around to leaving. His wife was buried here, and he saw no reason not to join her when the time came.

Calley fell silent so Dean and Stan could talk. Although Stan asked several questions about world affairs, he didn't seem particularly interested in Dean's answers. Calley guessed that living like this had made the rest of the world too far removed to be of much concern. He came to life when the conversation turned to a couple of bear cubs named Suzie and Bolinda. Calley's legs ached from being cramped all day in a kayak. She stretched them in front of Stan's wood stove and started rubbing them. Before she knew it, Dean was pulling her to her feet.

"You're snoring," Dean explained. "I think we better put you to bed."

Calley let Dean steer her toward a thick blanket-covered mattress in a corner of the room. The last thing she remembered was the distant yapping of puppies. Sometime later

Dean crawled in next to her. Calley molded her body to his, taking his warmth as her own.

She woke before dawn to the insistent cries of hungry young dogs. Beside her Dean stirred but didn't wake. Calley opened her eyes, watching as Stan pulled jeans over his weathered frame and stepped outside to tend to the dogs. She rose on her elbow and gazed down at Dean. The world of telephones and electricity seemed light-years away. No one except a gentle old man willing to share his cabin with them knew where they were.

"I love you, Dean Ramsey," Calley whispered. "I wonder if you'll ever know how happy you've made me."

Dean smiled in his sleep but didn't stir when Calley moved from his side. She dressed and stepped outside to use the ancient outhouse. She was starting back to the cabin when Stan called her. "I think you'll like to see this. I hope my babies didn't keep you awake last night."

A moment later Calley was too enchanted for words. Tumbling around a sturdy doghouse were a half-dozen blue-eyed Siberian husky puppies. Their mother sat half inside the doghouse as if seeking refuge from so much energy. Calley dropped to her knees and allowed the silky bundles of fur to engulf her. She picked up one charmer and held him up to her face. A pink tongue flicked out, wetting her nose. Calley needed only one look at the predominantly white face with a ring of black around the expressive eyes to come up with a name. "Bandit," she tried. "How do you like that?"

"I think he likes it fine." Stan grinned. "I get worn out trying to come up with names for all the creatures around here. What say we wake up that husband of yours and go see my other kids before you leave."

Calley was reluctant to leave the squealing, nipping puppies. Even when she returned to the cabin, her arms felt empty. "I'd take Bandit home in a minute," she admitted. "He's gentle and resourceful and strong, all at the same time."

"That precious puppy is going to weigh over sixty pounds in a few months," Dean observed. "Besides, if I know Stan, he isn't going to give up any of his kids."

Calley allowed herself to be distracted by the suggestion that they take a short walk to watch Stan's other "kids" feed in the creek. She had the feeling both Stan and Dean were watching her for her reaction, but she didn't think about the ramifications of what Stan had said until they were standing in a grove of evergreens less than a hundred feet from a trio of wild Alaskan brown bears.

"Oh, my—" Calley said, gripping Dean's arm for strength. A moment ago they'd had the forest to themselves. Now they were face-to-face with the creatures responsible for bringing them together.

Before Calley could think of anything else to say, Stan identified the bears, which barely gave the humans any notice. The one with the nick in its right ear was Brownie. The large female was named Edna Mae after Stan's late wife. The young male, who seemed most aware of the humans, was called Salmon after his favorite food.

"They don't give you any trouble?" Calley was incredulous. As though their surroundings were no protection if the bears decided to attack, Stan was leaning easily on his walking stick. "They let you come this close?"

Stan's look indicated that the question didn't deserve an answer. "Brownie's mother," Stan explained, "was Suzie. She and Bolinda were the orphans my wife and I raised when we first came here. Sometimes there's over thirty of them lounging around the cabin on a hot day."

Calley turned toward Dean. His eyes were on the massive creatures. He was watching their every movement not with fear but with the open curiosity of a trained researcher. "It's all right, isn't it?" Calley whispered. "The nightmares are gone."

Dean pulled Calley against him. "How can I have a nightmare when you're with me?"

Long before Calley was ready to leave, their guide had returned, and Dean was trying to get Calley to climb into the kayak without saying goodbye one more time to the Siberian puppies. "Take care of them for me," she pleaded with Stan. "They're precious. Everything about your place is fantastic."

"I think you said that before," Dean noted with a wink in Stan's direction. After promising to come back for a visit next spring, Calley and Dean were on their way.

They spent that night at the Alaskan Hotel; early the next morning Dean announced that they had one more place to visit before returning home. "I don't suppose you're going to tell me where you're taking me," Calley pressed.

"Be quiet and let me run things today," Dean warned as they were getting into the rented car. They left Juneau and headed north, finally connecting with the Alaska highway system. Near noon they reached Skagway. "I'll feed you pretty soon," Dean explained as they entered the city limits. "But we have one stop to make first."

By now Calley had reconciled herself to the fact that Dean had gone to considerable lengths to make the trip as special as possible. When he insisted that they visit a jewelry shop, she eagerly agreed. Calley wandered through the store, fascinated by the displays of hand-carved totem poles, hematite and jade while Dean pulled the clerk aside. A few minutes later he joined her, with a small box in his hand. "A souvenir," he explained. When she opened the box, she discovered three intricately carved grizzlies made out of stone. "Dean" was all she could manage to say in pure delight.

"Do you like them?"

"I love them." She clung to him for strength. "How did you know you'd find that here?"

"I didn't." Dean's grin was as beguiling as a young boy's. "I ordered it last month. I know the artist who did the carving."

"It's perfect. You're perfect," she whispered.

She paid little attention to where he took her for lunch. Calley was still in a romantic fog when they reached Whitehorse late in the day. She was struck by the bustle of the city that served as the capital of the Yukon but didn't object when Dean left the city and took a well-maintained road that ended at an isolated but modern campground complete with a restaurant. Dean would take care of her tonight. That was all she needed to know.

There seemed to be no end to the people Dean knew. Not only was the campground owner expecting them, but he explained that they were the only guests who wouldn't have to stay in the campgrounds. "I keep a bungalow for my personal friends," he told Calley. "You two let me know when you're ready for dinner and I'll have it brought to your room."

"Dean!" Calley exclaimed when he insisted on carrying her into the modern bedroom/living room combination behind the main building. "How many more surprises do you have in store for me?"

"Two. The first you'll discover later tonight. What would you like for dinner, milady?"

Dean made a great display of reading the menu and then eliminating every suggestion Calley made until she let him make the final decision. They sat cross-legged on a queen-size bed and ate Alaskan crab with their fingers, large napkins tucked down their fronts. "This is decadent," Calley said with a laugh. "I feel so pampered."

"That's what I wanted." The love pouring out of Dean's eyes took her breath away. "I won't get enough chances to pamper you."

"I don't care," she reassured him. "As long as I'm with you, I'm happy."

"Even if I wouldn't let you take that puppy home with you?"

Calley pretended to consider that possibility. "Bandit really was a sweetheart, wasn't he?" she admitted. "Do you think we'll see Stan again? I'd love to see how those puppies turned out."

"We'll see Stan," Dean said softly. "Sometimes I think he'll live forever. Alaska needs men like him. You know—" Dean drew out the words. He slipped off the bed, taking his plate with him. After placing it on the dresser, he turned toward Calley. "I don't think I want to talk about Stan anymore."

"Oh?" Calley started to tremble. Dean's eyes were telling her what she wanted to see. "What would you like to do?"

"I want to make love to my wife."

"And I want to make love to my husband."

With an effort Dean drew himself up straight. "But not here and not now," he whispered, his voice husky.

"More surprises?" she guessed.

"You could say that. Unfortunately we have to wait until about eleven o'clock."

Slowly Calley got to her feet. When she turned toward him, her fingers were aimed at his ribs. "You really know how to torture a woman, don't you?" she asked. "Well, what if I say no to that?" By reaching for the sensitive flesh under his arms, Calley was able to back him toward the bed.

Dean gave a sigh of reluctant surrender that didn't fool Calley. "I might not be ready for a repeat performance later," he pointed out as he collapsed onto the bed, pulling Calley down with him.

"Oh, I think you'll manage." Calley was on top, her legs stradling Dean's strong body.

They made love in the old bed and fell asleep to the sounds of vacationers outside. Calley had no idea what time it was when Dean shook her awake. She tried to bury herself under the blankets, but he pulled them off her. "You promised," he said petulantly.

"You're a hard man, Dean Ramsey," Calley said with a groan. Nevertheless, she dragged herself out of bed. She managed not to ask if he had taken leave of his senses when he helped her into a short terry bathrobe. "You want me to ask where we're going in the middle of the night dressed like this, don't you? Well, I'm not going to."

She didn't have to. After stepping outside, Dean led her to the swimming pool she'd taken scant notice of earlier in the day. It was deserted now, steam rising around the short slide. "They keep this heated?" she wondered aloud. "Doesn't that cost an awful lot?"

"You'd think so, wouldn't you." Dean's reply was noncommittal.

Calley was eyeing the slide. It had been years since she'd attempted one of those. "Are you sure we're going to have the place to ourselves?" she asked, mindful of her naked state under the robe.

"Positive. Well, Mrs. Ramsey, who gets in first?"

With a flourish she sincerely hoped no one but Dean would see, she threw off her robe and slid into the water. The moment she hit water, she knew this wasn't any ordinary swimming pool.

Naked, Dean joined her. He splashed water in her face before drawing her close to him under an Alaskan night sky. "What do you think?"

Thinking with Dean's wet body against hers was next to impossible. "What is it?" she managed to ask. "It's too warm to be a heated pool."

Dean gave her a wet kiss. "This is a natural hot springs."

"In the Yukon?" If it weren't for his expression, she would have thought he was putting her on. "Are you sure?"

"Sure I'm sure. There are several in the Yukon." Dean's legs were wrapped around hers. The combination of that and his tone of voice were responsible for her disorganized thoughts. Life couldn't be more perfect.

"Remind me to honeymoon with you more often," Calley whispered when they were standing in neck-deep water. "I like your ideas."

"Hmm. What if you come up with the next idea?" Dean's hands were making gentle inroads on what remained of Calley's senses. She closed her eyes and lifted her head skyward as his search centered around her breasts.

"Can't you guess?" she managed to say. "I want you to make love to me here. In a hot springs in Alaska."

IN THE MORNING they said a reluctant goodbye to their hosts before heading toward the plane that took them back to Montana. Although Calley had been ready to begin the journey south as a married woman, there was no denying the sense of melancholy she carried with her as they made the short trip from the airport back to their house. As she told Dean, she'd left a part of her heart in Alaska.

Dean was out of the car and around to open her door before she'd had time to move. "Come on, honey. Someone's waiting for us," he said.

First Calley saw Steve. The Indian was sitting on the front porch, his body hunched forward as if waiting for them was the only thing he had to do. Then she saw the puppy in his arms.

"Oh, Dean! Oh!" She hurried forward and dropped to her knees in front of Steve. The black-and-white bundle wriggled toward her, a soft pink tongue caressing her face. "Bandit," she breathed. "How did you get him here?"

Dean stood over her, smiling like a proud father on Christmas morning. "That's a long story. Do you like him?"

"Like him?" Calley lifted the puppy in her arms and rose to her feet in a single movement. She didn't care that Steve was witness to her happy tears. She fell into Dean's arms, the puppy cradled between them. "I love him. I love you."

Readers rave about Harlequin American Romance!

"...the best series of modern romances I have read...great, exciting, stupendous, wonderful."
—S.E.,* Coweta, Oklahoma

"...they are absolutely fantastic...going to be a smash hit and hard to keep on the bookshelves."
—P.D., Easton, Pennsylvania

"The American line is great. I've enjoyed every one I've read so far."
—W.M.K., Lansing, Illinois

"...the best stories I have read in a long time."
—R.H., Northport, New York

*Names available on request.

Harlequin American Romance

COMING NEXT MONTH

#185 STORMWALKER by Dallas Schulze

Sara Grant chose the wrong time to lie when she insisted that she knew all about horses and hiking. She badgered Cody Wolf into taking her on his search for the downed Cessna in the Rocky Mountains and Sara's missing nephew. Unfortunately she then had to prove she could be just as tough as her surefooted, half-Indian companion.

#186 BODY AND SOUL by Anne McAllister

Her mother had always said that disasters come in threes, and now Susan Rivers could attest to it. First her teenaged brother was thrust upon her for the summer. Then, she was evicted. And when Susan finally found another apartment in southern California, the unspeakable happened: Miles Cavanaugh moved in next door.

#187 ROUGE'S BARGAIN by Cathy Gillen Thacker

Only a scoundrel like Ben McCauley would have promised Lindsey Halloran three weeks of work on the idyllic island of Maui and then asked her to play a starring role in a high-stakes vendetta against a business rival. Pretending to go along with Ben's elaborate scheme, she plotted to beat the master at his own game. But what she didn't plan on was Ben's irresistible manly charm.

#188 A MATTER OF TIME by Noreen Brownlie

Jennifer Bradford thought that stress was an acceptable hazard of her job as a magazine editor in Los Angeles—that is until Dr. Julian Caldicott diagnosed her severe "type A" behavior. Although she resisted the efforts of the enticing doctor to defuse her, what should have been a simple procedure turned into a battle of wits and wills... and much more.

Janet Dailey Americana

A romantic tour of America with
Janet Dailey!

Enjoy two releases each month from this
collection of your favorite previously
published Janet Dailey titles, presented
alphabetically state by state.

Available NOW wherever paperback books
are sold.

HARLEQUIN HISTORICAL

Explore love with Harlequin in the Middle Ages, the Renaissance, in the Regency, the Victorian and other eras.

Relive within these books the endless ages of romance, set against authentic historical backgrounds. Two new historical love stories published each month.

Available now wherever paperback books are sold.

ATTRACTIVE, SPACE SAVING BOOK RACK

Display your most prized novels on this handsome and sturdy book rack. The hand-rubbed walnut finish will blend into your library decor with quiet elegance, providing a practical organizer for your favorite hard-or soft-covered books.

Only $9.95

Approximately 16" x 8" when assembled

Assembles in seconds!

To order, rush your name, address and zip code, along with a check or money order for $10.70 ($9.95 plus 75¢ postage and handling) (New York residents add appropriate sales tax), payable to *Harlequin Reader Service* to:

> In the U.S.
>
> Harlequin Reader Service
> Book Rack Offer
> 901 Fuhrmann Blvd.
> P.O. Box 1325
> Buffalo, NY 14269-1325
>
> *Offer not available in Canada.*